More Than Clickbait

PHILIPPA YOUNG

For content warnings, please visit my website:

www.philippayoungauthor.com

MORE THAN CLICKBAIT

Edited by Bryony Leah

PLAYLIST

Scan here to listen along:

For the ones who never get picked.

RECAP

More Than Clickbait is a continuation of More Than Shipmates. Skipping the first book will mean a few things go over your head, so I highly recommend you start at the very beginning. I hear it's a very good place to start. That said, here's a little catch-up to remind you what went down in More Than Shipmates…

Stand-up comedian Tom Parks and drama-school reject Eliza Chapman met on their first day on board the cruise ship Neptune, where they now work as entertainment hosts. Eliza said she wouldn't date a coworker, but the vibes were vibing between her and Tom and her resolve started to wane. He made her laugh and inspired her to let her hair down. Meanwhile, her charming British mentor, Oscar Harvey, encouraged Eliza to step out of her shell professionally and invited her to his secret musical theatre workshop nights, where Eliza built her confidence performing again.

When feelings started to grow, Tom and Oscar made an unofficial pact not to make a move on Eliza – but, ultimately, Eliza couldn't resist Oscar the theatre kid. They snuck around shagging everywhere except in their goddamn cabin while keeping their relationship a secret from Tom, who was working through the grief of losing his father by sleeping with half the crew.

Oscar got promoted to activities manager, which almost saw him working on another ship – *boooo* – but someone owed him a favour, so he came back to Neptune – yay! Oscar left for his six-week contract break, and Tom confessed his love for Eliza, inspired by an unrelated Oscar pep talk, only to be met with heartbreak.

There were a lot of tears, an unwanted reunion, and there *miiiight* have been some miscommunication, but eventually, Oscar and Eliza got their happily ever after, and she and Tom resolved their friendship. Still, Tom remains ambivalent towards Oscar.

Eliza's now got the best of both worlds – *don't sing it, don't sing it, don't sing it* – working as an entertainment host *and* occasional lounge singer.

Oh! And most people call Oscar by his surname, "Harvey", because his first name is code for "man overboard" and there have been some false alarms…

Now you're up to speed, I'd like to welcome you back on board the ship. It's good to *sea* you again.

(Sorry).

ONE

TOM

Four years. It took me *four years* to become an overnight success. I was happy – *more than* happy – just being a guy who entertained the people right in front of him, spreading the smiles one room at a time. But finding out I've made hundreds of thousands of people laugh with something I said in one small moment? That feels like magic. For all the stuff you hear about social media ruining lives and corrupting young minds, it has its positives too.

> I needed this today
>
> Not laughed like that in a while
>
> You've made my week

Everyone who works on a ship has to take a minimum of six weeks off between contracts, so before my last one ended, I applied for a few comedy gigs at the stops along the road trip I was planning with my twin brother, Bobby, and prayed someone was willing to take a chance on an unknown like me. While a couple of places did have slots, most didn't, but I was elated with whatever I could get.

The trip was about honouring and remembering our dad, and I can say without a doubt he was there with us every step of the way, because barely one week into it, someone's clip of me performing went viral on TikTok, and the next thing I knew I was being offered gigs left, right, and centre. One forty-five-second video posted from the right account, and suddenly I was a somebody.

I hope whoever runs that account knows they've changed my life. I mean, they should know by now – I've DM'd them a million thank-yous.

I got to play so many venues I could only ever dream of performing in before that viral clip, and Bobby filmed my sets, like a good roadie should, so I could make a bunch of clips from them to post online. Every gig felt like another opportunity to be discovered. Like at any minute the right person could see me, and it would change everything, again. It pushed me to write all kinds of new material and play with the audiences more than ever. I was confident when I first started doing stand-up, though not *that* confident, but with six months of constantly entertaining people under my belt, I could work the audience like a charm without worrying about how to link it back into my routine.

My shiny new TikTok account is making a killing already. I have ten thousand followers, with more joining every day. I still can't wrap my head around it. Though the attention will fizzle out soon, now I'm here. There's only so much footage from my gigs I can keep cutting down until I have nothing left to post. It's a shame for sure, but I've got no plans to end my cruising career anytime soon. Oh well, I can't think about disappointing all my "fans" right now, because I've got the two people who matter the most standing in front of me.

"I thought you abandoned me!" Eliza frets against my chest as she squeezes the life out of me in the crew bar.

I decided to extend my leave by one week to fit in some actual time with Mom after our trip ran long. *And* because I wanted to do a few final gigs in Chicago before disappearing for another six months. I knew Eliza would have some catching up to do with Harvey that first week, so it's not like I would have seen her much anyway.

"You're not getting rid of me that easily."

Eliza releases me and steps aside so I can hug the Big Friendly Giant lurking behind her.

"Jack!"

He takes a shy step forward, a huge grin breaking out on his face as his long arms wrap around me. I've been trying to catch him all day, but we kept missing each other in all the embarkation-day chaos. He was my roommate after Daniel, and even though we haven't known each other for very long, I'd say he's the best friend I've ever had. Male best friend, that is.

"What the hell is this?" I wiggle the knot of dirty-blond hair on top of his head. It was getting long before I left, but he always said he'd cut it before he had to tie it back.

"You can talk." He tips his chin at my hair. I've grown it out while I've been away – the curls are a little more defined than when it was short, but I *definitely* couldn't pull off a man bun.

"And what's with the *beard*?" I examine the thick stubble on his face.

"Someone said I looked like Thor, so I'm keeping it."

"Yeah, if he had a baby with the BFG."

Jack's part of the kids' entertainment team, and during a movie night on one of his first weeks here, all the kids pointed out that he was like the Big Friendly Giant onscreen. Taller than anything, talks funny – I mean, Brits who speak any differently from the way Eliza does are funny to us

Americans, but his Northern accent is *hilarious* – big ears, and he looks after children. So, yeah. Suffice to say I've never let him live it down.

As I pull out a chair at their table, Harvey strides in with *the most beautiful girl I have ever laid eyes on* (sorry, Eliza). She looks my way and it's as if time stops still. Her piercing blue eyes mesmerise me, and it's not until she breaks eye contact that I can breathe again.

What the hell was that?

They exchange a few words before splitting up, and to my disappointment, she doesn't head this way. She takes a centring breath as if she's frustrated and then walks over to another table. *How about that? There's someone else who doesn't fall at Oscar Harvey's feet...* Now I *really* wanna meet her.

"Harvey." I nod at him, extending my hand.

"Hey, Tom." He copies me, and we shake. "Nice to have you back." He studies me more. "You've bulked up a bit."

"Mm, I've got my brother to thank for that." We were on a tight schedule during our trip, but Bobby made sure to always fit in time for a workout. You'd think we were on a whistle-stop tour of all the fitness centres across the East Coast with the number of guest passes we got. And though I'm no stranger to the gym, Bobby's routine is on a whole other level. When you see what you're genetically capable of, there's no excuse not to try. That and I always aimed to do one more set than he could despite struggling to even match him at first. "Gym date soon?"

He straightens with surprise then smiles. "Sure."

Out of the corner of my eye, I notice Eliza's glowing more than usual. I know he and I have a...*chequered* history, but since he makes my favourite person happy, I'll play nice.

We're slowly joined by Sunshine, Louise, and a bunch of

other new faces I'll learn the names of eventually, but I can't take my eyes off Harvey's friend. Especially because I keep catching her looking over at *me*. I have the perfect view of her sitting a few tables over with the jocks and jockettes – otherwise known as the sports staff. She sits on the sidelines of their conversation, not contributing much from the looks of things. I've seen beautiful women, but she's in a league of her own. Her chestnut-brown hair is tied back in a high ponytail, and the cutest bangs almost hide her eyes. She's wearing the hell out of a cropped white tee and a short denim skirt. Casual, like she's trying to blend in, but she could never not stand out. Her skin glows with a subtle tan, her pink—

Harvey's huge shoulders block my view, so I take a sip of my Jack and Coke and lean the other way.

As I was saying, her pink, pouted lips look like they could beam the brightest smile, her button nose somehow points up a little when she turns to the side, and I can't see from here, but her arrival is already ingrained in my head, so I know she has long, slender legs and a slim figure. Assuming she's one of the jockettes, she's bound to be toned all over. And she has the most *incredible*—

"So how was your trip?" Harvey interrupts my train of thought.

"Yeah, great, thanks."

What was I—? Oh yeah, her breasts… *Sweet Jesus*, they could bring any guy to his knees. *Damn*. I've always considered myself an ass man, but I. Am. Hypnotised. Nope, *Titnotised.*

"Did you make it to New York?"

I'm reluctantly dragged back into the conversation by Harvey, so I indulge him in the details of my time off even though I'm sure he doesn't care, all the while keeping a less obvious eye on the girl behind him. She's a welcome distraction from the way Harvey's hand is secured to Eliza's thigh, his thumb never letting up from stroking her. It wasn't so long ago that it was my hand on Eliza under the table. How times have changed.

Don't get me wrong, I'm happy for them – meh, happy for her, ambivalent for him – and I don't want anything more than friendship with Eliza, but seeing them together still triggers me slightly. I got used to it, then I disappeared for two months, and now I have to get used to it all over again.

When the jockette walks up to the bar alone, my heart rate as good as triples. *What a woman.* I turn to Jack beside me. "Wanna get a drink?"

He looks at my mostly full glass on the table, smiles, then sweeps his gaze over to the bar. He knows our unspoken code: it's wingman time, no questions asked. But his grin turns into an amused warning as he glances back at me.

"*That…*"—he pauses for emphasis and drops his voice so only I can hear him—"is a *very* stupid idea."

"What? Taken?" It wouldn't be surprising. I'm sure half the guys on this ship are tripping over themselves to ask her out.

"Nope." He looks away from me, pretending to rejoin the conversation around the table. "Just a bad idea."

Hell, if I'm not curious now.

With trouble no doubt written all over my face, I stand despite his advice, and as I knew he would, Jack stands too and accompanies me.

People always talk about the struggles of getting their sea legs, but I had more of a problem rediscovering my land legs. The ship's steady for the most part; after a while you barely notice the mini adjustments you make every day while on board. But when I left the ship, I was all over the place for at least a week. Now I'm back, I feel like I'm finally able to walk straight.

I pick a spot along the bar near enough to her to be able to strike up a conversation naturally, but not so close that I'll encroach on her personal space.

"How's it been?" I ask Jack while we wait to be served.

"Quiet."

I'm on my second six-month contract, and he's on the third month of his first nine-month contract, so he's spent the past seven weeks without me. Though he has other friends, he's not as close with any of them as he is with me.

"I'm sure you found a way to keep things interesting."

Jack's a gentle soul, but he's no stranger to the more…*adventurous* activities ship life has to offer. Neither of us is.

Jack gives a wry smile. "Tiegan's having a few people over tonight."

Temptation warms my blood. Just a flashback to one of the theatre production manager's parties I went to before means I now can't think of a good enough reason to resist. Until I look to my right.

"I'll think about it."

My heart thumps in my chest while I wait for Harvey's friend to order. Do I look okay? Are my palms sweaty? Why am I so nervous? I know how to talk to women. I've hit on more than my fair share in the past. I'm out of practice, that's all.

Quit freaking out and shoot your shot, Parks.

"Hi."

She looks my way, and the blush that spreads over her cheeks, as well as the tiniest smile curling her lips, is positively adorable. "Hi," she says quietly before looking back down at her hands resting on the bar in front of her.

I place a hand on my chest and introduce myself in the hope she'll do the same. "Tom."

"I know who you are." Beautiful *and* British. Man, I guess I've got a type.

Wait – has my internet fame reached the UK? Or… *Shit.* Do I have *history* with her? No, I'd remember. But something about her is strangely familiar. I can't put my finger on what though.

I narrow my eyes as I attempt to figure it out. "Do I know you?"

At that, her slight smile falters and her whole body stiffens. "No."

"You sure? I feel like I know you from somewhere. What's your name?" It's not a line, but it sounds like one.

The bartender hands over her drink. Soda and lime. The only other person I know who willingly drinks that is Harvey.

"I'm sure."

Her words are blunt, I realise. To her, I'm probably another jerk acting like I'm entitled to her attention. She must get this all the time. When she doesn't tell me her name, I let it slide. I consider paying for her drink, but I get the sense it'd make her even more uncomfortable, so I hold back and place an order for the drinks Jack and I don't need.

"Have a good night." I offer her the get-out she must desperately want. For some reason, she looks disappointed, but she collects her drink and heads back over to her table.

Damn. There go all the hopes and dreams I wished up for us in the past hour.

"You've got no game." Jack mocks me once she's out of range.

"Shut up. You know I have game." I compose myself from the mild embarrassment, take our drinks, and head back to the table.

8

"Probably for the best," Jack consoles me.

"What do you mean?"

He settles back in his seat, pretending his focus is no longer on me, but I know it is. He always wants to be aware of his surroundings. "Don't worry about it."

After a little while, we call it a night and go our separate ways. Watching Harvey and Eliza head back to their room together stirs up something I don't want to put a name to, so I unpack quietly while Jack jumps in the shower, grateful he managed to secure us as roommates again. I'm sure the girl in charge of room selections is pretty grateful too, if I have to work out how he got in her favour.

"I thought you were over her," Jack says when I don't bombard him with a million thoughts like I usually do once he's out of the shower.

"I am." And that's God's honest truth. Eliza and I were always better off as friends. Took me a while to work that out, but… I just… I wish I had someone who wanted me the way she wants Harvey.

Jack pauses for thought before picking out a fresh T-shirt and pulling it on over his head. "Sure you're not coming tonight?"

"I said I'd think about it."

And I do think about it. No point pining for a path that isn't mine when there's a much easier route to take. It's been two long months, but now it's time to slip back into the role of ineligible bachelor I play so well. It's way more comfortable than putting myself out there for something more again.

We're the last ones to arrive at Tiegan's, narrowly beating the cut-off point because I took a second to freshen up. Tiegan's a little older than Jack and me, a little wiser too, and she holds officer status on the ship. The title comes with some hefty responsibility, but also a lot of perks. She has her own room a few decks above ours with a double bed and a whole-ass window, not just a porthole, that takes up pretty much the entirety of the back wall – though at 11 p.m. on embarkation day, there's not much to see. Between the bed and the window is a tiny round coffee table and two small armchairs, and by the door she's got a desk like the rest of us. But the real big-ticket item is her sofa bed, which is currently pulled out and made up so there are two double beds side by side. The only available floor space is by the door, at the bottom of the main bed, and in a tiny gap between the two beds.

I acquaint myself with who else made it tonight – mostly familiar faces, but there are a few new ones lit by the fairy lights strung up along both walls – as everyone talks and drinks over the chilled music coming from a speaker. It doesn't take many of us to fill the cabin, but it's not overly crowded. I guess there are almost twenty people in here, give or take, already paired off or mingling in their small groups. This is usually when I feel like a kid in a candy store, but tonight, something's not clicking.

Tiegan welcomes me back to the ship, gives Jack a knowing grin, and locks the door behind us. You can always leave if you need to, but everyone here knows to stay until the night comes to a natural end. And no one can arrive late. You can't relax into an orgy with the door opening and closing every five minutes.

Tiegan's parties are different from the others I've found myself at. Hers are organised and private. The spontaneous parties are the ones you've gotta watch out for. I only made that mistake once. The way people run their mouths after a one-off night like that makes my skin crawl. I might be an outgoing guy, but I like my privacy. And I also like that no one comes here unprepared; there are expectations for how to behave, and everyone respects them. The best thing, though, is that the ladies are in charge. Us guys can't initiate anything – we have to be invited. Everything is a question, never an assumption. Everyone's safe here, and when people feel safe, that's when the real fun can begin.

Before Tiegan can move away from the door, there's a quiet knock. Pleased, she unlocks it, smiles, and says, "I'm glad you could make it."

I have to suppress a gasp as the girl from the bar steps gingerly inside. *It's always the quiet ones.* Jack blows out a slow breath beside me, where we're now perched on the end of the sofa bed.

Tiegan locks the door again and struts towards her spot on the main bed. "You're a brave man, Tom," she muses.

Huh? *Me?* What did *I* do? And what is everyone's problem with this girl? Because whatever it is, no one's been bold enough to say. But what would it change if I asked? I know for a fact she won't be inviting me to play with her this evening. I need to pack my intrigue away and put it to one side.

It's clear the pot's been melting long enough for some indulgence to be a relief, and though I try not to watch, I notice the jockette's eyes popping outta her skull as lust descends upon the room. Why does she look so surprised? Who did she sleep with to be invited here, and why has that person not stepped up to welcome her in? Something's not right. No one comes here unprepared – I'm certain of that. Though I'm growing less and less certain by the second. It could simply be awe and wonder on her face instead of shock and horror. It's not. But I can't bother her again. She wouldn't want me to.

So when Naomi puts her hand on my shoulder and tells me she missed me, I should welcome her offer like I have done several times before, but my gut tells me to hold off a little longer to make sure Miss Innocent is okay. She's backed away, towards the door. Yep, she's not okay. I tell Naomi to carry on without me and get up to escort her out of here.

"Did no one tell you what kind of party this was?"

She shakes her head, unable to tear her eyes off the entanglement of limbs by the window. "I shouldn't be here."

Shouldn't. Interesting choice of word. "Why's that?"

"If people talk…"

"No one will talk. Cone of silence outside of these walls." She should know that, but Tiegan's obviously let her come here completely unprepared, so I catch her up to speed. "Which applies to you too. You can't repeat anything that happens here to anyone."

She gulps, shakes her head, and then finally looks at me with those big blue doe eyes of hers. "But what will people think?"

I don't take offence, because I have a hunch she didn't mean to slut-shame everybody in this room. "*These* people?" I hitch my thumb over my shoulder.

She nods, and I smile.

"It'd be pretty hypocritical of them to judge you, don't you think?"

Her brow crinkles. "I should go."

There it is again. Whenever a person says they "should" do something, it usually means they don't really want to.

"Do you *want* to go?"

She doesn't say no, though I'm not about to take the absence of that word as a yes. "Is that what you're here for?" She avoids the question.

I shrug by way of casual confirmation. Why else would I be here?

"You can go…join in or… Don't let me stop you."

"Is that you asking me to leave you alone, or are you just being polite?"

"Um…"

"You can't be vague in here. It's yes, no, or you go," I say softly, but my meaning is firm. I stay quiet as I watch her take in the rules for a moment. "It's okay to admit that you like it," I whisper, hoping my voice blends in with her thoughts.

"I was being polite," she confirms.

"Do you want to join in?"

"No," she says quickly. "Not tonight. I—"

"It's okay. You don't need an excuse."

"That's why I said you can go. I don't want…" – she looks over at a girl I've not had the pleasure of meeting yet, on her knees, switching her attention between one of the guys from the casino and one of the theatre techs – "to do *that* today."

"But you want to stay?"

"Am I allowed to if I'm not…?"

"I'm not gonna let anyone kick you out."

The tiniest crack of a smile breaks out on her lips. "So when will you—? Who will you—? How—?"

I head towards the now vacant desk and lean against it, patting the empty surface. "Come sit."

"I said I'm not—"

"I know, but if you're not going to come tonight, I at least want you to be comfortable."

She smiles again, and it makes my heart skip.

I decide not to cloud her already busy mind with conversation, so for a little while I let her watch the night unfold. *And I watch her.* I follow her line of vision to work out what her eyes linger on; what she's enjoying. I'm fascinated by her, but also kinda relieved to have her as a distraction. I used to get laid whenever I wanted and with whoever I wanted, for months on end, and then I was cut off for seven weeks. I should be jumping at the chance to blow off some steam, but for some reason, I'm not.

"Why aren't you joining in?" she asks.

"Maybe I don't want you to see me naked," I joke, but her features straighten with realisation, then embarrassment. "I'm kidding. I was on the fence."

The tension in her shoulders loosens again and she goes back to watching. "It's actually kind of beautiful."

I smile. Here I was, wishing I could crawl into her brain to figure her out, but she's already speaking her mind. "What is?"

"Her. Them." She looks at Naomi, who's lying on her side, sandwiched between two guys, kissing the one in front of her while the guy behind her fucks her slowly. I can't say it's not breathtaking, but I'm still happy I'm sitting it out.

"What do you like about it?" Anticipation makes goose bumps race along my skin.

"She looks like she's having fun."

I let out a small laugh. "Yeah, I think she probably is." I can't stop the next question that comes out of my mouth. "Is that what you think about at night?"

Her eyes lock on mine, though I don't miss the way they drop to my lips for a second.

I lower my voice so only she can hear. "Do you want to be shared?"

Contradicting everything I thought about her when she shied away earlier, she gives a tiny nod. *Shit.* There goes any chance I had of not immediately falling for another Brit on the first day again. It's like déjà vu. Fuck, what I'd give to help fulfil this girl's desires.

"What else do you want?" I ask, but after a period of silence, it's clear she's not going to answer. Either because she's too distracted by the various cries of pleasure or because she doesn't know. I'm so curious about her I can't stop myself from saying, "Tell me your secrets."

She turns her attention back to me, our faces inches apart. "You first."

Shoulda seen that coming. I take a deep breath and think of one. "Sometimes, if I see someone I know and I don't wanna talk, I pretend to be my twin brother."

She gasps and smiles. "That's amazing. I wish I was— Actually, it's probably a good thing I'm not a twin." She looks away, horrified, as if imagining a scene playing out in front of her.

"So you're a troublemaker?" I can't take my eyes off her lips.

"Depends on who you ask."

Sweet Jesus, I want to be the one she makes trouble with. "Your turn," I remind her.

She keeps her gaze on the room. "I feel safer here than I've felt anywhere in a long time."

Questions are quick to scramble themselves in my mind. Why doesn't she feel safe anywhere else? Why does she feel safe here? Is it because of me? "Why's that?"

For a moment she loses herself in her thoughts. "I think it's the first time I haven't been the most vulnerable person in the room."

Her answer only offers more questions, but if I'm not careful, I'll risk this becoming an inquisition and then some, because I could – and *would* – start a manhunt for whoever made her feel weak or small or *unsafe*.

I let her words sink in as we turn our attention back to the room. Naomi looks up at the ceiling in bliss, the glitter entwined in her braids shining as she bounces on top of one of her men. My competitive streak should be kicking in. I should want to be over there trying to make her scream even louder than everyone else. And yet I don't have the interest tonight. Not with anyone who isn't the woman beside me. But is she interested in me? At the bar it felt like an obvious no, but the longer we sit here together, the more I'm wondering if we just got off to an awkward start.

"I want another secret."

She looks over at me. "You know the price."

This one will put me out of my misery. She can reject me properly and I'll blow out the torch I'm currently carrying for her. Nerves rattle me, but I decide to say what I have to say anyway. "I know I shouldn't want you, but I do. And if that makes you feel…uncomfortable, you can tell me to—"

"It doesn't."

"It doesn't?"

She shakes her head. "I've fancied you for a very long time."

I laugh in disbelief. She can't mean that. *Can she?* "But you've only just met me."

"I know," she says, matter-of-fact.

"Is that your secret?"

She nods. *Shit*, I think she really does mean it. Her chest rises in shallow breaths, and her gaze drops down to my lips and back up to meet my eye again. It's so tempting to lean in. Her body language is all right, but I need her permission.

"Why haven't you kissed me yet?" she asks.

My grin spreads from ear to ear. "Because you haven't asked. In case you forgot the rules or were never told them in the first place, the ladies are in charge in here. As they always should be. Nothing happens without you requesting it. Also, that's not why I sat with you." Disappointment floods her eyes. "I just need you to know that. I wasn't sitting here waiting for you to want this. I only wanted to keep you company. I didn't have any expectations."

She studies my face for a second, the worry on her brow easing. "I know. Can I have a kiss, please? If you want to give me one."

Jack literally has a girl on his face and another riding his dick, and I'm over here trying not to burst my zipper because the hottest, cutest girl in the world wants me to kiss her.

With my pulse pounding in my ears, I run my thumb over her cheek and her breath hitches. I hold her and lean in slowly at the same time as she does, my lips finding hers, and she gifts me with the softest kiss imaginable. So delicate. So gentle. And finally, everything clicks into place.

I pull back to see her. I need to know if she's as affected by this as I am. Her eyes fill with need, and she reaches for my shirt, lightly pulling me back for more. I move to stand in front of her and plant another careful kiss on her lips, sighing at the relief of it, slowly chancing another and another. She welcomes a flick of my tongue against hers, and I have to fight not to combust with the hit of endorphins that shoots through me. *God, that felt good.* Another flick. *So good.*

She tastes sweet like lemonade, and I can't get enough. Losing ourselves in a crazy-hot make-out session, my hands roam free over her thighs, her body, her hair. I try to take her in, commit her to memory, because I'm scared that after tonight she'll be a thing of my dreams, and I would hate to not know what she feels like. She parts her legs for me to step in between them, and I pull at her thighs to shuffle her towards the edge of the desk. Her hands are on my chest and my waist, keeping me close as our kisses overlap again and again. We're in complete contradiction with the chaos of noise around us.

Does she taste this good all over? I have to know. I pull

back, unlocking her lips from mine, and lean in to kiss her neck only once. "Is this okay?"

"Yes," she moans, and she arches her neck to the side to encourage me.

I want to feast on her, but I hold myself back enough to wind her up, earning me tiny moans right in my ear that go straight to my dick. I could make out with her forever and never get bored.

Her. Are you kidding me? Where are my manners?

"I don't even know your name," I say between kisses.

"Gem— Meg. Megan."

I laugh. "Are you sure?"

"Uh…yeah. Sorry, my thoughts are all…backwards." She shakes her head as if to snap herself out of whatever daze she's in.

I made her forget her own name.

Delight surges through me. Tom and Megan. That has a nice ring to it.

She says my name, and it could easily be a chorus of angels calling out to me with the way it makes me float. Then she says it again, tapping my arm. *Huh?* I ground myself and realise she's trying to turn my attention to the casino guy and his friends, who are offering us their spot on the sofa bed. I look back to Megan, gauging her interest.

"Is that what you'd like?"

She nods nervously but then straightens her shoulders and says, "Yes," like I taught her to.

Heavenly Father, please give me the strength not to embarrass myself.

I take Megan's hand and trade places with the others, setting myself a mental reminder to thank them in my wedding speech. She lingers behind me, her hand tightening a little with what I assume is nerves. Noticing this, instead of lying down – which would be too much too fast – I sit at the back of the couch and invite her to straddle me, which she does with a coy smile. We aren't alone on the bed, but the activities of the others are nothing too obnoxious or potentially intimidating to Megan, I hope.

I cup her face and kiss her once. "We'll go at your pace, okay? Just because everyone else is having sex, it doesn't mean I expect that. You call the shots."

Her eyes swell with what I think is gratitude and she smiles. "Thank you."

"Just being near you feels like winning the lottery."

She hides her grin with her hands and shakes her head as if she doesn't believe me before diving in for another kiss. Her body rocks against mine, and she gasps, leaning back and staring at me with wide, wild eyes. Guess there's no hiding what she's doing to me now.

"Does that feel good?"

"Uh-huh." She nods.

"Good. Then use me."

I pull her into me and snatch her lips with mine. One hand nestles in her hair; the other guides her hips as she moves against me, gradually grinding harder. She breaks the kiss to moan, the noise startling her, and she peers around the room, worry twisting her mouth.

"You're safe in here. No one is judging you."

She takes a breath and lets the reality of my words restore her newfound confidence.

"Gem." I like her backwards name. "I promise this isn't some kind of move, and you can absolutely say no, but do you mind if I take my pants – nope, *trousers* – off? I think I'm gonna get a permanent zipper indent in my dick if not."

She giggles. "Yeah, sure." She gets off the bed so I can undo my zipper and wriggle free.

Ah man, that's better. I go to welcome her back, only to find she's removed her denim skirt and is in the process of lifting her T-shirt off, causing my jaw to drop wide open. She wasn't born; she was *sculpted.* Every muscle of hers has been conditioned and expertly defined, yet there's still a softness to her I can't wait to feel for myself. And *holy shit*, that's a *nice* bra she's got on. And the panties... *Talk about irresistible.*

I go to sit back on the bed, but she asks me to lie down, and once on top of me again, her warmth and wetness instantly soak my boxer briefs. *Damn*, I didn't think this through. I should have kept my pants on. I've gotta figure out a way to pace myself here.

I trace my thumb over the lace of her pink panties. "And you didn't know what kind of party this was?"

She shakes her head, taking a second to understand me. "All my underwear looks like this," she states, shrugging like it's nothing.

She's a girl with expensive taste. *Noted.* Wow, I really need my comedy career to take off, or to earn a pay raise, so I can spoil her *rotten.* I endeavour to kiss every inch of her bare skin as she works her hips on me, but I find myself getting lost in the sway of her breasts.

"Gem, can I—?"

Before I can finish my question, all the while struggling to take my eyes off her chest, she interrupts. "Anything."

This woman will be the death of me.

I don't hurry like I want to. I take great care pulling the lace down, exposing her right breast. My mouth catches it, latching onto her aroused nipple. I look up to check it's not too much, but she whimpers, digs her fingers into my hair, and treats me to a slow and heavy grind of her hips. I can't contain my excitement and release her other breast too, moving my mouth to that one while lightly teasing the other with my fingertips. *Jeez*, they're perfect. All boobs are perfect. But these… These deserve some kind of award.

"I can't believe this is happening." She beams.

"Right back at you."

I kiss her lips – why does it feel like so long since I last did that? – and then pull back to take her in. Where did she come from? And why does she want *me*?

She's more than a little worked up, rolling her hips over me with desperation.

"If you want more, you have to tell me," I remind her.

"Could you try to—?" She looks out at the people all around us – the ones I'd forgotten about – then lowers her voice and says, "Can you *touch* me?" Her eyes flash down briefly.

Try. As in, it hasn't been good before? Is she extra-sensitive? Could it be that vagi-mus-nis-itis-thing? Is it rude to ask? Would she want to explain with other people listening in?

Maybe. Maybe. *Maybe*. Probably. And probably not.

I'm kind of terrified to hurt her, but if that's what she wants, I'll be so damn gentle. "Anything." I repeat her words.

Doing my best not to disturb the couple next to us, I flip us over so she's under me. I think rushing to it would only overwhelm her, so I take my time, caressing her through her panties for so long that she releases her lips from the sweet spot on my neck and reaches for my hand to slip it down the front of the designer lace. *Fuck*. She's soaking-wet for me, and instantly, I know her pussy deserves to have every dollar in the world spent on it.

I stroke her carefully a few times, but she's having none of it.

"*Please,*" she begs. "I need more."

I circle my middle finger around her entrance, carefully

easing in my fingertip. I don't feel any tension or resistance, but I watch her closely to be sure her gasps are from pleasure, not pain. They seem to be, so I push all the way inside. I pull back and slide in again, and she whimpers, her whole face smoothing with relief.

"That okay?"

"Yes."

I curl my finger and stroke her, waiting for the moment she inhales sharply, and then I pulse the tip of my finger against that spot. She's like a stick of dynamite; the fuse has been burning for too long and she's ready to go off. Groaning and writhing against me, she arches her back and tightens around me as she comes. I'm so glad there are other people here to witness this, because her orgasm is my biggest achievement to date. I kiss her neck and her face while she cools down, her body occasionally trembling like waves crashing on the shore.

When she opens her eyes and finds me, she smiles, her breathing still laboured. She takes a second to remind herself where she is, and I look around with her. No one's making too big of a deal, but there are a few smiles aimed in our direction. Jack's smirking like I'm in trouble, and I know he's right. I'm in deep already.

"You like being watched, don't you?"

She bites the corner of her lip. "Yeah, I think I do."

"Did you know that before tonight?"

"I actually thought the complete opposite."

"How does it make you feel?"

"Powerful." I should have guessed that answer – it's radiating off her.

"Damn right." I kiss her, so impressed with the one-eighty she's done since the start of the evening. "You want to show everyone how much you like having me inside you again?"

The biggest grin spreads across her face. "Yes, please."

"So polite. Think you can handle two fingers?"

She nods eagerly, and I slip a second finger inside of her, still keeping an eye on her reactions, but she seems comfortable, so I build her up again, her body melting into the bed, lazily accepting my kisses. When I increase my pressure and speed up, yeses cascade from her lips before she completely breaks, unable to speak or even breathe. Her pussy squeezes my fingers tight as she loses herself in silent ecstasy.

She collapses back against the pillow and tries to recover. "I did not see my night going this way," she jokes.

I laugh with her, but something clenches my stomach. I can't help but feel like I've taken advantage somehow.

"I want more," she continues.

"Yeah? Describe more."

She grazes her fingers along the waistband of my boxers. "I think I want to have sex with you."

Oh man. I could jump at the chance if the word "think" wasn't in there and if I wasn't already questioning my ethics. I bide my time by kissing her neck. She didn't know what she was getting into; she's gotten caught up in a wild night of spontaneity; she was terrified and now she's got the lust-bug. She doesn't strike me as the type of person who goes into sex lightly. Has she had casual sex before? Do *I* want casual sex anymore? I might have come here willingly, but I was anything other than excited to be here when I arrived.

"Tom?"

"I don't think we should." I watch as the rejection lands on her face and act quickly to explain myself. "I just… I'm worried I've worn you down, and I really, *really* need you to know that when I came over to you, all I wanted to do was make sure you were okay."

"It's okay. I believe you."

"And I'm scared there's a chance you could wake up tomorrow and regret this."

"Will *you* regret this?"

I shake my head, carefully considering my next words to make sure they won't get misconstrued. "I would regret rushing this." I kiss her once to make extra-sure she knows I still want her. "Also, I think I'd be lucky to even last thirty seconds at this point, so…"

She giggles at my confession, and my concern eases a little.

"Can we keep kissing though?" she asks.

"Yeah. I'd like that."

TWO

TOM

I can't sleep. It's five-something a.m. and I've been lying here trying to calm myself down since two-something a.m. but it's not working. I don't have anything on until this afternoon, so at 6 a.m. I give up completely and sneak out to the gym in the hope some exercise will clear my head and tire me out.

I've been thinking about it for a while, but only last night did I believe it. I don't want to fuck around anymore. I want more from my interactions with the opposite sex. I want more for myself. I wasn't ready for a relationship before. I would have been a terrible boyfriend for Eliza. I had some healing and growing up to do, and now I've come back feeling like something's different. Like *I'm* different. I've evolved. I'm not the hothead I used to be, and I've got therapy to thank for that. Bobby started the moment Dad died, Mom a little bit before, but with my psych studies behind me, I thought I was above it; thought I was immune from needing help. In reality, I was too close to my problems to even see they were there. Or, maybe more truthfully, I chose not to see them.

"Could I take you out sometime, like for coffee or a smoothie or something?"

Yeah. That's good. I've been spitballing ideas of what to say to Megan when I see her today so I'll have something ready to go. Failing to prepare is preparing to fail. Has she been as restless as I've been, or was she out like a light after the night we had? I wanted to go back to hers, snuggle up with her and stroke her hair until she fell asleep. I wanna be the kind of guy who takes care of his girl. I want her to want me to be her guy. Or does she already?

"I've fancied you for a very long time."

That *was* a joke, wasn't it? A cute thing she said in the moment. I can't see how else she'd know me. Unless my viral video really did worm its way into her algorithm.

Not a euphemism.

Thirty minutes down and I'm still not tired. In fact, I seem to gain more energy every time I think about Megan. But then my happy bubble pops when Harvey enters the gym. I'm surprised he'd rather be here than curled up in bed with Eliza.

Fuck. How did I forget about whatever mysterious ties Megan has with him? I know how, but...

"Up early, or did you never go to bed?" he asks with a mischievous look.

"I went to bed." *Eventually.*

His lips form a tight, patronising smile as if he doesn't believe me. I mean, he'd be right not to, but fuck him for being so quick to judge.

"What?" I challenge him.

He arches a brow and glances down at my neck. "You might need to get creative with how you cover that up."

I wipe my neck, not sure what he means, but when he smirks and shakes his head, I step over to the back wall to inspect myself in the mirror. Ohhh, *that's* why he was so cocky: Megan gave me a hickey. I head back over to my "boss", who's giving me a side-eye as if to say, "Already?" Yeah, okay, it's not a great look, but I can't find it in myself to be mad at her. She's marked her territory, and now I'm even more excited to see her again so I can mark mine.

I jump on the shoulder press opposite Harvey and keep going with my routine. "What's got *you* up so early?"

"Couldn't fall back to sleep."

"Something on your mind?"

"There's just been a lot going on lately."

It's only then I really register the state of him. He looks…*tired*. And maybe not from the early start. Thinking back, he was a little withdrawn last night.

"Everything all right?" Worry unnerves me – not just because I'm suddenly concerned Eliza's tangled up in whatever's bothering him, but because I'm concerned for him too, which I didn't see coming. It's as if I'm feeling the weight on his shoulders simply by looking at him. "You and Eliza still good? Not liking the job?"

"Oh, yeah, no, all fine on those fronts. It's…" He finishes his last rep and exhales. "Family stuff."

"You wanna talk about it?"

He takes a sip of water and then takes a few tries to get his words out. "Actually, I came here to *not* think about it for five minutes, if that's okay?"

"Yeah, man, no problem. But I'm here if you ever wanna talk." See? *Evolved.*

"How's internet fame?"

I shrug and move over to the leg press. "Fizzling out."

"Oh. I thought things were going well?"

"Yeah, they are, I guess, but I'm here now, not gigging, so it's not like I'm gonna have anything to post for the next six months." It's unfortunate, because I found a way to help people like I always wanted to, but on a way bigger scale. It's fine though. Stand-up and TikTok will be there waiting for me when I finish this contract.

"Have you considered any other kinds of content?"

"Nah, I wouldn't even know where to start." I've never been a social media person, always preferring to live in the moment than tell everyone about it. Then I had everything going on with Dad, and the last thing I wanted was to be glued to my phone.

"You should speak to my sister."

"You have a *sister*?"

He laughs. "Yep."

Huh, I never knew that. Or maybe never listened if he mentioned her before. "How come?"

"She…just knows what she's doing where all that's concerned."

A conversation couldn't hurt, I guess. It might not work, but it could be worth a try. "Yeah, okay. Thanks. I'd appreciate that."

I stick around after my workout to keep him company through his, and then we make our way below deck together.

"Oh! There she is," he chimes.

"Who?"

Like the mirage she is, I spot Megan down the hall. Excitement thrums through me until I realise whose door she's waiting outside of. *His*. What the hell is she doing near his *bedroom*?

"My sister."

Oh no.

"Sorry. Give me five minutes to shower and we'll go," he says to her.

Oh no, no, no, no, no.

Megan's eyes dart between me and her *brother*. I should

have known she couldn't be one hundred percent perfect. Something had to give. Of course she's a *Harvey*.

"This is Tom."

"Oh yeah, from the photo stream. Hi." She gives a curt wave.

Photo stream? I look between them and finally see the resemblance. I *knew* there was something familiar about her.

"Hi." I put on my most casual front, acting like I didn't have my hand down her panties only a few hours ago.

"Tom's trying to come up with ideas for TikTok content. Thought you might be able to help him." Harvey taps his key card on the sensor to his big-boy cabin. "I'll be quick, promise." Before he goes, he takes one look back at me, his eyes dropping down to my neck. "I'll see if Eliza has some concealer you can borrow."

The crash of the heavy door swinging shut wakes us both up from this nightmare. I move us away from the door so there's no chance of Harvey hearing us through it.

"Gem. *Megan.* I— If I had—" *Fuck!* "He can never find out about last night," I say as quietly as possible.

Megan shakes her head with gut-wrenching fear in her eyes. "Never."

I'm on his photo stream. I heard him mention it once or twice before, but I never would have connected the dots. So she knew who I was last night? She knew the drama this could cause, and she still went along with it?

"You shoulda told me."

"You didn't know?" Her brow twists in confusion. "I thought someone would have told you. And you said you shouldn't... How did you *not* know? Everyone knows and I've never told a soul."

It all makes sense now. Jack and Tiegan's comments, why no one would greet her at the party... They all know who she's related to and didn't fancy losing their jobs over her.

"If I did, don't you think I woulda got you outta there?"

She looks down at the ground. "I'm so sorry," she mumbles, practically drowning in shame and guilt. Suddenly, I hear my words back and I hate myself. Who the fuck am I to make her feel bad for going to a sex party? "I just wanted one night without Oscar watching over me."

My whole soul deflates. She's come here for whatever reason and now she's stuck hiding in his shadow. If anyone understands what that's like, it's me. She's her own person, not some boring clone of his – why shouldn't she be allowed to have her fun? I see now how easy it is to fall into the same pattern everyone else used to with me and Bobby.

"Hey, it's okay." I take her hand, and she looks up at me with scared puppy-dog eyes. "We got carried away together. It'll be our secret."

She relaxes at that.

"But it can't happen again."

She shakes her head in agreement.

"Besides, we didn't do anything. Not really, if you think about it."

She swallows. "Yeah. It was no big deal." She lets go of my hand.

I'm already grieving all the dates we'll never get to go on, all the mornings we won't get to have, all the orgasms I'll never get to give her… I've made a real point to work on my friendship with Harvey, and I'm pretty sure messing around with his sister would ruin all of that.

I look back over my shoulder to make sure the coast is still clear. "Are you okay?"

"Yeah. Um, thank you for not…uh…letting things escalate last night."

I frown. "I'm sad you feel the need to thank me for that." *Which pushy asshole have I gotta punch around here? Say the word and I'll deal with them.*

"You were right. I would have regretted it," she says earnestly, and it makes my heart sink with panic.

"Do you regret anything we *did* do?"

"Oh, no. I mean with this whole…*thing*—"

The door opens and Harvey appears in nothing but a towel. *Ew.* He waves a shiny stick of something in the air, which I take from him, before he shuts himself away again.

"What do you need concealer for?" Megan asks.

I turn my head to the side to reveal the mark she left behind.

Her eyes widen. "I'm so sorry!"

"Don't sweat it."

When I realise the silence is only going to grow more uncomfortable, I make a move. "Guess I'll see you around."

We part ways, and I traipse back to my cabin for a shower. Jack's getting ready when I arrive. All it takes is one look my way for him to understand my mood.

"You worked it out then?"

I only have it in me to glare at him.

"I told you it was a stupid idea."

"Would it have *killed you* to be more specific?"

THREE

GEMMA

I came here to escape how awful it is to be me, but instead I've become a whole new type of public outcast. My brother's some big cheese around here, and I'm like a Babybel that's been forgotten at the back of the fridge. I love Oscar, and I owe him *everything* for helping me to get this job, and so quickly too. But…I thought I was coming on board to hide, and more importantly, for a fresh start. New hair. New name. New career. My plan was to blend in with every other crew member, have no notable quirks or backstory, and simply coast through the next six months as plain old unsuspecting *Megan*. And then he went and made it abundantly clear we're related. I get it. He thought it would give me some kind of "in," but so far, it's only given everyone a reason to push me out. No one seems to be able to relax around me, as if they think I'll report any bad behaviour straight to the top. Even my mentor, Matt, who I'm *convinced* would chat up his own reflection given half the chance, wants nothing to do with me.

I guess I can't really complain though. Beggars can't be choosers and whatnot. I have to take any opportunity for normalcy I can get, because that's the reality of my situation now. At least here I'm safe – and distracted – which is more than can be said for being back home. And while I may be unhappy with how this escape has panned out, no one recognises me. Most of the passengers are American, and whatever crew that are on here from the UK haven't had access to national television since I was stupid enough to feature on it, so that's something.

Eliza holds my brother's hand ahead of me as we walk along the beach, two of her steps matching one of his. There was talk of Tom tagging along today, but it's ended up only being the three of us, and I'm a weird mix of relieved and disappointed. Relieved because even though it's been two weeks since we met, I still can't stop my cheeks from flushing at the sight of him or the mention of his name, and I'm terrified of someone catching on to what happened between us. And disappointed because I have this *stupidly* enormous crush on him – have done ever since he started appearing on Oscar's photo stream – and I want to spend time with him.

He's the hottest guy I've ever laid eyes on – even more so in person. And his *personality*? His *charisma*? It's extraordinary, and something you rarely come across in British guys – on that level anyway. And his accent… *That accent…* Talk about *sexy*. He's like one of the hot Disney Channel actors I used to fancy as a girl. I've been on the receiving end of plenty of parasocial relationships before, but I never thought I'd be unhinged enough to fall into one myself. *And then I met him.* And it was like every fantasy come to life – besides the room full of people having sex. Though that wasn't the vibe killer it should have been…

I completely mistimed my "you need to let me make my own connections" speech to Oscar, because the day after I gave it, Tom arrived, and when I tried to back out of spending time with my colleagues, Oscar brought it up again and I lost my chance at a natural introduction. I couldn't exactly explain to my brother why I was suddenly so keen to sit at his table after complaining about it less than twenty-four hours earlier. He'd have a meltdown if he knew the fantasies I've concocted about his friend. That and I'm stubborn. Then my nerves and paranoia completely ruined mine and Tom's eventual meet-cute and I was desperate for a do-over. I was terrified I'd been spotted, and I couldn't think rationally, but after some reflection, I assumed he must have recognised the family resemblance, not the face of the most hated woman in the UK. Cue the most out-of-character sequence of events ever: tracking down one of Oscar and Eliza's friends I'd only met once, accidentally inviting myself to her sex party by lying about who invited me (Tom), then actively – and more than willingly – engaging in foreplay with the guy I've been fangirling over since last September. Gemma would *never* do anything of the sort, but Megan? She lives on the edge, and I like it.

Lord, maybe I really am as crazy as people think. I've created an alter-ego I actually prefer. Oh no. What if Gemma feels like she's being replaced and starts acting out? I've never read Jekyll and Hyde, but I'm pretty sure it doesn't end well.

We're not too far down the beach when a hand slips into mine. Not just anyone's hand – *Tom's*. I tense and check that my brother and Eliza, now a few steps ahead, aren't looking our way. *What happened to us pretending we aren't romantically involved?* When I try to pull away, Tom doesn't let me; instead he's in a standoff with a group of neanderthal lowlifes on sun loungers beside us, who are laughing among one another and leering at me. Yes, I noticed them, but once I realised they didn't know who I was – they would have their phones out if they did – I went back to doing what I always do with catcallers and unwanted attention: I ignored it.

"I have watched every head on this beach turn for you," Tom informs me once the creeps are behind us, his voice low and…possessive?

And with one sentence he so easily undoes all the hard work I put into convincing myself we don't have a future.

Don't blush. Don't swoon. Don't freak out.

The day I realised I was pretty, I discovered what my value was. I could be smarter than everyone in my school year, the captain of every sports team, but my looks were the only thing people ever commented on. The attention I got was always for the way my blouse fit tighter than the other girls', or because I had "blow job lips," or because my skirt looked shorter than everyone else's due to my never-ending growth spurts. It wasn't until I had to start thinking about further education that I realised, ironically, the smartest thing I could do to be successful was to use my looks. Within a year, I was earning more money in a month through sportswear brand deals alone than my classmates would earn in their future graduate jobs, alongside running a successful charity.

"You should probably let go." I make a point of glancing over at my brother.

Tom's protective hand slips from mine, and he holds both up like he's under arrest. "Yep, sorry. Just wanted those assholes to stop staring."

Before I'm left alone with my thoughts for too long, we arrive at Oscar's favourite ice-cream place. Tom makes a beeline for the glass counter, forgetting me behind him, and I can't hide my smile. I've met the man, but today I'm seeing the boy.

They've got the quirkiest selection of flavours: Jamaican

rum cake, s'mores, and coconut plantain. Then there are sorbets: pink lemonade and Ting, which piques my interest. My mouth salivates, and just as I think I might be brave enough to get one, I remember why I can't. It'd be bad enough getting recognised, but getting recognised *pigging out on ice cream*? I'd be crucified.

The shop owner with grey curls and smile lines hands Tom a cup overflowing with pink lemonade sorbet before sticking a colourful spoon into the side of the slush. Eliza gets a cone of piña colada-flavoured ice cream, and Oscar one of candy floss. He throws a hopeful, supportive look my way while the other two are distracted, but I shake my head.

"Wait up – Megan hasn't ordered hers yet!" Tom calls to the others as we head out of the shop and back onto the beach.

I wave him off. "Oh, no, I'm fine."

We continue our walk, but Tom takes a few seconds before following. "Are you lactose intolerant?"

"No." I shrug casually even as awkwardness claws at my insides.

"You know they'd offer you a sample to help you pick which one to get. Wanna try some of mine?" He uses his spoon to point at his pot.

Yes.

"Nah, I'm good. Thank you though."

"How's your plan for world domination coming along?" Oscar steals Tom's attention.

Tom shrugs. "Meh, I gave up. I'm not savvy enough to keep up with all that."

"Megan's advice didn't get you anywhere?"

Ah, I forgot I was supposed to have helped him. Though, if I'm completely honest, I'm relieved he didn't bring it up. The last thing I ever want to see again is a social media app.

"I'm way past saving. Wasn't gonna waste your time." Tom covers for us, and gratitude warms me. He's going for casual, but there's a tinge of defeat in his eyes.

Nothing he could ask of me would be a waste of my time. I might find it triggering, but if I could save his page and subsequently make him happy, I'd do it in a heartbeat, even if it would be to my detriment.

"What's your niche?" I ask.

"My *what*?"

"Your niche. Your specialty."

"Oh, my *nitch*."

"You're saying that wrong, but yes, your *nitch*. You're a comedian, right?" I ask as if I don't absolutely know the answer to that already.

He sucks on his spoon, and I cannot take my eyes off his lips. "Mm-hmm." He finishes his mouthful. "I was posting clips from my sets. Which I can't exactly do now."

"Maybe not, though there's nothing stopping you from reposting the content that works every now and then. But also, there are so many other ways to make comedy content without gigging."

"Yeah?"

I've spent years watching others try and fail to become vloggers, all of them making the same mistakes. They film and edit some great material but then completely give up when it comes to getting their videos in front of the right people. Why bother putting in all that time and effort if you're not going to do it properly? It's like a chef making a five-star meal and throwing it at the wall.

"You've just got to work with what you have. You have one of the most unique lifestyles in the world, which means you've got something over everyone else trying to film day-in-the-life videos simply by being here, so use that. People back home have to film themselves *opening their curtains* and *brushing their teeth* as if that's some groundbreaking event that needs to be publicised. Take a look around you – what's there not to show off about?"

Instead of shifting his focus to our surroundings with a new appreciation like I thought he would, he stares at me in horror. "You want me to start a *vlog*? What about the comedy?"

"Not a vlog necessarily. But like, film little bits of your day, edit them together, and record a comedic voice-over once you're done. So yes, I guess that's a vlog, but you do it your way. Tailor it to your ideal demographic. Do you know the best time of day to post for your audience?"

Tom shakes his head as if I'm speaking in tongues.

"That's okay. We can figure it out. How long have you been posting for?"

He looks up thoughtfully as he does some time-math in his head. "Six…ish weeks, I think. Before I gave up."

"Oh wow, not long. There should be some stats to look over though. If you're up for it, I can take a look at some good hashtags for you too, and then—"

"Are you some kind of influencer?"

It dawns on me suddenly how utterly idiotic I've been. I was meant to be keeping my cards close to my chest, and here I am, giving him more than a peek at my hand. I have no choice but to lie.

"No. I, uh…just used to run the social media accounts for one." Technically true. Jekyll would probably speak of Hyde as if he were an entirely separate person too… "How many followers do you have?" I put the attention back onto him.

"Just over ten thousand," Tom reveals, and I'm taken aback. It's hard to get to *one* thousand in a couple of *months*, let alone *ten* in only *weeks*. "I had a head start," he clarifies. "How about you, on the accounts you were running?"

"I can't actually remember…"

"Combined, 1.5," Oscar inserts, turning around with that "proud big brother" smile on his face. He's been trying to build my confidence back up ever since the event that knocked it all down, and that's great and all, but could I not have kept it vague? Also, I could have done without the "point five" reminder. I had one million when I went on that show. Why couldn't that have been enough for me? Gaining 500 *thousand* followers in five weeks is only a good thing if they like you.

"Thousand? Nice." Tom nods as if he's happy for me, but I can tell he's dismissing all my advice. If he doesn't see me as credible, he won't try what I've suggested, and then he'll always feel a little bit downtrodden. And he shouldn't ever not have a smile on his face.

There's also a *teeny-tiny* part of me that's desperate to impress him.

"Million." I correct him.

Tom chokes on his sorbet. "Holy shit! Are you serious?"

I don't miss the fact he doesn't look to the others for clarification. He's only looking at me, ready to take me at my word. For some stupid reason, it makes me emotional. I've spent the past month being gaslit, having my words twisted and used to turn my followers against me, so I could be portrayed as someone I'm not by a whole team of TV executives. *And the entire country believed them.* Yet Tom's here admiring me as if there isn't a single chance I'm not telling the truth.

Bloody hell, I need therapy.

"That's insane! Damn, I shoulda been taking notes. Okay,

so I film little clips throughout the day, edit them, make some jokes over the top, and then post it."

"No, then come to *me* and I'll make sure you post it the right way."

He nods seriously, then he grins again. "Thank you so much. Whoa, okay, this feels manageable." He glows for a moment and then dulls. "My Wi-Fi bill's gonna be huge."

The downside of having one of the most unique lifestyles in the world.

"I mean, if you haven't posted for a while already, I think there's no harm in taking this next week to film as much as you can. Then we can get you a scheduling app and upload everything for the coming week at a café, ahead of time."

"Yes, ma'am."

He takes a spoonful of sorbet, his eyes closing as he takes a second to really enjoy it. Is that the same face he'd make if I touched him?

Why didn't I touch him?

"Ice creams in, everyone!" I shout. I get my phone set up ready to record, then I hand it over to Tom. I look over his shoulder and direct them all to hold up their ice creams – or what's left of them – with the ocean as the backdrop. Five seconds or so is all he needs, one lap of the waves on the shore, and that's it. "It's as easy as that."

His eyebrows rise. "Seriously?"

"Seriously."

Oscar takes Eliza's hand again, and they walk ahead of us. Tom finishes the rest of his sorbet in cheerful silence beside me.

"How can you not like ice cream?" He can't seem to drop it.

"I never said I didn't like it."

"So why—?"

"I can't eat sugar."

All Tom does is blink. "What? How? *Why?* Is that a *medical condition*? Nope, that's a rude question... I take it back, sorry."

I chuckle. "No, not a medical condition. I just...try not to have it."

"But everything's okay in moderation."

I believe that too, but after they set me up as some junk food-hating lunatic on that show, I can't take the risk of eating it anymore – not in public, at least. "Except Brussels sprouts. Those are never okay," I deflect.

A giggle bursts out of Tom. "Okay, yeah, except Brussels sprouts. But imagine if all that delicious ice cream back there was sugar-free – what flavour would you pick?"

"Why does it matter?"

"Because I can tell a lot about a person based on their favourite ice cream flavour."

"What a load of twaddle." I call him out.

"*All right*, all right, I'm just curious!"

"S'mores," I say, having considered it at length in the shop.

He smirks at me. "Didn't have you down as a campfire girl. You ever had real s'mores?"

"Once, on a school camping trip. They made so much mess, but they were *delicious*." Oh, to be that girl again...

We reach the end of the beach and begin to walk back on ourselves. Halfway home, Tom jogs ahead and draws a line in the sand, insisting we race to the big palm tree maybe four hundred metres away. Eliza's up for it straight away, Oscar talks Tom down from adding any kind of stakes, and I don't waste time with smack talk because I know I'm going to win.

"On your marks..." Tom calls out, crouching down,

pretending he's a sprinter. "Get set…" He sticks his bum in the air. "Go!"

We launch ourselves over the starting line, kicking up sand behind us. My brother's all strength and no speed. Eliza hates running, only ever exercising to keep fit but never to train. Regardless, she squeals as she tries to keep up with Oscar. And Tom is like a Jelly Baby, one happy ball of energy, the sugar rush from the ice cream evident as he flies ahead of the others. The thing none of them have, though, is the combination of my speed and stamina. Tom begins to crash and burn, and he keeps trying to push through, but I'm way out in front and he knows he can't catch up. I make it to the palm tree with enough time to pull out my phone and film the rest of them crossing the "finish line".

Everything's an opportunity to make content.

"Damn, you've got some speed on you, Gem."

Gem. I want nothing more than for him to call me that, but I can't risk him being overheard. "You know it's Megan, right?" I say as casually as I can.

"I know." He smiles to himself.

We catch our breaths and continue on. Eliza and I chat for a while, and when I look back, Tom's nowhere to be seen. I scan the area, noticing the ice-cream shop, and inside, Tom's back at the counter laughing with the owner about something. It's so endearing how happy he is all the time, and how happy he makes everyone else around him.

I slow down so he can catch up when he's ready to, but then he calls out to me.

"Megan! Come take a video of this!"

He's getting the hang of it already.

Eliza and Oscar carry on as I go find Tom. The owner watches my arrival, reaches for a mini spoon from a pot on top of the counter, and dips it into a metal tub behind the glass, handing it to Tom.

"What am I filming?" I put my hand out for his phone.

"Oh, nothing. That was just to get you in here."

"Huh?"

"Okay, so you're *forcing* me to vlog."

"*Forcing* you?"

"Shh, okay, encouraging. Which means I get to *encourage* you to have a little bit of sugar. Some would even say a moderate amount." There's that boyish grin again. He holds out the taster scoop for me. Mini toasted marshmallows and small chunks of biscuit stick out of the chocolate ice cream, and my tongue starts to feel like it's dripping.

I look around the shop full of couples, friends, and families enjoying their sundaes. Safe enough, if you're fine with playing fast and loose with your reputation. But if any of these people see through my disguise, or if they take a picture that later gets uploaded onto their socials and *someone else* sees me in the background, I'm *screwed*.

"What's the worst thing that's gonna happen?"

I could quite literally list a million consequences. I can't handle more public shaming than I've already faced.

"What will people think?" I mumble.

Fraud. Sham. Liar.

Worry mars Tom's face. "What people?" he asks gently.

"I shouldn't."

His worry melts away and is replaced by something else. "No one's watching you."

I scan the room again. He's right. I know he is. But then I look at the owner, confused but with a warm, grandfatherly smile on his lips.

"Jamal, please close your eyes," Tom requests.

Jamal's smile grows, and he does.

Tom leans in closer to me. "Sometimes it's fun to do the things you shouldn't." His voice is so low it rumbles through me, awakening the part of me that wants to take risks around him. The part that feels safe enough in his presence that I can.

I take the spoon and Tom closes his eyes tight. With the spoon in my mouth, my own eyes close as the taste I've been craving hits the spot. It tastes so delicious I actually moan. When I swallow and open my eyes, Tom's peeking at me, his mouth agape.

"Good?"

All I can do is nod like some ice cream-drunk fool. He and Jamal laugh softly.

"Can we get a taster of pink lemonade too, please?" Tom flashes a cheeky smile at Jamal, and he gladly obliges.

"Oh, no, Tom, I can't. Please—"

"Relax. This one's for me." He sucks the spoon into his mouth, pulling it out from his lips so slowly it's like he's filming some kind of erotic advert, and it makes my pulse deepen a little.

He leaves a note in Jamal's tip jar and floats out of the shop.

"I'll see you next week, my friends," Jamal says after us.

"Yes, you will," Tom confirms over his shoulder, his smile about ready to burst his cheeks.

FOUR

TOM

Megan's been tip-tapping away at some search engine Optimus Prime thingy on her phone since we got here, while I've been double-checking my seven videos are ready to upload. As a thank-you, I got her a smoothie, but she didn't pick some tasty tropical thing like I did – she got *the forbidden green juice*. While mine is made with pineapples and bananas, hers has vegetables and *demons* in it. God knows how, but she doesn't even wince when she drinks it. Who is this sugar-free sadist I'm obsessed with?

I've installed some app that I can program to upload my videos to the right place at the right time with all the captions and hashtags ready to go. It was a couple of dollars, but that's nothing compared to my internet bill if I bought a Wi-Fi pass every day.

"Okay, let's see what you've got."

I'm so excited to show her my videos. I've already learnt what not to do from putting my previous videos up, and even though this new style is alien to me, I think I've nailed it. I've never bothered to do the algorithm-hacking stuff properly before. I mean, I've seen videos of those overenthusiastic social-media gurus telling you the basics: use hashtags, but not too many; write a caption; ask a question; blah blah blah. I've followed those few steps, but anything past that is too much for my brain to handle.

I eagerly study her expression, but she gives nothing away. She'd smile if she liked it, right? *Aw, shit.* I wait another agonising minute before stopping her from watching any more.

"They suck, don't they?"

"They'll be fine." She gives me a placating smile, the disappointment behind it more than obvious.

"I don't want them to be *fine* – I want them to be perfect! What did I do wrong?"

"They're funny, and you know how to hold a camera and edit stuff. You made some good choices with the music. But the actual footage… It's… People will enjoy it, but no one will remember it."

"Cor, don't beat around the bush."

"Why are you talking like you're in 'Mary Poppins'?"

"Something Eliza says."

She bobs her head as if she's saying to herself, "Yeah, that tracks." "Sorry…but other than the clip of you guys running, you're not in any of them. To the people who don't already follow you, they could think this is Oscar's page."

I'm going to drown myself in the sea.

"I don't think you realise *you're* what people really watch the videos for. Ship life, absolutely, but they want to see you living it."

"Are you saying I'm nice to look at?" I flirt.

She blushes, but her smile matches mine. "Sure." Yeah, she's trying not to give anything away, but she's a terrible liar. "Also, the algorithm likes faces."

I sigh, dragging a hand over my stupid face as I sink into my chair.

"Okay, so let me send you these captions, and then we can get uploading to—"

"Wait – we're not gonna scrap all this and start again next week?"

"No point letting it go to waste. Like I said, it's not *bad*, it just isn't groundbreaking. Consider this part of your landing page."

"My *what*?"

She pauses, realising she needs to dumb it down for me. "When a future video takes off, people will go to your profile to see what else you've posted, so having a backlist of stuff to watch is always useful."

Okay, it makes me feel a little better knowing it's not been a *complete* waste of time.

"One more thing though."

I hold my breath, waiting for the blow.

"You can't tell people to like the video to help you. No one ever wants to help you – not unless it helps them."

"That's what Youtubers do."

"Yeah, and how many of them wake up one day to a million views? Sure, different platform, different viewing style, but growth over there is slow because it means something different. On TikTok, it can happen in the blink of an eye, and you need to be ready for it."

The reality of that scares me a little. I've already seen firsthand how sudden it can be, and that was when I *wasn't* in the driver's seat.

After some more masterminding on Megan's part, we upload all my crappy videos, along with her certified-to-succeed captions and hashtags. As we go, she talks me through each step so I can do it all by myself in the future.

But then it hits me. If she teaches me how to do all this, I'll lose my excuse to hang out with her alone. And I can't let that happen.

Well-intentioned weaponised incompetence: *on*.

What does that button say? "Privacy – Only me." *Click.* "Schedule posts for 1 a.m." *Click.* "Cancel upload?" *Cli—*

"Maybe I should do this bit."

I'm pretty sure us toxic boys are supposed to refuse to admit we're wrong…

"No, no, I got it."

"You don't. Hand it over."

It's like getting in trouble with the hot substitute teacher. I'm both intimidated and a little turned-on. She finishes the upload for me while I daydream about the sound she made when she tried that ice cream last week. *Crap*, now I'm sporting a semi again.

"All done. Can you show me your schedule? I'll try to film some bits for you when I can."

"I'll show you mine if you show me yours."

I will never get bored of the way her cheeks pinken when I hit on her.

She snaps a picture of my schedule, then she goes to some other app and hands her phone over. *What is it with this girl and all these organisation apps? Whoa* – everything's colour-coded and planned to the minute, including her free time. *She makes free time an appointment.* Yep, she's definitely a Harvey. All work and no play. I wonder what would happen if something didn't go according to her diary. She's even got this little meet-up in there, which apparently ends in five minutes. And here I was, hoping for more time.

"What does orange mean?" I notice it's mostly in the evenings, all staff activities and events from the looks of things.

"Things I don't want to do but probably should."

Oh. That makes me sad, and I spiral with all the reasons why. "But these are all fun things. Why wouldn't you want to do them?"

She takes a deep breath. "I'm not a particularly sociable person anymore."

I don't miss how quiet that last word is.

"And what's the colour for things you want to do?"

"Blue."

I tap the staff volleyball tournament tonight and change its colour from orange to blue. I figure she'll at least put up a fight, but she sits back and lets me tamper with it.

"Now you have to come, because I'm going, and I need you to film me."

I refuse to lose. It's almost midnight and we're busting our asses to win the second semi-final against "the Shoppies". My wrists are red-raw and stinging, but we have to win this match if we want a chance to knock the sports staff off their perch. We only need to keep our lead for a minute or so longer, and then it's ours.

All the departments who've been knocked out already have stayed to spectate and cheer on anyone who isn't a jock. It's a good thing the guests aren't allowed out this way tonight, because it's getting *rowdy*. Where the sports staff have succeeded by using real skill and athleticism, we on the entertainment team have succeeded on our energy levels alone. We're used to giving our all to fast-paced activities – something that can't be said for the zen, gentle-natured spa girls who were never going to get this far in the tournament.

We almost have it when a Shoppies' serve doesn't get the

power it needs, but then one of the guys manages to dig it out for his teammate to spike it over the net to us. Cora, who's brand-new to the entertainment team this week, is light on her feet and gets to the ball impossibly fast, but we're all caught off-guard, not as ready as we should be for the assist, because we didn't think it'd get onto our side. Sunshine makes an insane dive to save us when the ball almost hits the sand, and I'm right there next to her, smacking it high for her buddy Finn to jump and ground it on the other side *just* as the whistle blows.

Yes! We did it!

We all bask in the glory for a moment, then we take five to catch our breaths before the final round, and I go find my sexy PR manager-turned-rival as she heads over to the water station.

"If I win…" I begin, and her attention turns to me as mine turns to the drops of water on her lips. I wasn't that thirsty when I came over here, but now I'm *parched*. "You have to let me take you out sometime."

She tries to suppress her grin. "What about my brother finding out?"

I know it's against Bro Code, but I can't shake the feeling there's something here worth exploring. "Then we tell him it's for TikTok, like we did earlier today," I reply and take a sip from my cup to quench my sudden thirst.

She bites down on her lip, but her smile shines through regardless. "Okay."

"And what would you want *if* – and that's a big 'if' – you win?"

She takes a second to consider it, her eyes scanning my body, and suddenly I'm very excited about where her thoughts are running off to. "One more secret?"

She says it so sweetly, but the meaning behind her request

is nothing but dirty. *Oh fuck.* I don't know what I was expecting her to say, but it wasn't that. Every fibre in my being tingles at the thought of having her against me, moaning my name.

"Deal."

A mischievous grin twists her lips. "May the best player win."

I'm trying my hardest to throw this thing, but everyone around me, now with the chance of beating the sports staff at their own game, is suddenly giving an Olympic medal-worthy performance. Jack's filming from the sidelines, and right now he's capturing nothing but evidence of me failing to rig this game. What also isn't playing into my favour is that the jocks who've subbed in keep getting distracted by the view of their own teammates in front of them.

Pigs.

As if I'm not also guilty of ogling one player in particular... But still, she smiles when she notices me staring, so it's fine.

The sports staff all huddle together after losing yet another point to my teammates' hard work. The guys are sent off the pitch with their tails between their legs, three new ladies walking on in their place. Perfect. They're reinvigorating their team with players full of energy who won't spend more time staring at the asses in front of them than the ball. I pretend to care, but I'm one step closer to losing my bet and I couldn't be happier.

They go to break the circle, but one of the girls calls them back. We watch on as a nod spreads around the ring and they disperse. It's their serve, and I prepare myself to dive completely the wrong way, but one of the fresh-faced jock-ettes puts the ball on the ground instead. A conspiring glance passes between them all and then, in unison, they all strip off their tops, leaving them in only their bras and shorts.

Megan is yet again proving she's capable of so much naughtiness when she's not being babysat. She stands there, full of mischief, in her no doubt designer sports bra, which is doing the Lord's work keeping her boobs in place.

Oh boy, what I wouldn't give to have them smother me.

I want to thank each and every one of them for this stroke of genius.

Their strategy works almost instantly. Their serve flies over the net, hitting Finn square in the face while he's distracted by the view.

"Aw, come on, man!" I shout at him, faking disap-pointment.

I look back at Megan and her previous confidence seems to be waning. Her eyes scan the crowd, and I can sense her self-consciousness rising.

Don't worry, Gem. I'll get the attention off you.

"I'm not going down without a fight!" I pull my T-shirt off and toss it to the side of the court, earning a bunch of wolf-whistles and cheers from the other departments. Without hesitation, the other men on the team join me.

"Now, now, children. Keep it clean." Sunshine mothers us.

"All right, easy. Nothing below the belt!" the crew activi-ties manager shouts over the noise, and I turn to see Finn pulling his shorts back up, a cheeky smile filling his cheeks.

I insist I'm trying out a "don't let them know your next move" strategy that just isn't paying off yet when Cora scolds me for letting the ball drop a third time. It'll never pay off. Or rather, it will…but not for my teammates.

The professionals gain points fast. *Surprise, surprise.* Though not entirely because of my intentional fuck-ups, nor their missing clothes. They're athletic and agile, and *holy shit*, Megan looks *so hot* right now, competitive and almost naked. I'm so glad she came along to this.

Thwack.

The ball hits my chest then falls to the floor, and the whistle blows. That was the match point I just cost us, and for the first time it wasn't actually intentional. There's laughter from the stand and praise for the girls for clawing their way back to first place.

Sunshine tuts. "Boy, get your head on straight."

"Sorry, Mom." I wind her up.

She smiles as she struts off with the rest of my crestfallen teammates.

"Yeah, yeah, I know. I'm sorry," I say to everyone else, but I can't wipe the grin off my face. It feels as if a swarm of bees has entered my bloodstream. But, like, happy honey-bees. There's no stinging, only a fantastic buzz, as I wonder what secret Megan and I will be keeping after tonight.

I head over to Jack, collect my shirt, and put it back on, feeling Megan shadowing me.

"Congratulations."

"Thank you. Commiserations. Looks like you lost your bet."

"Yeah, it's been a rough night."

We glance at each other out the corners of our eyes as we wipe the sand off our bodies, and something unspoken passes between us. Is she as excited for this as I am? I watched her fight to win this game. If she didn't want to win our bet, she would have done what I did and sat back.

"Want me to walk you back?" I offer.

"Sure."

Jack has the impressive ability to seem a million miles away from a conversation happening right next to him while still paying close attention to every subtle detail. It's a skill he picked up while moving from home to home in the care system, and though it makes me sad to think he had to live like that, now, it's as if he has superpowers.

He glances at me, no need to say what he's going to do next.

There are enough sports staff around to assist with the tidy-up, though it seems the trio of jocks with wandering eyes is doing most of the work, so the three of us grab the last of our things and follow the crowd. People begin to break off, but as we get closer to her cabin, Megan notices Jack still walking with us.

"To stop people talking," I tell her.

She settles with that, maybe not realising how quickly we'd get found out if people watched me follow her back to her cabin alone.

When we get to her door, there are too many people still walking around, so all three of us enter her room. She flicks the light on, the door closing behind us, and when she turns around she startles at Jack's presence, clearly expecting him to have stayed in the hall.

"Just until the coast clears," he says.

She worries her lip but proceeds to remove her trainers and clap the sand off them over the bin like we were taught. I do the same after her.

"No way did you get a Jack-and-Jill cabin." Jack marvels at her room. It's single occupancy, only one bed against the wall with no bunk above it. There's another room exactly like it through the other side of a shared bathroom. These rooms are typically reserved for actors or headline entertainers. They're still shoeboxes, but they're private shoeboxes.

"It's the cabin I was assigned when I got here." She shrugs as if she doesn't realise the significance.

We don't need to ask who got her bumped up to a better cabin. I'm jealous for past me, who had to put up with loud (but lovely) Daniel, though I'm not jealous for the me who found Jack, and I'm not jealous for the me who's about to enjoy all this privacy.

Jack picks his moment to go, and I hope our efforts to stay inconspicuous have worked. It's not exactly something I've done before, but while it's this busy in the hall, and given who Megan is related to, it couldn't have hurt to have him escort us like some untouched innocents from Bridgerton.

The tension between me and Megan is palpable. We're both covered in sand and sweat, and judging by how neat and tidy her room is, I don't think she'll appreciate us getting it dirty. But something in the air tells me asking for a shower might be a little too forward. From what I know of her so far, she's an "act now, think later" kinda girl, and maybe her mouth was a little bolder earlier than she actually wants to be.

I take her hand in mine. "What does one more secret mean to you?"

"Stay here tonight?" she requests like it's a question.

She pulls my hand towards her, and I accept her offer with a kiss. My hands go to her waist as she snatches my lips with hers, the taste of her making my mouth water. *So much better than sorbet.*

She pulls back for a second. "I'd really like to shower though."

A soft laugh leaves my lips. "Yeah, me too."

"Do you want to go first?"

First. Not together.

"You go ahead. Just don't use up all the hot water." I smile, and she slips off to the bathroom.

Alone in her cabin, I take it all in. Exactly like her diary, it's expertly organised. We have weekly inspections, but the next one isn't for another few days, and it's not like she knew she'd invite me back tonight, so does she keep her room like this permanently?

I pass the time by peeking at the photos on her wall. And then the question I haven't had a moment to ask resurfaces: what's on her brother's photo stream? Whatever it is, it's clearly flattering if it made her have a crush on me all this time. Not knowing is killing me.

On the wall is a cute photo of her with her dog, and next to that, there's a picture of a little girl in a hospital bed. She's hooked up to oxygen and wearing a colourful wrap around her head. She's got the brightest gap-toothed grin as a princess holds her tightly and poses for the camera too. Looking closer, I realise the princess is Megan.

Emotions I wasn't ready for overtake me. Was that her job before coming here? No – she ran social media accounts. Some voluntary charity work then? *What a woman.* What a brave and kind and *strong—*

The shower cuts off and I panic, feeling like I'm about to get caught looking at something maybe I shouldn't have seen. I flap for a second before perching on the end of her bed and pretending to check my phone until she comes out.

She looks as sexy as hell in a short pink towelling robe, a hairbrush in her hand ready to go through her wet hair. But despite how insanely attractive she is, I don't feel uncontrollably horny. Instead I want to snuggle and swap stories with her, because learning about who she is matters more to me now.

"All yours."

She passes me a clean towel and a spare toothbrush from

her closet, and I head to the shower, but not before turning back and stealing a quick kiss.

There's so much I don't know about her. She has a whole life off this ship, and up until today, I haven't had the chance to talk to her about it unsupervised. I only know bits and pieces, like what she's good at, and I know her energy. But I don't know *her*.

"I would have regretted it."

Her words cut me all over again. But I'm back here. She didn't regret what happened, only what *could* have happened… Yeah, I can't let us get carried away tonight. Without prying eyes and eavesdropping ears, I want to get to know her.

When I come back out of the bathroom, she's changed into the cutest little silk shorts-and-shirt combo. The big light's off and her reading light is on.

"I, uh…didn't think about not having any clothes to change into," I explain, gesturing to the towel wrapped around my waist.

She gets up from where she was sitting on her bed and guides me to the end of it, my pulse quickening as she sits me down. She straddles me, and my plan for a get-to-know-you session is momentarily forgotten.

"Thank you for making me come tonight," she says.

"*Already?* Jeez, that must be some kind of record!"

"Tom!" She giggles, and the way her body vibrates against mine as she does feels out of this world.

"Oh, come *on*, that was the perfect setup – you can't blame me for jumping on it."

She smiles and strokes my damp hair.

"I'm glad you had a good time," I say with more sincerity.

Her mouth finds mine and I sink into the sensation. The

pull slowly intensifies, and when I feel us about to fall backwards onto the bed, I take it as my cue to break the kiss.

"So, are we gonna talk about the fact you knew who I was?"

She pulls in her lips so they form a line. "Depends. Did you think it was cute or creepy?"

"Are you *kidding*? It was the *best* news I ever heard! I've been dying to find out what exactly it was that made you so *obsessed* with me."

She buries her blushing face in her hands and groans. "Oh *Godddd*."

"Don't be shy. The truth's out now. I don't see what other choice you have but to own it." I gently pull her hands away from her eyes. "So go on – tell me. What did you see? Or has your brother talked about me too? You know what? Start from the top. Tell me everything you have on me."

She takes a deep, meditative breath. "I knew you did comedy."

"Mm…" I lean back on one of my hands and reposition my other on her waist so I can remind myself how soft her skin is under her shirt.

"I knew you were Eliza's best friend." She runs her finger lightly along my cheekbone.

"So I'm not your brother's best friend?" I'm pulling her leg. I already know the answer.

She raises one eyebrow at me. "*Are* you?"

"Not his best, no… What else? Oh! Did you see me in drag?" I sure hope she did.

She straightens with delight, trying to imagine it. "What? No! When were you in drag?"

"Staff talent show. I'll find the clip for you tomorrow, but you'd better prepare yourself, because I looked *hot*."

"I believe it." She smiles and I kiss her, because I need to feel it against my lips.

I let us fall backwards this time, allowing us a moment to enjoy each other before I get back to business. "So, what should I know about you?"

"I knew one more thing."

I'm pleased she's still sharing. "Oh yeah?"

"I knew that at one point…you liked Eliza…as more than a friend."

I take what I said about being pleased back. My hands still where they were stroking her. *Did it just get hot in here?* I try to laugh it off. "Came up in conversation, did it?"

"Kind of. We were picking on Oscar about the new girl in his photos for a while, and then one day, he had enough and said you guys were an item. But then the next thing we know, they're together, so…"

I swallow my embarrassment, not letting myself dwell on what wasn't meant to be and has since worked out for the best. *So Megan knew that, and yet she still wanted me when I arrived? Still wants me now?*

"Can I ask, did you guys ever—?"

"I don't think it's fair for me to share the details about our *very brief* fling."

She reflects on that answer for a second, agreeing.

"But what we *didn't* do was sleep together, if that's what you were wondering."

I assume her momentary silence is from the relief of learning this, but it doesn't show.

"Do you still like her like that?" She's not asking for her brother.

"Not like that, no."

Whatever worry was in the back of her mind seems to ease, because she strokes my hair again and kisses me.

"Did you know I kissed your brother?" I admit, just to lighten the mood.

She sits up straight in horror. "*What?* Ew! Why would you do that?"

"Because I clearly have a thing for Harveys."

"That's *disgusting.*"

"You can't say that – it's almost Pride Month!"

"No, stupid, not because— *Ugh*, you know what I meant."

I giggle and pull her back down. "Relax. It was for a party game." I kiss her again, but she's as stiff as a board.

"So gross."

"Hey, don't kiss me and then say *gross!*" I roll myself on top of her, enjoying the sound of her laughter as she looks up at me.

"So tell me, what should I know about you?" I repeat, not missing the way she tenses.

"There's nothing really to know about me." She shrugs innocently enough, but I can sense something's off.

"Okay… So what made you come work on a ship?"

Her cheeks begin to flush. "Uh…I just felt like it, I guess."

"Cool. And what were you doing before?"

"Nothing noteworthy."

"I thought you were managing social media for someone."

"Oh, yes, I was doing that. You're right."

This wasn't meant to be an interrogation, but it's quickly become one. *What could she possibly not want me to know?* She kisses me, her hands reaching between us to where my towel is wrapped around my waist. If there was ever a diversion tactic to stop a guy talking, it would be this. *What is she hiding?*

"I wanna know you, Gem," I implore.

"There's nothing to know about me."

It's starting to hurt, how desperate she is to keep me in the dark. "Is there nothing to know, or nothing you want me to know?" The words are out before I can rephrase them a little more graciously.

Suddenly seeming so small, she looks away and reaches for the water bottle on the nightstand. I shift onto my side to let her sit up, and she drinks for too long. I can't see her face, but I know she's thinking of a way out of this conversation.

"Megan?"

"Mm?" She makes no move to turn back.

"Look at me."

Defeated, she glances my way, revealing teary eyes, and my heart breaks. Holding my towel, I carefully but quickly move to comfort her.

"Hey, hey, I'm sorry. I didn't mean to upset you. I wanna get to know you, that's all."

"You would hate me if you knew me." A tear falls down her cheek, but she wipes it away.

"What do you mean? Of course I wouldn't. Why would I hate you?" I wrap my arm around her and wait for her to know that she can count on me.

"Because everybody does."

I ache hearing her say something so awful about herself. "I really don't think that's true. What possible reason could they have to hate you?"

Her bottom lip trembles. I really don't want to push her, but I have to find out what she means, because I *know* it can't be as bad as she thinks it is, and I want to make it all better.

She shakes her head. "Tom, I can't. I came here to start over."

I wait a few more seconds to see if she'll change her mind, but she doesn't.

"Okay." I'm not entitled to her story, no matter how much I want to be a part of it.

As she puts her water back on the nightstand, her phone lights up, revealing how late it is.

"Do you still want me to stay?" I ask.

"Do you want to go?" she counters. There's so much pain in her eyes, but her tone is understanding.

I never want to leave her side. "No."

"Then I'd like you to stay."

She heads to the bathroom to wash her face of tears, and I find my boxers to put on, because being naked feels inappropriate now.

We get settled into bed together, her as the little spoon, and I let her fall asleep while my mind races with all the possibilities of what happened to her before she came here. I wonder what could be so awful that she can't tell a soul. Not even me.

I'd always keep your secrets, Gem.

FIVE

GEMMA

Waking up in Tom's arms is the best thing to happen to me in a long time.

In the week following our secret sleepover, I assume the tension between us will fizzle out – on his end anyway – or that he'll decide he doesn't need my help anymore and we'll drift apart, but that's not the case at all. As an added bonus, he doesn't bring up my mysterious past again. I hope that's out of respect and not because he's satiated his curiosity by getting Eliza to break her promise to me and Oscar not to tell a soul.

Some days, I feel like I could come out and tell him and it'd be okay. But I don't let myself act on the impulse. He didn't see me on my pedestal, and he didn't see me fall from it, and I'd like to keep it that way.

My watch vibrates, signalling my shift on the surf simulator is over, so I wrap up the last session, but I don't hurry to grab my towel and pack up. When I got here a month ago, I would have jumped at the chance to finish for the day and disappear off to my cabin, but the new me doesn't want to pass up the opportunity to be outside and watch the sun set while I'm doing something I love.

Thrill-seeking Megan is at it again…

I'm allowed to surf as much as I'd like on this shift whenever there aren't guests booked in, because it drums up interest and subsequently makes the company money. So, instead of shutting everything down, I hop on a board and ride the artificial waves to my heart's content.

Fake waves. Fake life.

I would marvel at the symbolism of that if it didn't fuel the tiny voice in the back of my head saying, "Everyone was right – maybe I am a fraud after all."

Even though coming here was my only option – if I don't count never leaving the house again, which Mum, Nan, and Oscar said *wasn't* an option – I'm surprised by how much I'm enjoying it now. There are definitely parts that still aren't my thing, but this moment right here, the wind in my hair, the water skimming my legs, it helps me to forget all the not-so-good bits.

"You make it look so easy!"

I smile. He helps me to forget about those bits too. I look over to see Tom watching me with the biggest grin on his face.

"Because it is." I reach out my hand in invitation even though he's too far away to touch. "Come have a go."

"No, thanks. I've tried and failed before," he shouts over the noise of the waves.

"But you haven't had me as a teacher." I can see his resolve waning. "It'd be good content…" I suggest tunefully.

He takes a second more to mull it over, then he gives in. "Fine, but only if you hold my hand."

"If I have to." I pretend it's a chore.

He lets himself into the now closed area at the bottom of

the simulator and strips his top off, causing me to almost wipe out. I just about manage not to embarrass myself as I come to a stop.

"The camera's not rolling yet." I make fun of him, and the smirk that earns me is phenomenal.

"Hey, not all of us have those fancy rash guards you jocks have."

"Rash *vests*." Another day, another funny Americanism I get to laugh about with him.

He sets his phone up to record on one of the viewing benches and takes the board from me.

I've told Tom I don't want to be in his videos, and he's never asked me why or tried to convince me otherwise, which I appreciate. But this is the first time I've been in front of the camera, and I'm nervous he'll use a shot where I can be recognised, which would cause the floodgates of hell to open. I make a mental note to check his videos carefully the next time we go to upload them.

I brief Tom the same way I would brief anyone else, explaining the basics about balance, what to feel for, and how to avoid serious injury in the highly likely event he falls over. He's brave and reckless, and he wants nothing more than to show off, but that isn't enough to make his first attempt a success. Nor his second. Yet, like the eternal optimist he is, he blindly backs himself despite having none of the ability to achieve the results, and I have to admire him for his willingness to keep trying, especially when each of his falls would make anyone else give up and blame the machine for not working properly.

The second he manages to stay on unaided by me for more than three seconds, he screams in celebration while I cheer him on from the sidelines. Once I'm certain he's steady on his feet, I step away and pick up his phone to get some better footage of him.

Ugh, he's so fit.

I tear my eyes off the screen to get a look at him in the flesh. Tanned, ripped, and beaming with glee.

"I'm a natural!" His confidence is intoxicating. Unfortunately, his triumph lasts for all of ten seconds before disaster strikes. "Hey, Megan, check this out!"

"Check wha—?"

"Spin move!"

"Tom, no!" I yell, but my warning comes too late.

He sticks out his elbows and flings the top half of his body behind him, expecting to do a 360, but what he doesn't realise is, by not leading with his feet and keeping his knees bent, the board can only betray him and knock him off. The strong current sweeps him up to the top of the slope, and he's pummelled by waves as he tries to recover from his awkward landing.

Phone down. Run. Get his head out of the water. Big brown eyes gaze into mine. *He's conscious.* Breathe. Check for signs of concussion as I was taught to do during training. Scan his body for any limbs bending the wrong way or bones sticking out. No blood.

"I'm good, Princess."

"You're okay?" I keep cradling his head as if he could still go limp on me any second. *Did he just call me Princess?*

"I'm okay."

Relief kicks in, and the sound of his laughter eases all the stress coursing through my veins, making me laugh too.

"You have to admit, that woulda been *awesome* if I'd pulled it off."

We giggle harder, both of us replaying the moment over and over in our heads, until there are tears in our eyes and my stomach hurts. I can't remember the last time I laughed like this.

"What were you *thinking*? This isn't an immersive 'Jackass' experience!"

He points his fingers at me like a tipsy person trying to get their point across. "You miss one hundred percent of the shots you don't take."

"No!" I tell him off playfully. "You could have really hurt yourself. I was terrified you *had*!"

"Sorry." He pinches his lips together and glances to the side the same way my dog, Tilly, does when she's in trouble. "Do you still fancy me?" That word sounds so funny in his accent. "I don't think my ego could take it if you didn't."

A smile breaks out on my face. "I still fancy you, Knoxville."

Neither of us can look away, and the mood turns heated fast. His eyes drop to my lips first, and then my gaze does the same.

"Not here, Princess. We'll lose our jobs."

I study the way his bare chest rises and falls. "Yeah," I agree wistfully.

He subconsciously grazes his bottom lip with his teeth. "Wanna go back to yours and pretend to make content?"

I swallow and try to deepen my now shallow breaths. "Yes, please."

Standing up, I give him a helping hand back to his feet. He takes a few tense steps, shaking off any aches, but then he stops, and I worry again that maybe he did hurt himself.

"I should've known you'd be at the centre of a laughing fit."

I look up to find my brother smiling at Tom. Then he peers over at me. *Has he been here this whole time?* There's nothing sinister in his smile, but panic rises in me nonetheless as my brain whirrs with thoughts of how to downplay the situation. He couldn't have heard us over the water... *Could he?*

I power down the machine while Tom dries off.

"Manage to make it up this time?" Oscar asks him.

"Yep, for, like, five minutes!"

"More like one." I correct him jovially before I hear what that sounds like and cringe at myself.

Oscar makes no move to go, so Tom heads off, unfortunately, leaving me with the cockblock of the century.

"I know I should have shut the sim down earlier, but I was having fun and—"

"I don't have a problem with you sticking around for a bit. You weren't doing anything wrong."

"So why does it feel like you're about to tell me off?"

"I'm not." Oscar relaxes his posture. "You doing okay? I haven't seen you as much this week."

I can't blame him for checking in on me. I didn't exactly have a great time settling in, but I'm fine now. He should know that.

"All good. Just been busy."

"Mm-hmm..." He bobs his head, and his mouth twists a little. "It's good to hear you laughing again."

Ever since the show, I've developed a sixth sense for people mincing their words, and right now, my radar is going haywire.

"Oscar." I level my stare. "You clearly have something to say, so say it."

He hesitates, but he knows I need him to be honest. "Be careful, okay?"

I don't reply, because playing dumb would only make me a hypocrite. But I also refuse to confirm his suspicions.

"I know him. He's not... I don't want him to hurt you,

that's all. He won't mean to, but he will. I've been through it with Eliza once before, and I don't need to go through it with you too."

"I'm only helping him with his social media – which *you* asked me to do, I might add."

"I know, and I'm really grateful you're helping out my friend, but—"

His friend. Not mine.

"—I feel like I'm watching history repeat itself for…a number of reasons."

He's scared I'll give someone the power to destroy me again. And as much as I hate to admit it, he might be onto something, because my feelings for Tom are already quite intense. And even though being wrong about Tom can't ruin me on the same scale as "Love Lodge" did, it could ruin the one place I'm safe. And I need this ship. I need it more than I need someone I've only known for a few weeks.

My brother tried to warn me about the risks of going onto what ended up being one of the nation's most popular new dating shows, and here he is, trying to warn me again now. I ignored him before and I lost everything.

"I'll be careful."

The orange block in my diary looms over me. There's some kind of Blind Date thing going on tonight for the crew, and I can think of a million other things I'd rather do than watch people flirt with each other for entertainment. Like eat glass. I told Oscar it would be too distressing, and to be fair, he didn't put up a fight when I mentioned skipping it. But…Eliza's going, which means Tom probably is too, and seeing him will make all the discomfort worth it.

I've barely seen him these past few days. Not properly. Whenever I've managed to track him down, he's either been rushing off somewhere or in the middle of an activity. Where possible, I've filmed a quick clip of him in action, but I still haven't had the chance to AirDrop anything over. It's probably a good thing we haven't had any moments alone given what I promised Oscar. But I do miss his company. And tonight would be safe enough, right? That's the only thought that gets me changed and out the door.

I arrive at the crew bar to find Oscar and Eliza at a table with some other entertainment hosts. The two of them look surprised to see me, but they make space for me to join them.

"You sure you want to be here?" Oscar asks.

I nod, and he goes up to get me a drink. I've told him a million times I can get my own, but when the bar's busy like this, he never lets me.

Up on the small platform at the front of the room, a glittery partition wall divides the stage. Three chairs on one side and one on the other, behind another glittery partition wall. I spot a pair of heels peeking out at the bottom, so the poor girl must already be back there.

Frankie Valli's "Can't Take My Eyes Off You" comes on through the speakers, and the lights dim over the audience while colourful hues brighten the stage. The crew activities manager, Grace, jumps onto the platform and welcomes everyone to the show before inviting up "the three most eligible bachelors on the ship". My heart sinks as Tom steps up onto the platform and takes his seat at the end of the row.

Why's he taking part in this? I thought—

I got it wrong.

This is exactly what Oscar warned me would happen, and yet I'm still surprised.

I turn to him and Eliza in the hope that by the time I look

back at the stage, I'll discover it's not Tom at all, and it's actually because I'm so freakishly consumed by him that I've seen him in the face of someone else. I catch them shooting each other worried glances, and then they both cast their eyes over to me but quickly turn their attention back to the show.

Grace goes down the line of guys and asks them all questions about themselves. There's Gus, a security guard who's built like a brick wall and keeps a stern face throughout the mini-interview, and Matt, who, unfortunately for me, was my mentor when I first joined the ship. He's the most annoying person I've ever met, and as of recently, that's *really* bloody saying something. A proper lad's lad, he lives to get as drunk as he's allowed to in the bar, boasts about his conquests each morning, and always talks over me. How he got picked for this, I have no idea, because even if he was the last man on earth, I still wouldn't describe him as "eligible".

There's a deep thumping in my chest when it's Tom's turn.

"Tom! Good to see you up here."

"Happy to be here."

Ouch.

He's in his showman mood – I recognise it from seeing him in action around the ship. He's still the life of the party when he's not working, but it's a different kind of energy.

Why is he performing?

"We couldn't not invite one of the sexiest guys on the ship up here, could we, folks?" Cheers go off around the room. "So tell us a bit about yourself, for those who haven't had the pleasure of your company yet." Her tone drips with suggestion.

"I'm Tom, part of the entertainment team. I spend most of my time trying to—"

"Top shagger!" a girl heckles from the crowd, and other

whistles and noises of agreement go off around the room, causing my cheeks to heat up. How do I expect to stand out on a ship literally full of other women he's liked at one point or another? Is this what he does – has little flings and then disappears on them?

Despite that thought, something protective overcomes me as he laughs nervously and looks up at the ceiling, trying to shut out the noise until it dies down. He looks about as uncomfortable as I feel.

"I think our lucky lady is going to have a tough time picking only one of you tonight. Shall we meet her?" Grace addresses the crowd.

Music plays again and the front partition wall is rolled away, revealing a beautiful girl to the audience only. She's short, with long dark hair and olive skin, enviable curves, and a big smile. Everything about her is elegant and preened.

"Carmen! What a treat we've got in store for you tonight. As you could hear, the boys are very excited to meet you, so why don't you go ahead and introduce yourself?"

"Hi, I'm Carmen, and I'm a guest services specialist from Puerto Rico!"

There's a big holler from the guest services staff and the other Puerto Ricans in the bar.

"And how would you describe your dream man?"

"Oh, you know, kind and caring, good manners, emotionally intelligent, good sense of humour..." She lists the traits off, her natural inflection sounding almost like a song.

So he just has to be a decent human being then? Ugh, the bar for men is so low.

I choose to focus on that injustice rather than the fact Tom is all of those things *and more* and, of her three options, he's obviously going to win the date with her.

"Really going for personality over looks there, Carmen."

"If I was all about the looks, I'd be the wrong woman for this game. *But* it wouldn't hurt if he was handsome too…" A smirk plays on her lips, and the crowd eggs her on.

"There it is! Good stuff. Now, you've prepared some questions for the boys to help you decide, haven't you?" Grace gestures to the cards in Carmen's hand.

She waves the cards in the air. "I sure have!"

"Then let's not keep them waiting any longer. Hit us with your first question!"

"Okay, so in my job, I have to be patient and polite no matter what, because 'the customer is always right' even when they are very, very wrong…" She gives the audience a cheeky side-eye, which gets her some laughs.

Of course she's funny too. *Tom's going to love that.* In fact, he does – he's already laughing.

"How would you help me let off steam after a long, *frustrating* day?"

"We'll go to single man number one first. Gus, fire away."

He considers his answer briefly. "We have a zero-tolerance policy when it comes to harassment of a staff member, and so I'd take no issue with confronting or even detaining anyone found to be doing so." A dark grin cracks his stern exterior. "And I'll let you watch."

"Wow, okay. Matt, can you beat that answer?"

Needing no time at all, he immediately shows the room exactly who he is. "If you kept your little uniform on, I'd let you do anything you wanted to me. I've got a pretty active job, but I don't tire easily. You have a bad day, I'll give you a good night."

Grace's eyebrows shoot up as Carmen's mouth hangs open a little, though she doesn't look horrified.

"Moving quickly on… Single man number three, Tom, how would you help Carmen let off steam?"

"Stress is a silent killer, but laughter is the best medicine. So consider me your own private dispensary, because I will stop at nothing to put a smile on your face."

The crowd cheers for him as they did for the other two, but he gets extra support in the form of shrieks and whoops from his ex-lovers.

"Hold up. Tom, are you saying you could save her *life*?"

"I mean, if the shoe fits…" Already proving his point, he effortlessly amuses the audience.

"All right, Carmen, so we've got 'The Purge', 'Indecent Proposal', and 'Whose Line Is It Anyway?' Think one of those is a bit of you?"

"Oh, absolutely!"

"Excellent! Why don't you go ahead and hit us with your next question?"

Carmen looks down at the second card in her hand and reads from it. "My love language is words of affirmation, so I like compliments, love letters, being told what a good girl I am…"

People wolf-whistle as she flaunts her seductive smirk once again. She's so confident and sexy, and I'm about as sensual as a worm. I know I'm attractive, but I don't have the same kind of *allure* as she does. Tom probably figured it out and that's why he gave up on me.

"What's your love language, and how do you like to use it?"

Shocking absolutely no one, Matt's is physical touch and Gus's is acts of service. Tom's turns out to be quality time, and while he doesn't make that sound dirty, everyone else around him does.

"And finally, Carmen, please can we get your third question for the guys?"

"You know what I'm looking for in a man – what are you looking for in a woman?"

Matt essentially wants anything with a pulse, Gus wants a rule-breaker to keep him busy, and Tom wants someone he can take home to his mum.

Funny, dedicated, and family-oriented. He's the whole package. It's not because I can't have him that I want him so much; he is quite literally my dream man.

"Now, Carmen, based on all the answers you've been given, which guy are you leaning towards?"

She covers her face with her cards. "Ahh, I have no idea!"

"It's going to be tough to pick, huh? You know, what might make your decision a little easier is if we narrow down your options from three to two." The colourful lights suddenly change to bright white on the guys, and tense music plays. "Gorgeous Carmen, out of our three mystery men, who isn't floating your boat?"

Carmen winces as she tries to decide, the crowd adding to her panic as they shout out different names for her to pick.

"I'm so sorry, but Tom."

Everyone makes noises of sympathy and support for Tom while I make the most of being able to breathe again. He's invited past the partition wall to meet Carmen. She gives him a hug, and he's applauded as he steps off the stage to Céline Dion's version of "All By Myself".

It's a good thing he can take a joke. That would've mortified me.

SIX

TOM

The lights are too bright. I can't hear anything except the sound of my own blood pumping. Is this what stage fright is? It's as if I'm standing still while the world carries on around me. *Laugh it off, Tom. Smile and get off the stage without embarrassing yourself any further.* I cross my fingers, hoping the ground will swallow me up on my way over to Jack and his colleagues. *Play it cool. It's no big deal. It was just a game show. Light entertainment for the evening, nothing serious.*

I went up for content, for a joke. Yep, I'm just one big joke. The idea I might want to find love is so inconceivable it's hilarious.

I can't run away. I can't let it show that I'm falling apart.

I find Jack, pretend the humiliation isn't eating me up from the inside, and excuse myself for a bathroom break as the game continues onstage. I lock myself in the cubicle and lean against the wall.

I can't fucking *breathe*. Why can't I breathe? It's like the more I try, the harder it gets.

I can handle rejection, I swear. I've been rejected a bunch

of times and never cared before. But when girls turn me down, it's the sex they're turning down, not me. But this is me. All me. There could be a million reasons someone might turn down sex: I'm not their type or they're in a "shipuationship" or they could plainly not want to have sex. Great. Easy. But to put myself out there and be rejected for my personality, and to come last to a guy like *Matt*? That hurts like hell.

I didn't even want to do this. I was asked, and Jack thought it might be a good idea to help me get over Megan because I can't have her.

I just *had* to leave my phone behind the other day. It *had* to still be recording. And I *had* to hear everything Harvey said about me. And how easily Megan agreed. I thought there was something special going on between us, but looking back, was she ever gonna let me in?

I've got so much love to give, and nobody ever wants it.

The door to the bathroom opens, and I still my erratic breathing so no one will hear me and mistake my shuddering breaths as furious masturbation. I've done so much work to be better, to be someone worth loving. I've gotten better at controlling my anger, but it's turned me into a crier. I'm not ashamed of it, but I sure as fuck don't want anyone to know about it. Harvey got one thing right: I held in too much before, and it wasn't healthy.

"You doing okay in there?"

Jack.

I release a painful breath. "Yeah," I call back, sounding anything other than okay.

He knocks on the door.

If it were anyone else, I'd keep them shut out, but it's Jack. We've met each other's darkness, and I have no shame when it comes to him. I unlock the stall and he slips in, locking it again behind him. He takes in the sight of me, and from the sympathy in his eyes, I know I must look like a pathetic piece of crap hiding in here.

"When's it gonna be my turn?" I ask, seconds before I'm bundled into his chest in a tight hug.

Hearing the words out loud makes me feel like even more of a loser. It's a question Jack has no doubt asked himself a million times before, watching all his friends find their forever homes while his stay would only ever be temporary. And here I am, throwing myself a pity party over not landing a date.

I wouldn't even hug my own brother like this, but Jack is my person. No other way to describe it. It's such a shame I'm not even a little bit gay, because I love this guy so much more than it's normal to love a friend.

Jack lets go of me. "Rather it be the right one late than the wrong one early."

How does he always know exactly what to say?

"You'll find her one day, I promise."

The door to the bathroom creaks, and Grace's voice gets louder and then fades out again as the door swings shut. The two of us freeze, knowing we're going to have to wait this guy out, but a few seconds pass and I don't hear him shuffling around to use the urinal.

"Hey, quit sucking each other off in there! I gotta go."

"It's *so big*! I can't get it all in!" Jack quips back.

That fire right there is exactly why we're friends. I may have a twin, but Jack's my platonic twin flame.

I decide to play along. "Relax your throat. That's it. Oh *shit*, you're good at that. Don't stop." I make all kinds of noises to piss off that guy even further.

"Oh, for fuck's sake." Whoever it is huffs and leaves.

"I can't go back out there," I admit.

"Because you want to be fake-gay in here with me some

more?" Jack eyes me with curiosity, then he shrugs it off. "Bit weird, but okay."

With his stupid joke, he inadvertently gifts me with the choice to either smile or stay sad. And choosing to stay sad is how depression starts, so...

"If anyone can handle this, it's you. We're going back out there, and we're gonna do it looking like the happiest guys on earth. Don't show those fuckers they won."

I take a deep breath, and we exit the bathroom stall.

"I won't leave your side," he assures me.

Every person in the bar might as well be watching me right now, because that's what it feels like. It doesn't matter that it's not true. In the time I've been gone, Carmen has made her choice – Gus – and they're now doing some kind of game to decide their date location. There's a shout for my name, but I ignore it, hoping the fact it's so loud and crowded in here will pass as an excuse for my rudeness.

The person calls out again, and I realise it's Megan. *Of course* she's here. Of course she had to witness the most humbling moment of my life. You know what? I don't care. *She's here*. And I need her.

I turn around, and my stress vanishes upon seeing her.

"Hey, do you have your phone on you?" She gets straight to the point, and it puts me back on edge.

I fumble around in my pocket to get it out. "Uh, yeah. Why?"

"Can you turn your AirDrop on? I've got stuff for you to put into this week's videos."

The last thing I want is evidence of what happened tonight, but I comply because I know she's only trying to be helpful. She AirDrops over a whole bunch of clips, checks I got them okay, and then immediately deletes them from her phone. *Weird.* I've not seen her do that before.

"Are you running low on storage space?"

"No," she answers, a little confused.

Great, so she's deleting everything featuring me from her phone. That's a sucker punch I could do without tonight.

No – she's cutting me out because *I* cut *her* out. Which I guess is fair, but it sucks all the same.

She says her goodbyes and walks away, leaving me with Jack and my worsening mood. I look down at what she sent me. *Whoa.* She's been a fly on the wall in so many places this week. I spotted her once or twice, but only now do I realise the effort she went to even though I've been avoiding her for days. I'm grateful to discover that she didn't film any of this evening. The idea of watching it back, let alone posting it for the world to see, is my worst nightmare.

Jack bumps my shoulder with his and escorts me out of the bar once again. Outside, I spot Megan right down the end of the hall.

"Gem!" I call out, unable to stop myself.

She halts and turns towards us. "Yeah?"

"I'm gonna need help uploading this again. Think you can slot me in sometime?"

It's hard to see the little changes in her expression from this far away, but after a moment, she says, "Okay."

"When?" I press, because if she's cut me out of her photo album, then she's cut me out of her diary, and I hate that thought.

She unlocks her phone, and I root around in my pocket for my schedule. "Tuesday morning?" she shouts.

"Works for me." I wait for her to finish programming it in. "Good night." I turn and walk in the direction of mine and Jack's room.

"Why did you take part in that?" Her voice sounds small, and it's not necessarily because of the distance between us.

I take a second to pull my thoughts together, not sure how to tell her about the recording, but I know I'm gonna have to.

"I signed him up." Jack steps forward. "I thought—" He checks we're still alone. "I thought it might help with…optics."

It's the truth. Maybe not all of it, but that's one of the reasons I agreed to it in the end.

She nods thoughtfully. "Good night."

We head our separate ways, but I can't resist turning back once more.

"What colour have you made my appointment?" I shout.

"Blue," she confesses, and suddenly my whole world feels brighter.

The second we arrive at the juice bar Megan gets down to business. I hand over my phone so she can watch the videos I made this week and see what she's working with, then I head to get us smoothies.

I slow my steps on the way back when I spot her giggling to herself. She must be watching the surfing incident. Oh yeah, the bruises I got are totally worth it to see that smile.

Accepting her devil drink, which I've kept at arm's length, she notices the disgust on my face and rushes to defend it. "It's not *that* bad!"

"So it's a little bad?"

She looks down at it and tips her head to the side. "It's fine."

"How can you be happy with 'fine'?"

"Because that's my life now." Her regret is instantly clear.

I tread carefully because I never want to make her cry again. "Can I ask you more about that?"

"I'd rather you didn't," she says quickly, with a straight face.

"Okay then." I change the subject even though my head is full of burning questions. "I'm pretty sure one sip of that would kill me."

"Don't knock it till you've tried it."

My nose wrinkles at the thought.

"Yeah, you probably couldn't handle it."

I waggle my finger at her. "Don't you reverse-psychology me, young lady!"

She pushes the glass across the table towards me. "But you couldn't, could you?"

This shouldn't be working. "I could. But I'm not going to."

"Because you couldn't handle it."

Oh, she's a youngest sibling all right.

She leaves the drink where it is and gets back to watching my videos. The froth floating on the top of it taunts me. I can't let her think I'm weak. *Ah, screw it.* In a swift movement I grab the drink and suck on the straw before I can back out. I swallow, but it takes an effort to keep from gagging, bits of green assaulting my throat on the way down.

Gross. "Call a doctor." I clutch my chest as I struggle.

She snickers. "So you can't handle it?"

I bolt upright, snapping out of my little charade. "No! That was the opposite of the point I was— I did it! I handled it!"

She cocks an eyebrow with all the words she isn't saying and then looks back down at my phone, tutting. "If you say so."

Dammit. I take a few long sips of my tropical smoothie to regulate my system while she watches the last video.

When I get my phone back, I catch up with the family group chat. With me living on a ship, Bobby reinventing himself, and Mom keeping busy, it's less of a "Hey, how are you?" thing and more of a group journal. We each share what we got up to that day – or in my case, that week – and reply when we can. In grief counselling, we learnt about continuing bonds and allowing yourself to hold space for the person you lost, and we've all found it immensely helpful in finding peace again. So Dad's still in the chat, quite literally ghosting us, but we're okay with that. All the photos we've ever shared and his messages are all still here if we ever want to look back at them, and I often do.

Mom, Tom's stripping on the internet.

I can hear the playful whine in Bobby's voice as I read one of his messages. So he's seen the short clip of me playing volleyball where I took my top off. Sure, that wasn't the *only* clip from volleyball Jack captured, but I don't work hard on my body to hide it away.

I read through the rest of their messages and then share some highlights from my week, interrupting myself to ask Megan a question. "What's this thing you're doing right now called again—? Wait, no, I got it. Search…Thomas the Tank Engine…optimisation," I mumble as I type it out, keeping one eye on Megan.

She shakes her head, a smile on her perfect lips.

After I hit send, I head over to TikTok. Notifications haven't been popping up, and there's no red-numbered dot on the corner of the app icon either. That briefly concerns me. Maybe the scheduling app didn't work this week. But when everything loads up, I know that isn't the case at all. It's the exact opposite.

"Holy shit." I feel as if hot coffee has been injected into my veins. "This can't be… Did we…? Gem, we did it!"

Megan looks over my shoulder, but I can't think straight enough to linger on how good it feels to have her so close to me again, because staring back at me are thousands of comments, likes, follows, and DMs. I can't bring myself to click on any of them, because I'm scared the second I touch them they'll disappear and I'll realise this is actually a demon juice-induced hallucination.

"Help," I whimper.

Megan shakes my shoulders with excited hands. "Oh my God, congratulations!"

Reality finally catches up to me and I let go of all my tension with a wave of laughter. I drop my phone on the table and wrap my arms around her tightly in celebration.

"Thank you so much, Gem." I pull away and do everything in my power not to kiss her face with appreciation.

"I'm so happy for you." She smiles softly.

Now would be a *great* time to kiss…but I restrain myself, breaking eye contact and getting to work on breathing normally again. It happened. We got my name out there. I can make so many people happ—

Oh no.

What if I went viral for something bad? What if there's a word that's become problematic this week, and I didn't know because I live in the middle of the ocean with rare access to the internet, and I've used it and offended an entire minority group?

"What are you waiting for?" Megan asks while I stare into space.

"I'm too scared to look."

"Want me to do it?"

I nod enthusiastically. "Yes, please." I give her back my

phone, and she begins analysing everything. "Have I been cancelled?"

She looks up at me, confused. "What? No. Why would you get cancelled?"

"Just a new fear I've unlocked in the past thirty seconds."

After another minute or two spent scrolling, she looks up and gives me a reassuring smile. "No, you haven't been cancelled. Everybody loves you."

I let out a huge sigh of relief.

"Some people *really* love you." Her eyes bulge suggestively.

"What do you mean?"

"You have at least a hundred proposals." She scrolls some more. "Fifty percent of which I'd say aren't exactly for your hand in marriage…"

"What?"

She passes back my phone so I can read the comments:

Stand up? More like sit down. On my face.

I choke on my smoothie.

"You okay?" Megan pats me on the back.

"Yeah, fine. I mean, I wasn't expecting…*that*." I flash her the screen. "How…? Why would…? *Is that even a thing?*"

"In the words of Bo Burnham, 'welcome to the internet'," she says with a sarcastic smile.

I brace myself and continue reading.

Do you have a girlfriend?

I've got something else he can smack and it isn't a volleyball…

Marry me! I'll organise everything, you only have to turn up!

> SO HOT!

> Pleeaaassseee tell me he's single. Actually, I don't even care if he is, I'm willing to share.

> Hands up if you're looking up cruise jobs right now to be his ship-wife!

> He's a seaman, and what do you know I like—

"*Jeeeesus Christ.* Why is everybody so horny?"

"It could be worse. You could be a woman on the internet," she remarks light-heartedly, but all at once, things start to slot into place.

1.5 million followers.

Everybody hates her.

She came here to start over.

This is her life now.

She wasn't running an account for someone else, was she? I mean, look at her – it would make complete sense if she was some kind of model or influencer. Was *she* cancelled? And if she was, will I ever find out what for?

Megan goes back to finishing off her very important work while I revel in all the attention. Even though the number of likes on that ship-wife comment raises a few concerns for my privacy – my safety too – I can't lie: it feels really good to be wanted for a change.

I click on a notification that says I've been tagged in a video and my jaw hits the floor. "You've gotta be kidding me." Someone's actually made a thirst trap using a sloweddown clip of me taking off my shirt. The video flashes in black-and-white while music plays that makes you think about staying up all night fucking.

I shoot Megan a look of absolute shock, and she looks up from the video with a smirk.

"That's what happens when you show a bit of skin online, Tom. Get used to it."

"Are you trying to say I was asking for it?" I pretend to be offended.

She narrows her eyes and leans in with the cutest, most playful smile on her lips. "How does it feel?"

"Fucking awesome! Why do women complain about being sexualised all the time? This is *great*!" I purposely wind her up.

We burst out laughing, and I swipe off the video before it gets to my head. *There's no way this is happening.* I go back to my own content and start scrolling through comments, deciding which ones I can reply to without encouraging a potential stalker.

"Okay, ready to upload? What are you doing?" There's an edge of panic to her voice.

"Replying to comments to get my engagement up. I'm telling these ladies to first of all buy me dinner, and I'm confirming that I am in fact single." It's so lame that I'm trying to bait her like this, but all I want is for her to stop me and tell me I'm not single. That she wants me. She was clearly upset I took part in Blind Date – as was I – but in the few days since then, even though I've stopped avoiding her, nothing's changed.

Get jealous over me again, Princess. Please.

She puts her hand on my arm, looking serious.

Yes – it's happening!

"Don't say a word."

A grin tugs at the corner of my lips. "Why not?"

Come on, tell me I'm taken. Tell me I'm yours.

"This is a perfect opportunity." *To declare your love for me.* "You need engagement, absolutely, but nothing brings engagement more than people wanting to be right about something or to point out that someone else is wrong. You tell them upfront and it's over."

Oh...

It takes a genuine effort to hide my disappointment. "So I just ignore it?"

"Could do. Or...you could really lean into it."

"And how do I do that?"

She checks her watch. "Let me think about it. I need to get these uploaded for you first."

My PR manager has spoken. She sends her notes over to my phone and then starts copy-and-pasting all her SEO-approved jargon into my app with each of my videos. I take mental notes on what she's doing, because I came danger-ously close to needing to do this all on my own, and I realise now how badly I'd have failed without her help. But I pretend to watch the world go by as she taps away, just so she can't decide I'm capable of going solo and that I don't need to hang out with her like this each week.

She finishes up, checks her watch again, and sips the last of her drink.

"Somewhere to be?"

"Some of the sports staff are going out for lunch. Thought I'd join them."

I can't hide how happy I am for her. A few weeks ago, she'd never willingly do something like that, and yet here she is, looking actually excited to go.

"Mind if I walk you there so we can talk game plan? I have no idea where to start when it comes to chairing a debate in the comments."

"Sure." She smiles, and I follow her out.

"So...I shouldn't tell people I'm single."

"Correct."

"But surely people will get bored of not knowing."

"Not if we do it right. Have you heard of controlled controversy?"

I shake my head.

"See it as an umbrella term for this kind of marketing strategy. Most content like this can be split into three categories. First, you've got Feather Rufflers. They're the ones who actively make polarising content trying to divide everyone. These creators don't care if they're hated by half the population – in fact, they thrive on it. They've got half their viewers supporting them because their opinions align, while the other half of their engagement comes from people spouting hate, either to them or about them. The reason these creators don't care is because at the end of the day, they're getting views, getting paid, and – most importantly for these types of influencers – gaining notoriety."

"Right."

"Then you've got Hansels and Gretels."

"Are these official terms?"

She looks away, sheepish. "No, just mine."

Damn, she's cute when she nerds out about marketing. "Sorry, continue."

"Hansels and Gretels leave little breadcrumbs in their videos for sharp-eyed viewers to pick up. So they might misspell a word, get a small fact wrong, or have something odd in the background that people can point out."

"Okay, and what's the third category?"

"Men with podcasts."

My laugh gets caught in my throat. "Of course it is. And let me guess, they're the ones who do all this completely by accident because they're straight up terrible people?"

"Exactly." She hits me with the cheekiest of smiles.

"Isn't all this just a fancy way of saying 'clickbait'?"

She grabs my arm and veers off-path, taking cover behind

a palm tree and looking around as if I've revealed classified military secrets. "Shh! Keep your voice down."

I smirk at her farce. "Is that a dirty word?" I ask quietly, too close to her now to resist breathing her in.

"It's like saying 'Shakespeare's overrated' to a drama teacher," she says in a hushed tone, looking around. Once she deems the coast is clear, we continue walking to the restaurant.

I consider all this new information. "So I don't want to pit people against each other – least of all *me*. My skin's not thick enough to handle that. And I am *not* starting a podcast. You've already pushed my limit by getting me to *vlog*."

She giggles. "Don't worry, we're going for the other strategy. If you want to, that is."

"Hey, you've gotten me this far – I'm down for trying it. But I'll need you to tell me what to do."

"I'll brainstorm some ideas later, but the main thing is, it has to be really, really small."

"But surely if it's *too* small, no one will notice?" I don't know why I'm challenging her when she so clearly knows what she's doing, but I don't want to mess this up.

"You're severely underestimating what women are capable of finding out about a guy online."

That thought alone would be enough to scare me if I'd ever bothered with social media before this. I almost feel lucky I kept away from it while I was growing up, because now no one has anything to dig up.

"And *if* no one notices?"

"Then you've lost nothing. You'll still be putting out your usual content."

We arrive at the restaurant to find it heaving with people. We both scan the tables, looking for her team, but they're nowhere to be seen. Megan connects her phone to the Wi-Fi, faffs for a second, and then sighs, looking crushed.

"What's up?"

"They couldn't get a table, so they've gone to some burger bar instead."

"Oh, I know where that is." I begin to head in the direction of it, but she stays where she is and takes a deep breath.

"No, it's okay. Let's head back."

"Why? It's not too far from here. Five minutes, tops."

"Honestly, it's fine."

Oh, hell no. I have no idea what's caused the sudden change of heart, but there's no doubt it probably took her a lot to agree to attend this thing, and I'm not gonna let her give up. I catch up to her, already a few steps away from me, and grab her hand. It's a feeling I could get lost in, if only she'd hold my hand back and wouldn't keep walking away from me.

"The food's really good there." I continue my sales pitch.

"I'll grab lunch on the ship."

I tug her some more. "I think you'll have a good time."

"It's fine. I'd really rather go back."

I stop dead and use my new muscles to prevent her from walking any further. "Gem, you wanted to go. I really think—"

Her hand slips from my grasp as she turns back to me abruptly. "I can't go!" she snaps, and I can already feel the heat scalding my cheeks. "I can't… It's not…" Her strength weakens as helplessness takes over. "I can't do spontaneous. There are too many unknowns. I wouldn't know how to get back to the ship alone if I had to. I still don't know these people very well. I don't trust them, and I don't know what to expect from them. That was meant to be the one uncontrollable thing I'd have to tolerate, but now…it's *everything*.

They'll have already sat down, so I'll probably have to drag a chair over and disrupt everyone, or sit on the end where I can't hear anything and get left out, or I'll have to sit on a table by myself, *or* I'll get put next to *Matt*, and I honestly couldn't tell you which of those options would be worse."

Being next to Matt. Definitely.

"I don't know if they'll have something I'll like on the menu, and if they don't and I wing it and hate it then the food will get wasted, but if I don't order anything at all I'll look like some freak who went out to lunch but didn't eat, and people will start speculating I have some kind of eating disorder – I don't, by the way – which will only mean they'll monitor me more closely over the next few weeks or even months when I just want to lie low. I know this all sounds stupid. *Believe me*, I hear it. It's *exhausting* living like this, and I'd honestly rather not exist, but I *do*, so I have to endure all this *nonsense*, but I'll pick missing out again over having to put myself through that. It's too much stress, and I don't want to go."

Her neck is flushed and her chest is heaving as she catches her breath. *Princess.* I knew she was shy. I knew she had her secrets. But knowing she's so tortured by anxiety crushes me. I hate that she'd prefer to miss out than ask for help and get to have a good time.

Guilt wracks me for having caused some kind of spiral, or maybe contributing to one that was already happening, and I have to find a way to fix it. I can't let her feel like she's alone in this. And I can't in good conscience stand by and let her anxiety win without trying one last thing. I get my phone out and look up the burger bar's menu before handing it to her.

"I said—"

"I know, but you can look for next time. While I have Wi-Fi," I bargain.

Surprising me again, she actually looks at it.

"The jerk chicken burger with pineapple salsa is awesome. Though I think you'll wanna skip on the salsa – might be too sweet if you're not used to having actual flavour in your food." It's a bold joke to make right now, but her lip quirks into a tiny smile.

"Think they'd do it without the bun?"

"I'm sure they would, but if they don't, I'd eat it." Because I'm absolutely going to be there with her whenever she's feeling up to it.

When she makes no move to walk off again, I click off the menu and tap the button to get directions so she can see where it is in relation to the ship. "It's a ten-minute walk back. Mostly along this same route we've already done. I'd leave with you, however suddenly, and take you back if you needed to go. I'd finish whatever you don't like so there's no waste. I wouldn't ever let you eat alone or get shoved on the end or *put next to Matt*. If—"

"Why would you do that? Any of it? Why do you care if I go or not?"

"Because I care about *you*."

Her whole aura shifts as she processes my words.

"And you're helping me with something I find hard that you find easy, so I want to return the favour."

"Thank you," she says softly, staring down at the ground.

"You wanna give it a try?"

She nods.

"Come on then." I take her hand and lead the way.

I'm not met with the usual smug feeling I get when I win something. I just feel good, because while she might not trust anyone else, she's beginning to trust me.

SEVEN

TOM

"Tell me again why you couldn't have given me a real one," I ask while I check over the video Megan took of me, making sure I can see enough – but not *too much* – of the fake hickey Eliza painted on my neck with her special effects makeup.

Megan's mouth twists like she's trying not to smile. "Because if it isn't there tomorrow, people will have even more to argue about."

For more than a week she's been coordinating all kinds of little calculated shots, such as slipping hair ties onto my wrist one minute, then making a point of getting Jack in frame with his long locks the next. I swear she's some kind of evil genius.

I dart my eyes around the indoor pool, checking for anyone I wouldn't want to overhear me. "But I like your ones so much better…" I skim my eyes over her flawless body, her bathing suit making it so hard to focus, then I watch her try to hide her giddy grin.

She's always so beautifully awkward when it comes to flirting. I mean, she should be a pro by now, given that's all we've done since her brother made her more wary of me.

Jack turns up finally, his gaze landing straight on my neck. "You have *got* to be more careful."

"*Relax*, it's fake." I turn back to Megan. "Can I wash it off now?"

She takes a sip of her drink. "If you're done filming for tonight, sure."

"Great. Just think it ruins my street cred, you know?"

"Didn't have any to begin with," Jack mumbles, and I give him the stink eye as I get up to go to the bathroom.

"Marco Polo!" some guy bellows before bombing into the pool.

"*Yes!* Come on – put your drink down! Quick!" I grab Megan's hand and pull her along behind me. We hurry among the chaos to get into the pool to avoid being the last ones standing.

Resurfacing, she giggles and studies the people jumping in all around us. "What's happening?"

Before I can answer, Jack grabs me by the crook of my arm and drags me away from her. "Don't get caught!" is all I can say before the sound of splashing is too loud to shout over.

The rules are simple: you get caught, you get kissed.

The last person who made it into the pool when the game was announced is assigned Marco, and the rest of us scramble to get out of their firing line for when we have to shout "Polo". The DJ turns down the music so we can hear each other, but the party lights are still flashing around the dark room.

For some reason, Harvey and Eliza stay *in* the pool rather than get out of it, so I guess they're playing too – which is a weird move, but okay. Maybe it's so Harvey can feel like a big, strong man playing bodyguard to both of them. Whatever. Jack was right to get me as far away as possible from the two women on here who'd get me decapitated if I caught or got caught by them. Because unsupervised, I'd definitely be stupid enough to risk it when it comes to one of those women.

"Marco!" the straggler shouts with his eyes shut tight.

Everyone replies with a loud "Polo!" no matter how near or far they are.

"Marco" lurches forward, scarcely catching the arm of a passing player. He opens his eyes, grins upon realising who he touched, and then kisses her. We all count down from five – else this game would never end – and then the girl shuts her eyes tight and shouts, "Marco!" beginning the next round.

Jack tries his usual stealth move of climbing out of the pool and speed-walking to the deep end along the edge, earning him a scowl from the lifeguards. But the split second before he goes to jump in, "Marco" yells, "Fish out of water!" and catches him in the act.

Jack tips his head back with a groan, accepting defeat, then tracks her down, gives her a kiss, and takes over. His long limbs are definitely an advantage in this game – he can catch anyone with much less difficulty than everyone else. But that advantage is completely wasted on him, because girls purposely swim into his path. Jack has a certain reputation on this ship – a very good one, to say the least – and I can't blame them for wanting his attention. I've seen him in action. I've taken notes.

Megan keeps up with Eliza and Harvey, using them as human shields. I see how she watches each capture, though, fascinated by it, and then her eyes find their way to me before she quickly looks up at Harvey and then down at nothing. I could finally kiss her again tonight, if only her stupid brother wasn't here.

A hand brushes against my back. *Oh fuck.* How long have I been standing here watching her?

The guy who caught me tries to back out of it, much to the protest of the other players. He looks like he could drop-kick me overboard, but that doesn't stop me from toying with him.

"Come on. Rules are rules, big guy."

"I'm not *gay*."

"So you don't need to worry about one kiss turning you then," I challenge. I won't push it further, but I hate people being so aggressive with their straightness.

He grumbles and reluctantly presses his lips against mine until the countdown runs out.

We're given plenty of attention when we break apart, and I give him a little wink before shutting my eyes tight to shout, "Marco!"

I let the "Polos" sing around me before disappearing underwater, pushing my feet off the edge of the pool and launching into the noise. My tactic panics people – they can't determine which way I'll propel myself, and it causes them to make erratic choices. I reappear, catch my breath, and shout once more. There's movement so close to me that all I have to do is reach a little to the right to tag someone. I open my eyes.

Oh crap. I swear I didn't cheat, but somehow I have my hand on Megan's shoulder, where Eliza's holding onto her. It's like I have some kind of death wish. Harvey may have a poker face, but I know he's as good as glaring at me. I shoot him a look as if to say, "Take your pick," but there's no way in hell I'm kissing Eliza. I try to minimise my smile as Eliza distances herself, and I take a few steps back with Megan, because I'm not letting this moment be ruined by Harvey breathing down my neck.

"Better make this good, Gem."

"Why?"

"Because I'm a dead man after this."

In one quick motion, I pull her in and claim her lips. Flashbacks to that first night we met hit me like a truck. Her sighs, her requests, her secrets. *Damn*, this girl has no idea the power she has over me. One of her hands rests on my chest and the other squeezes my waist tight. Her almost-naked body slides against my bare skin. The feel of her boobs pressing against me? *Unbelievable.* The sensation of her drifting over my hard-on with each new kiss? *Insane.* Her tongue skims the tip of mine. *Jesus fucking Christ.* I can't keep myself restrained any longer. I need everything from this girl. I let my tongue get completely tangled with hers, because if this is the last kiss I'm ever gonna have, it's one I'm gonna be proud to go out on.

"Tom…" Harvey's warning grates on me like nails down a chalkboard, snapping me out of the moment.

Everyone's watching us.

Shit. I didn't even hear the countdown start, let alone end.

Megan stares at me, breathless, but then her face turns stoic again. How did I not figure out the resemblance straight away? She's frozen still, unable to turn to her brother, who's standing behind her.

"I think you say 'Marco' now," I tell her.

Grateful for the guidance, she nods once, collects herself, shuts her eyes, and then shouts into the room. Harvey's annoyingly defined chest rises and falls with barely composed anger.

I put my hands in the air, surrendering. "It's just a game, man. Chill."

This is anything other than a game.

Jack gets himself in her way. Dazed and confused, Megan

stumbles into him, and he makes sure to lay the biggest possible kiss on her, taking a bullet for me in the process. He's not only giving Harvey another guy to put on his watch-list, but he's also making sure she's mine by keeping her away from any other players who might try their luck at being caught by her. I love that man more than I know how to put into words. I'm not worried about their kiss. I'm never worried when it comes to Jack. I'm the most competitive guy on earth, and yet with him it disappears. We're a team.

To my surprise, Megan doesn't back down from his enthusiastic kiss; she rises to it. Exactly like when he escorted me to her room that night, she's quick to catch on to our unspoken plan. Another surprise: watching the two of them together makes my heart beat *very* fast. That's…new.

I steal my eyes away to clock Harvey's jaw ticking, then I sense a new pair of eyes on me. Elizabeth. She knows what I look like when I'm pining for someone. She was on the receiving end for long enough to recognise it. Her gaze turns serious with a plea or a warning – I can't tell which – as she shakes her head. *Don't go there*, she's saying.

I think it's too late for that, Queenie.

Jack and I keep our distance from the three musketeers for the rest of the party, and it doesn't seem like a smart idea to remind Harvey we exist as the night wraps up, so we leave without saying good night. But a low voice from behind stops me in my tracks.

"Tom."

Damn. Looks like I'm not gonna get off so easy.

I turn back to Harvey, whose eyes are trained on me as he cocks his head to the side, beckoning me to join him. Jack hangs back, and I follow Harvey to a quiet part of the room. We stand in silence for a second, and his Adam's apple bobs with all the things he's not saying.

"Come on – hit me with it."

He breathes a heavy sigh. "She doesn't need this, Tom."

"And what's 'this', exactly?"

He takes another deep breath. "I have done nothing but help you." He skirts around the question.

Yeah, helped himself to the first girl I ever loved, behind my back, after making promises he couldn't keep. Then helped steer his sister away from me before I had the chance to be loved by her. *Thanks for the reminder*.

Rage begins to bubble up inside of me. I'm sick and tired of this guy trying to control me. I was willing to ignore his warning to Megan, but to actually *confront* me about getting close to her… Who does he think he is? Or rather, who does he think *we* are – his *puppets*? I've had enough of him calling the shots when it comes to my love life.

"I heard what you said to her," I reveal, not letting him get away with this hero façade of his. "That day we were surfing."

His confusion is only brief, but regret sinks in a second later. "Tom, you don't—"

"Nope, don't wanna hear it. Just get on with your life and stop talking shit about me." I go to walk away, knowing if I don't, I'll boil over.

"Think before you act, okay? Please," he implores behind me.

"Oh, I've thought about it." The words are out of my mouth before I can stop them. I'm better than this. But having him lecture me, giving me the same holier-than-thou bullshit speech he's given a thousand times before, makes me childish.

"Who do you want to be?" His words from last year echo loudly inside my head.

His worst fucking nightmare. That's who.

His gaze hardens, and I don't let myself back down. I've said it now – might as well own it. No take-backs.

"Do not…fuck…my sister," he warns before walking away.

"Want me to get Jack for you? He put his tongue down her throat too!" I call out, aware I'm poking the bear with the wrong stick. But it's still a poke.

"Thanks, mate." Jack tuts as he approaches.

I march out the room, and he follows closely. When we get below deck and I turn the wrong way down the "I-95", I sense him stop, but I keep going, my path set on Megan's room because I *need* to ask her if she wants this too. I'm sick of letting her brother speak for her. And if she wants me, I'm gonna make sure her brother doesn't miss a second of the inevitable torture that'll ensue.

"Twenty-four hours." Jack's voice echoes down the hall.

"God dammit," I huff under my breath, knowing I have to listen to him. I don't walk any further, but I'm not ready to retreat yet.

"Sleep it off. If you feel the same tomorrow, I'll stand by you."

His words hit harder as I really take in the distance he's put between us. Jack knows reckless impulsivity better than anyone, so he can spot it from a mile off. If someone else called me out on it, I wouldn't listen, but it's Jack… If I insisted, he wouldn't stop me, but his opinion has been stated. He's letting the choice be mine.

I look up to the ceiling and release all the burning air in my lungs before spinning around and returning to him. We walk to our cabin together, and he lifts his wrist to his mouth.

"Hey, Siri, set a timer for twenty-four hours."

Eliza's waiting for me outside my room when I head to breakfast the next morning.

"Nice to see he's promoted you to hall monitor, Elizabeth."

She gives me her trademark eye roll while fighting a smile. "Quiet, you."

Without questioning it further, I follow her to the crew mess. Weekend breakfasts are a routine we know well. I get a Full English, while she gets American pancakes with syrup and berries. Except this morning, she piles a few strips of bacon on top of the stack.

"Hungry?"

"*Starving*," she says without realising what she's admitting to. She's worked up an appetite with that overbearing, frustrated jungle-gym of a boyfriend.

I grind my teeth, the unfairness of it all weighing me down. Not because I want to be the reason she needs to refuel, but because he always finds a way to gatekeep my exploits while holding the master key to come and go as he pleases.

We each take a sip of our tea and coffee in loaded silence, the tension building with every second that passes. I delay the inevitable conversation by taking a quick video of our full plates, noting that having Eliza's manicured hand in shot is no bad thing. I put my phone down, but still, she doesn't say anything.

I have so much love for Eliza, but things are different now she's in a relationship. Whenever we hang out, I either have to tolerate Harvey and feel like a third wheel or I'm crushed by this enormous guilt that I'm taking up time she could otherwise be spending with him. Not that she's ever said as much.

"I guess we should address the elephant in the room." I give in.

"She's a really special girl, Tom."

Keep yourself in check. She's only the messenger.

"And I can't date special girls because Boat Daddy says so? Like always."

"Boat…Daddy…?" She blinks slowly, taking in my new nickname for him. "No, that's not what I was going to say, actually."

I frown. What angle is she playing here? "Oh, I get it. You're the good cop."

"No… I only wanted to make sure you're doing this because you like her, not because you have an axe to grind with Oscar."

"I'm not. I don't." I'm quick to defend myself. I should be hurt by her assumption that I'm the kind of guy to toy with a woman's heart like that, but after the shit I said last night, I can't exactly blame her.

"Still…maybe give it a minute. Make sure you actually want her and not the fight that comes with it."

Damn all of Harvey's stupid wisdom for rubbing off on her. *Don't finish that thought.*

"Because if she breaks your heart, Thomas, Oscar's not going to like the side I pick."

I laugh at her joke, but it only creates a destination for the paranoid train of thought that set off a while ago. Eliza wouldn't pick me – not really. It would cause her too much grief. So if I fuck this up, I'm out for good.

Looks like I need to distance myself from Megan. *Again.* Not for Harvey – he can go fuck himself – but because I'd never forgive myself if I ruined my friendship with Eliza in all this.

Speak of the devil... Harvey sets his tray down next to Eliza and pulls out a chair. I want to Gretchen Wieners his ass and tell him he can't sit with us, but that's not going to do me any favours in the long run. "Keep your enemies close" and all that. The silver lining to his appearance, though, is that Megan's never far behind. She pulls up a seat next to me, her perfume briefly coaxing me out of my bad mood.

"Morning!" Eliza greets her with a bright, musical tone.

"Morning." Megan smiles back.

For too long, no one says anything more. We pretend we're busy with our breakfasts, but I can feel everyone waiting for someone else to break the tension.

"How did you sleep?" Harvey finally asks his sister.

"Fine, thanks. You?" she replies.

"All right, thank you. Could have done with a few more hours."

Gross.

"Always the way."

Isn't this quaint? We're like one big passive-aggressive family.

Ignoring the tension all around us, Megan gets next week's schedule out and starts adding everything into the app on her phone. "Have you got yours yet?" she asks me.

Is she really asking to hang out with me so openly? She's sure braver than me.

My gaze flashes briefly to Eliza, who watches us closely. "It's okay. You've helped so much already. I think I can take it from here."

Confusion distorts Megan's face. She doesn't understand why I'm suddenly pushing her away. *Shit.* Now I'm faced with my very own weird version of the trolley problem. Stay on this track and hurt Megan or pull the lever and risk losing Eliza in the fallout.

But…this will only ruin our friendship if Megan and I don't work out. What if we *do* work out? What if we give this a real shot and fall madly in love? I want that. I want *her*.

Fuck it, consider the lever pulled. It's time to prioritise myself for a change. I have to take a leap of faith that mine and Eliza's bond is strong enough to survive whatever happens next. I fish the schedule out of my pocket and hand it to Megan.

I'm gonna get the girl this time.

But to prove to everyone that I want to be with Megan for who she is, and not to spite who she's related to, I'll wait for her to make the first move.

EIGHT

TOM

I've been on my best behaviour for weeks. *Weeks.* The same can't be said for Megan, however. Her plans always seem to end up with us either alone in my room or with me wishing we were. Like when she had to be the one to put a bottle of micellar water and some cotton pads in *exactly the right spot* in my bathroom for when I film myself walking in there to start my day, or the time she planted a pair of her lacy "knick-ers" in my laundry basket. They're barely noticeable in the clip of me throwing my clothes in the dryer, but apparently, it's enough. It's as if she's trying to test me. *Or break me.* It's exhausting being this restrained around her, but she hasn't explicitly told me she's interested in more than friendship with me, so I haven't given in to whatever vibes I've been picking up. I've had another few videos go semi-viral, and my average views are way up since we started making click-bait. No one's cottoned on to our tricks yet, but Megan assures me it'll pay off in no time, and she's been right about everything else so far, so I'm not going to question it.

I've been going out of my way to reassure everyone this is about the content, and the content only, even more so than before. I've limited all our interactions and only spent time with her behind closed doors when we've absolutely needed to. It sucks, but it's what has to be done. It's not enough though – not to scratch whatever itch I've had since we met. I literally count down the hours until I can see her every day, and the time never goes fast enough. Until we're together, and then it goes by way too fast. Which is how I've found myself lurking outside on a balcony watching the end of her sunrise yoga class. I could have paced in my room waiting for her to show up, but why would I do that when I could be out here enjoying the view? If I can't touch, I'm sure as hell gonna look.

She's got an easy smile as she runs a group of people through a slow, fluid motion of stretches. I've noticed at the start of each new cruise she's always on edge, checking over her shoulder wherever we go, looking out for what, I'm not sure. But with today being the start of the weekend, she's pretty zen. I'm sure the yoga helps with that.

Eventually, Megan brings her hands together in front of her and bows to the class, who do the same back. After accepting a few words of thanks, she checks her watch and gets straight to packing up – rushing, for some reason, even though she finished right on time. I come out of hiding to lend a hand by rolling up one of the mats while she collects the hard foam blocks.

She spots me, surprised by my appearance. "Oh, hey! What are you doing out here? I was just about to come find you."

"Had some time to kill. Thought I'd see if you needed a hand."

She smiles to herself, and it's enough to make my week. "Thanks."

"What trick have you got up your sleeve today?"

Her eyes sweep the area around us. "I'll tell you in a minute."

So it's inappropriate? Now I'm *really* excited. I've never moved so quickly in all my life. Before long, we're entering my empty cabin, alone, and her sneakiness, along with her yoga pants, makes me think about a lot of things I shouldn't be. *Aw, man. Today might be the day I give in.*

"You gonna keep me waiting in suspense, or…?"

"Have you got a condom?"

Forgive me, Father, for I think I'm about to sin.

"Uhhh…yeah, I have a whole pack. Why—?"

She holds out her palm expectantly, so, with shaky hands, I head to my closet and root around for them, eventually finding the box right at the bottom of my belongings.

"It's full. I haven't— The pack's only open because of, uh…Tiegan's party." What am I *saying*? I find the unused single at the top and hand it over to her. "Which I didn't really wanna get involved with anyway – it was just in case."

She tears it open.

Fuck. Me.

Megan heads over to the bed, leans down, and places the opened foil on the alcove shelf beside my pillow.

"What's the reasoning behind this one?"

She takes a second to answer. "To make it look like you had sex last night."

Oh. Disappointment envelops me. With the wrapper torn, no one would think it was full. "And is that for Team Single or Team Taken?"

"You could argue it's fuel for both fires. Either you're sleeping around and being careful or you have a girlfriend who isn't ruining her body for the sake of making a minimal difference to a man's orgasm."

Damn, I love it when her feisty feminist side comes out. I'm putty for a confident woman who won't take any shit.

"Great point. So what should I film with it now?" I know we've set up a lot of things, but it's only ever to add a tiny bit of background detail to what I'm already doing. I don't wanna start creating fake scenarios; I want my videos to be as genuine as possible, with only a sprinkle of marketing mischief in them.

"I thought it'd be good to plant there for when you film yourself going to bed or something."

"Sure." There's a vibe in the room that's not exactly sexual – it's more awkward than that. I check my watch and quickly come up with an excuse to get us out of here. "I think Jack—"

"Can I use your bathroom?"

"Yeah, go for it."

She disappears, running the tap the second the door's locked, and I busy myself by putting the box of condoms back in the closet. I'm pleased with how long I've managed to keep it full. And honestly surprised. I really thought I would have gone back to my old ways by now, but casual sex hasn't even crossed my mind.

The tap shuts off and Megan comes back out. She's breathing faster than normal, and her brow is creased with stress.

"Are you all right there?"

"Nothing's going to plan," she frets.

"What do you mean?"

"I had a plan. I was gonna run back to mine, change, and tidy myself up a bit. Then, when I got here, I was going to ask you if you had a condom, and you'd say, 'Yes,' and then I'd say, 'Good,' and then I'd kiss you. But I wimped out, and now I'm annoyed because yet *another* move of mine hasn't worked."

"You've been making *moves*?"

"Yes!" she sighs at the ceiling as if she can't believe she has to spell it out.

I take a step towards her, pointing my finger. "I knew it!"

"So why haven't you done anything?"

"Because I've been waiting for you to ask!"

"Will you please, please *kiss me?"*

I don't think; I just jump. And then I'm devouring every ounce of her desperation, consuming it until there's none left. She pulls me into her even closer and kisses me with everything she's got, and I kiss her back with just as much. It's *earth-shatteringly* good, and all I want is *more*. Without letting up, I move us over to the desk so I can set her on top of it.

"Ow!" She reaches behind her to remove a ginormous pair of sunglasses from last night's themed party. I need to return those.

I apologise before claiming her lips again, letting her pull me in as she shuffles back further.

"Ah!" She breaks away, retrieving a bag of candy from under her.

Yeah, okay, my room needs a tidy. Oh, who cares? I sweep all my clutter off the desk and onto the floor, making a truckload of mess, but I'm too turned-on to care. *Shit*, that felt good. I've always wanted to do that, and it's exactly as satisfying as I thought it would be.

She looks at me, panting. "That was *so* hot."

"Right?"

I dive in for her neck, and she makes the sweetest sound while I feast on her skin, stopping only to lift her tight sports shirt off. My hands roam until I find the zip on the front of her sports bra, and I wait for her to give me permission before unzipping it. Her heavy breasts fall out.

"Help," I whimper, accepting the little kisses she keeps giving me.

"Help?"

"I think I'm gonna pass out. I'm too excited."

She giggles. "Please don't pass out. I've been waiting for this moment for too long."

I push through my elation-induced dizziness to make sure I can live up to her daydreams. I taste her nipples one at a time, grinding against her slowly. She arches her back and then reaches forward with one of her hands to tug at the waistband of my shorts. She takes ahold of me and the whole world stops spinning. *Hell*, I've wanted her to do that since we met. She strokes me in slow movements while I continue to play with the sensitive peaks of her breasts.

"I wanna take this slow, but I don't think I can wait," I admit.

"Me either. Go get the condom."

"Yes, ma'am."

I rush to retrieve it from my bedside, and when I turn back, she's up, stripping off her yoga pants, now in only her panties. *Holy shit.* She gets back on the desk, and I hand the condom over while I take off my clothes. I kiss her the moment I'm done, because spending barely a few seconds with my lips off her is agonising.

She looks bowled over when she sees me totally undressed. "That's bigger than I was expecting."

Consider my ego boosted. "Thanks. I grew it myself."

She snickers at my joke, and I laugh with her. I don't have a big dick. I have a boyfriend dick – at least that's what I've been told – and the irony that I've never been a boyfriend before isn't lost on me. Not too long, not too thick, *just right*. Right enough that you can take it on the regular and not worry about – as Ariana Grande so delicately put it – walking side to side.

"Hold on – what were you expecting? Do I give off small dick energy or—?"

"No, no! I… I don't know." She laughs nervously. "It just surprised me."

I kiss what I decide is a compliment off her lips and slide my hand over her warm, wet panties, rubbing gentle circles through them. I know she was happy with me touching her before, but I still want to err on the side of caution.

The wrapper scratches my side as she holds me. "Do you wanna put it on?" I offer, because I've been with some women who prefer to do it themselves so they know it's on properly.

Something changes in the kiss. "Can you do it?" she asks.

"Sure." I take the condom from her, but I don't get it out of the foil yet. I don't know why, but a weird feeling overcomes me.

"I would have regretted it."

"Are you sure you want this? You can change your mind, it's okay. We can forget about this whole thing."

Her brow crinkles. Determined, she grips my waist tighter. "I *really* want this."

"Okay." I try to settle my uneasiness, but something's still gnawing at me.

She must sense it, because she goes on. "I've never used one before, that's all. I don't want to break it or anything."

I keep my face neutral as I look down at the foil, but inside I'm freaking out, because that opens up a whole world of questions I now need the answer to.

"Are you on birth control?"

She shakes her head.

Shit. But she's still not telling me straight what I think I've pieced together.

"When were you last tested? Outside of work medicals."

She stares up at me with a lost look in her eyes, confirming my growing fear that she has no answer to give me.

"Gem, have you done this before?" I ask softly, my hand on her cheek.

Her eyes begin to glisten with tears. Biting her lip, she shakes her head again.

Oh, man. I can't let this be her first time. A quickie with me on a desk when I haven't even had the decency to warm her up properly. You always remember your first, and I don't want hers to be remembered like this. Rushed. Uncomfortable. And, let's be honest, over very fast.

"Please say something," she whispers.

"This isn't how a first time should go. I'm so sorry, Gem. If I'd have known—"

She sinks, defeated. "You wouldn't have touched me. Yeah—"

"No. I would have made a lot more effort."

"I want to do this with you. You're not *taking* anything from me. I'm not *losing* anything. You're not *defiling* me or whatever other bloody thing people say about virginity. I'm not *a virgin* – I'm just someone who hasn't had sex yet."

"I know, but it still means something."

"It's just sex. I'm not precious about it."

Her words hit like a punch to the gut. Yeah, that's all this is, isn't it? *Just sex.* A quick fuck to get it out of our systems and no strings. But I want strings. I want a whole Michaels store worth of string. I'm not brave enough to say that out loud, though, and I take so much time working out what to say instead that she gets up and rushes to put her clothes back on.

"Gem, I'm sorry. I—"

"Don't bother." Her defences snap up. She stuffs her feet into her sneakers and heads to the door. She presses down on the handle but turns back, one tear falling down her cheek as she holds back a million more. "I really thought you were different."

The door slams behind her and I'm left naked and alone to feel the sting of her words as they cut me. I curse at myself, throw on my underwear, toss the condom in the trash but keep hold of the wrapper, then get to tidying up the mess I made.

The door startles me as it opens, and even though Megan doesn't have a key, I'm disappointed when it's Jack and not her.

"Hey, man, do you know why Meg—?" He takes in the state of the room. "Ah. I think I can put two and two together. Tom…"

"I know, I know. You can spare me the lecture."

"You wanna tell me what happened?"

I would *never* talk about this with anyone else, but I can count on Jack not to repeat anything. And I think if I keep this to myself right now, I'll burst.

"That was almost her first time."

His eyebrows rise in surprise. "And why wasn't it?"

"I didn't know before and I freaked out."

He pulls his lips in tight, not hiding his disappointment. "I hear virgins really like it when you do that."

"Thanks, asshole."

He gets to his knees and helps me pick up the stray Skittles that fell out of the opened packet. "Why did you freak out?"

"I don't know." I shrug off his question.

"Yes, you do."

How does he always see through me? We throw the candy in the trash, and I return everything to its rightful spot – *not* on the desk. I fold my clothes and place them on the end of my bed, then I take a seat ready to wallow in regret. Jack watches me quietly, not letting me shut down and end the conversation.

I sigh. "Being her first isn't important to me, but I want to at least stand a chance at being her last."

"Then I guess you have to go fix it."

NINE

GEMMA

Half the crew look like descendants of unicorns, all thanks to Eliza's glitter and face-paint station. Every department is involved in this evening's Pride parade on the bustling promenade deck, either marching flags or pushing floats or dancing. There's not one person in this room who isn't having fun, and yet I feel a million miles away.

I look up to one of the balconies and watch Oscar survey the room with a smile on his face. We'd always go to Pride back home – the parade was practically on our front doorstep – but he'd only wear a rainbow flag. Even on a day devoted to celebrating his sexuality, he still wanted to blend in. Tonight, however, he has a stripe of bi flag colours on his cheekbone, and I'm so glad he finally wants to flaunt it. He's worked flat out this week to make sure everything runs smoothly – most weeks are busy, but event weeks are crazy – and hopefully, after tonight, he can relax a little.

I wish I was in the mood to join him and Eliza at the crew party that's about to start, but after the day I've had, I hurry to disappear the second the show is over.

"Gem, can we talk?"

Dread sinks in as I realise Tom's found me.

"It's fine," I throw over my shoulder, because if I look him in the eye, I'll cry. I thought public embarrassment was bad, but private embarrassment with *him*, the guy I've spent an unhealthy amount of time crushing on, is a million times worse.

The unfortunate side effect of becoming an influencer is that you quickly see the worst side of men. The comments, the DMs, the unsolicited photos. Especially after I was naïve enough to take part in a campaign for a lingerie brand. Just because I did it for other backbreaking-busted girls like me, it doesn't mean they were the only ones who saw it. Countless times a day, my inbox requests would run rampant with the *dregs* of the opposite sex describing the things they wanted to do to me – not *with* me – in vulgar detail, whether I liked it or not. And I'm not talking about whether I liked getting the messages themselves – I mean within the scenarios they'd dream up. So is it any surprise I've never had an interest in sex before, when I know the capacity for hate and disrespect and pain some men are capable of and fantasise about inflicting?

It wasn't until the opportunity arose to go on a reality TV dating show that I had any interest in trying to find someone. It felt weirdly like the safest option, because we'd be supervised and monitored while we were there, and once in the real world, any wrong step and their life would come crashing down around them – I'd make sure of it. But things didn't pan out the way I thought they would, and I figured that was it for me. Then I saw how fun sex seemed at Tiegan's party, how gentle men could be, that men as good as Tom existed, and the part of me I'd long thought was broken began to heal. Until Tom dropped me the second he found out I was *untouched.*

"No, it's not," he shouts over the noise, but his tone is kind.

We're pressed against the wall by all the moving bodies around us, our tight position made even more claustrophobic by the passengers coming out of one of the lifts right next to me.

"Megan, I didn't mean to—" He's right behind me, not deliberately pressing against me, but his hand is gentle on my waist.

I turn my head to talk to him. Remorse is written all over his face. "Please don't. It doesn't matter." I bite my lip to stop it shaking.

I know he wants to make it right. I'm not denying him that because I'm a bitch, but because I really can't bear to bring the subject up again. Especially not here.

"It matters to *me*."

The next thing I know, I'm being pulled into the empty glass lift as the doors close.

"Tom! We're not allowed in here!"

"You are in an emergency." He jams his finger against the "close door" button repeatedly, reactivating the doors after we interrupted them, and then he presses the highest number possible.

"It's quite literally the opposite."

"We can debate that later, but right now—"

"I don't want to talk about it."

"That's fine, but please listen. I didn't freak out because you're—because you haven't had sex yet. I freaked out because you said it didn't mean anything. I've never had sex that meant something, and I want that – more than I want five minutes of fun with you. Or with *anyone*. I couldn't get my words out fast enough earlier, and I know that gave you the wrong idea, and I'm so sorry. But *that's* what was going through my mind, not anything about your lack of experience. It's not just sex. Not to me. And if you don't want it to mean anything, that's fine, but then I can't be the guy for you."

The lift stops earlier than it should and the doors open to a family of five. I step into the back corner, away from Tom, to make room, but he slides up next to me, allowing the family to stand together. The kids are all hyped up from the parade. The parents tell them off for bouncing on the balls of their feet as they ask each other if they saw the drag queens and fight over which one looked best.

Does he mean that? Does he really not care that I'm a virgin? Does he not think there must be something wrong with me? Does he really like me more than that?

The family get out on the top floor, and Tom goes to follow them. I hold him back and press the button for the lowest level. He doesn't resist, letting the doors shut in silence.

"I only told you what I thought you wanted to hear."

"And what *wouldn't* I have wanted to hear?"

Opening up only gives people the opportunity to use your weaknesses to their advantage, but Tom wearing his heart on his sleeve makes me want to bare mine too.

"That I wanted it to mean something. *I* wanted to mean something."

My pulse thumps in my ears as he sits with my confession for only as long as it takes to descend one floor, but it feels like a lifetime.

He takes my hand. "You mean something to me."

Surely he's just saying that. There's a large part of me that doesn't believe anyone anymore, but a small – though equally significant – part that always believes *him*. I tighten my fingers around his hand, watching the floors count down. *Ten. Nine.*

"So that's settled. If it happens, it means something," he says resolutely.

"*When* it happens," I correct him.

He smirks. "*When* it happens, it means something."

Four floors to go. Three.

"And when is it happening?" I ask before we arrive back on the ground floor.

"Not everything needs to be an appointment in your diary." He smirks. "I'm not going anywhere. We've got time."

The lift settles and the doors open. A bunch of people are waiting to get in, so going back up again to iron out these details isn't an option.

Tom tries to break away, but I can't leave his side without knowing when we're going to get a do-over.

"How about tonight?"

When he turns back to face me, he has the most delicious smile on his lips and a dimple on his cheek I want to kiss. "Sure, I can come over tonight."

Excitement flurries through my body.

"Give me a chance to get this glitter off, and I'll meet you at yours."

"I'll schedule it in."

TEN

TOM

She didn't say it back.

She said it means something and she was quick to invite me over. But she didn't say *I* mean something to her. Doesn't matter – not tonight anyway – because I'm on a mission. And it's slightly different from hers.

With everyone out celebrating the gays, the hallways are virtually empty, but I rush down them nonetheless to get to her door, knocking fast when I arrive. Her door opens a moment later and all urgency leaves my body. Cancel my mission. She's standing there in matching pink lacy under-wear, her nipples visible through the intricate pattern on the bra. A reminder of having them in my mouth barely a few hours ago stops every other part of my brain from function-ing. The sweet smell of her shower gel drifts past me. *I bet it smells even better on her skin.*

"Holy…"

"Get in, get in!" She tugs my arm and shuts the door behind me.

I take a quick glance around the room before returning

my attention to her. It's clear her appearance isn't all she's put thought into. There's music playing – laid-back, sexy, nothing I've heard before, but I like it. And her fairy lights are the only thing illuminating the private room. It's not just sexy; it's romantic.

Though barely clothed, she's not shy. She's giddy. Her smile is radiant and infectious. After letting me take her in for a generous amount of time, she pulls me in to kiss her.

Don't get distracted. Stick to the task at hand. I have a duty. *A responsibility.*

I tear myself away from her. "Gem."

She steals her name from my lips with another kiss. "Mmm?"

Holy shit. Maybe I can delay the task for another night. *But by then it will be too late.* Oh hell, just rip the Band-Aid off.

"We can't have sex tonight."

She stills in my arms. "*What?* Why? But you said— And you're—"

"I know. *But*...I got to thinking in the shower that if you've not had sex, then maybe you've missed out on all the fun things that *aren't* sex."

"What do you mean?"

"Has anyone ever touched you the way I did the night we met?"

"Uh...once, a very long time ago. Or rather, they tried to, but it wasn't... They couldn't... I was too...tense."

"Okay, and have you ever touched a guy? Before today?" I'm not shy with my words. People are awkward when it comes to talking about sex but not about getting down to it, and it's a complete paradox. It's not a taboo; talking is good. It's exciting. It's safe.

She shrinks a little, and I rub my thumb over her naked waist to encourage her.

"There's no wrong answer. I just wanna know what you're comfortable with."

She considers her answer, or maybe whether she's even going to answer me, for a few seconds. "I've given someone a hand job – again, a very long time ago, back in sixth form – but nothing more."

"Okay, cool." Now I have something to work with. "So there's a certain rite of passage any…non-sexually act—"

"You can say 'virgin'. I was just angry and making a point earlier."

"Good to know. So there's a certain rite of passage any virgin has to embark on before they can have sex."

"Right, so what—?"

"Have you ever seen the movie 'Anchorman'?"

She stares at me blankly. "Yes, I've seen 'Anchorman'."

"Great, so you're not gonna be mad if we don't watch it." I'm already heading over to the TV on the wall to plug my hard drive in.

"Tom—"

I point two cheesy finger-guns at her. "Welcome to a night of Netflix and chill with your special guest host – me." I point both my thumbs at my chest. "Tom Parks."

She blinks and looks confused as hell, but a smile breaks out on her face. "*What* is happening?"

"I'm gonna put this movie on, wait an embarrassingly short amount of time before I make a move on you, and then I'm gonna make you come about a thousand times before Jack Black's even kicked a dog off a bridge. Sound good?"

She shakes her head with a titter. "Sounds great."

I could spend eternity with my head between Megan's thighs. Marvel could drop the trailer for a secret new project or I could be offered my own stand-up special on Comedy Central and I still wouldn't budge. The joy I get from the sounds she makes, the way she writhes when she's almost there, and how her thighs tremble against my ears when she is, makes me certain this is my new life purpose. I let her ride the wave once again, my fingers massaging her G-spot while I suck on her clit, and I wait until the tension in her legs has eased and the panting has begun before slowing down.

She lets out a long, satisfied sigh. I look up and take in her flushed cheeks, the sheen of sweat glistening on her skin, and the most satisfied smile I've ever seen.

"You want more?"

"Yes."

Her wish is my command. I begin to kiss my way back down her thigh.

"No, no – of you. I want more of *you*. Come here." She reaches forward and pulls me up to her, and my body settles on top of hers while her legs tighten around me. My tormented hard-on, trapped in my underwear, rubs against her naked, warm pussy as we make out. It feels so right to be with her. To be doing *this* with her.

"I can't wait to have sex with you, Gem," I confess.

"So don't wait."

Stay strong, Thomas.

"I promise I'm ready." She holds me tighter, the friction driving me crazy.

"Soon. Just not tonight." I kiss her to stop myself from saying what I really want to say, which is "fuck it".

"Tell me again why we can't."

"I honestly don't remember anymore."

I grind harder with her encouragement, both of us

moaning as we pick up the pace. *Fuck*, I love dry-humping. I've never allowed the time for it before. Why did I ever rush to the finish line when the race is the best part?

"No, I remember. I remember. Because I wanted you to experience everything, and sexual frustration is one of those things."

"I've experienced it. Thank you. I'm good."

I hum against her lips as I kiss her once more.

"Ooh! What if we did that thing Mormons do? Wetting or something."

"You mean soaking?"

"Yeah, that's it. You could just pop it in, and I'll cough a few times, or you could put out a Bat-Signal to Jack and he could come wiggle the mattress."

"I'm pretty sure that would count."

She throws her head back with frustration. "Ugh. Fine. It would, but don't tell the Mormons."

I laugh at her adorable attempts to bed me. "If there's one thing you need to know about me, it's that I'm stubborn," I admit between kisses on her neck. "So no matter how much you beg me to, I'm not gonna cave."

"Interesting. Thing is, I don't think you're as stubborn as I am. So, respectfully, and only ever with your consent—"

"Of course."

"I'm going to make you cave."

Defiance looks fantastic on her.

"I'd love to see you try."

Her grin matches mine as she squeezes me between her thighs and flips us over so she's on top, naked and hopelessly horny. She trails kisses down from my neck to my chest and stomach until she's at the waistband of my boxers, and that's where her confidence diminishes.

"Tell me what you're thinking."

She sits up and rests on her heels. "Given where we ended up that first night we met, I imagine this isn't your first time getting a blow job."

I'm surprised by her candour but still happy she feels she can speak freely. "Does it bother you?"

"*No*, but I... I'm not going to be as good as whoever's done it before, and..."

"Let me stop you there. There is *quite literally* no way to give a bad blow job. I mean, if you're using your teeth... you're doing something wrong. But otherwise, just putting it in your mouth feels *awesome*. But do you want to do that? I don't expect—"

"I want to. I'm just embarrassed and I don't think I'd cope with...notes."

"Nope, not allowed to be embarrassed. And I promise not to give you any notes."

She smiles, her nerves easing a little. "Could you maybe, like...guide me? *Gently*."

As if I'd be rough with *anyone*, let alone her. I haven't got it in me, much to the disappointment of the ladies I've been with in the past who like it a little rougher.

"If that would help you."

She nods, so I place my hand on her cheek and lean forward for a kiss. I stare into her big blue eyes, which I realise now are a unique combination with her brown hair. I've never met someone who looks like her, and she's even more beautiful because of it.

"There's no end goal. You stop when you wanna stop, okay?"

"Okay."

She kisses me again as I relieve myself of my tight under-wear, then I lean back and wait for her to decide when she's ready. I block out Ron Burgundy and the gang singing "Afternoon Delight" as Megan takes hold of me and leans in. I reach for her face, but I have no intention of guiding her movement – my hand is only there to calm her nerves. She licks her lips, and the anticipation alone could make me come at this point. She runs an explorative tongue up the length of my shaft and then slowly lowers her lips around me, making my eyes roll into the back of my head. *Oh shit, that's good.* She doesn't suck too hard or too soft; she's just right. There's a Goldilocks joke in there somewhere, her actions with my "just right" dick, but I can't think straight enough to piece it together. The combination of her hand pumping me, the warmth of her mouth, the movement of her tongue as she tries out different things, *and* seeing her on her knees pleasing me, has me on the edge way sooner than I'd hoped.

"Come up, baby," I say when I can't hold off any longer, but she keeps going. "Gem," I say louder. *Oh fuck, I'm gonna come. "Gem!"* I pull her up, my hand tightening into a fist around myself as I spill onto my stomach with an ache from holding off my orgasm for a few seconds too long. My whole body rocks with pleasure, and I come down from the high.

"Sorry, I didn't hear you." Megan bites her bottom lip, looking so pleased with herself she could burst.

"You're okay. I just didn't wanna…you know."

"Thank you." Her gratitude hits a melancholy note, which I put a pin in for later.

"Would you mind getting me some tissues from the bathroom?"

"Oh! Yeah, sure." Her breasts bounce as she walks away, and I collapse back on my pillow. *How did I get so lucky?*

Once we've cleaned up and hydrated a little, we tuck ourselves into bed. She wears cute little panties and an oversized shirt, and I throw on my boxers. She picks out another movie from my selection and we snuggle up together. I think this is the Sunday kind of feeling people get with their partners that I've always secretly wanted.

"Show me your schedule," I request.

She smirks. "I will if you say it properly."

"Sorry, *schhh*edule." I overemphasise the British pronunciation.

Grinning, she reaches across me to grab her phone off the nightstand and opens up her app. Perfect – we both have the morning off. I poke around for a while, trying to figure out how it works, until I'm finally able to program in a new block of time.

"What are we doing then?"

"I'm gonna take you on a date."

The most tremendous smile spreads across her lips. "Do you have somewhere in mind?"

"I do." I shuffle onto my side to see her.

"Where—?"

I brush a soft strand of hair behind her ear. "I'd really like to keep it a surprise, if that's okay?"

She considers it briefly, then she nods. "Okay."

I lie back on the pillow, pleased with myself, and then the dread kicks in. "Your brother's gonna kill me."

She groans with me because she knows he will. "We could keep it quiet?"

I turn back to her. "You deserve to be so much more than someone's secret."

She loses herself in another thought. "I've spent a big chunk of time living very publicly. I'm more than okay with having something that's just mine for a while."

My heart glows. *She shared with me.* And it potentially

confirms my suspicions of her being some kind of influencer—

Nope. Her past doesn't matter, and I'm not gonna mess this up by focusing on it. As long as I get her present, and maybe even her future, I'm the happiest man alive.

ELEVEN

GEMMA

Even with a whole team of professionals spending hours setting them up, the ridiculously idealistic dates on "Love Lodge" have *nothing* on my perfect morning with Tom. He doesn't tell me much about where we're going, but he does clue me in on what I'll need and how we'll get there and back, and he shows me a cropped screenshot of a menu – not that the name means anything to me. He takes us to some kind of swanky hotel a short taxi ride away. He's never been, but he's always wanted an excuse to come here.

We're kicking back on our deckchairs, enjoying the view from high up on the island, having spent most of the morning in the infinity pool, where Tom kept us afloat while I clung to him like a weightless koala. It's so quiet here, and the few people around aren't of the demographic I need to worry about. We've made the most of having a few hours to ourselves where we don't need to hide, talking about every-thing and anything, as well as engaging in an ungodly amount of PDA. This man kisses the same way he works: with great enthusiasm and genuine skill.

I'm enjoying my breakfast soul bowl while Tom digs into

his chocolate milkshake and "fries" like the big kid he is. It's a "special occasion", which means he can order whatever he wants, and I can't argue with that reasoning. I never would anyway. I'm actually a little envious, because even though my choice is nice, his looks…*nice*.

"Sure you don't want one?" He holds out a thin chip.

"Sure you don't want to try *mine*?" I deflect.

"Quinoa is my Kryptonite – you know this," he says, pronouncing it "key-no-wah".

"*Keen-wah*," I correct him playfully, "doesn't taste of anything, so it's probably the one thing you'd survive trying."

"Still rather not take the risk. You know what *does* taste of something…?" He holds out a new chip for me.

Temptation makes my mouth water and I take a quick look around. *Jesus, I can't believe I'm actually considering it.* Stuff it, we're safe here. I lean forward and steal the chip from his hand with my teeth. *So worth it*. And the smile that greets me when I come to from my foodgasm? Also worth it.

Even though this was a spontaneous trip, it's clear a lot of thought went into it. What Tom couldn't have planned for, though, was the massive horde of rowdy holidaymakers turning up and instantly disturbing the peace with their caterwauling. Judging by the matching orange towels, they're from our rival cruise liner, which must've recently docked next to ours. Where Neptune is a family ship, catering to all age ranges, theirs is adults-only and very much targeted at a younger crowd who want to let their hair down.

With the noise momentarily forcing us into silence, I take Tom's phone from the small table between us and pull the camera up. I film a panoramic shot of him admiring the view in his swim trunks – while I admire *that* view for a moment – then I follow his gaze to the pool and the island beyond it.

I'm about to hand his phone back when a better idea strikes me.

"Wait! Look at me. Tip your head down. Tiny bit more. Perfect." I let a few seconds tick by and then stop recording.

"Did you just film the reflection of your boobs in my shades?"

"Maybe."

He laughs and shakes his head, taking his phone back from me. "Gretel's allowed a day off, you know."

"I know, sorry. I saw an opportunity and I had to take it."

"On that note…" Tom gets up and takes a seat next to me. With our backs to the view, he holds the phone up in front of us to take a video, and I shift away, out of the frame.

"Don't worry – it's not for them. It's for the grandkids." He wraps an arm around me and I sidle up next to him.

Tom has no idea how much I'd *love* to have a photo of the two of us together. But he also has no idea how much power he'd have in taking it.

Noticing I'm not exactly champing at the bit, he lowers the phone and looks at me. "What, you don't want them to have pictures to go along with the story of how we fell in love? 'Cause that's kind of a dealbreaker."

It's impossible not to smile when he says stuff like that. *Grandkids*. He's such a wally. I shake my head with a smile, trying to downplay how happy the thought of a future with him makes me.

"Oh, is it now?" My eyes are drawn to the cheeky smile on his lips that mine are now matching.

"Mm-hmm." His eyes drop to my mouth too.

"Take the picture," I say, replacing my lips on his.

He snaps a selfie of us kissing. "All right, that one's solely for us. Everyone knows grandparents kissing is gross.

Now a PG version for them," he directs, and we both smile for the photo.

My chest feels like it's vibrating with all the little butterflies floating around inside of it. I've had millions of photos taken of me, but this one will forever be my favourite.

I take a sip of my water and enjoy watching him look through the photos, his dimple prominent on his cheek as he smiles to himself.

"Have you always been such a forward-thinker?"

"No, not always." He nibbles on another chip.

"What changed?"

"You don't know?"

I shake my head, not understanding.

"Oh, you always seem to know all kinds of stuff about me that I never told you," he teases before taking a moment to think before he speaks again. "So I lost my dad a year and a half ago. He was sick for a long while before that, and I spent all that time living for just one more year, one more month, one more week. I was stuck in that headspace until only recently. I had to really force myself to work out what I wanted long-term. And I'm living for it now."

A lump forms in my throat. I can't reply. Can't work out what to say that would be the right thing. Instead, I take his hand and give him a smile that says, "I'm sorry, and I'm here for you." Nan always says, "Find someone who's known loss and they'll hold you tighter than anyone else can."

"Can I ask you something?"

I nod.

"I saw that photo of you dressed as a princess in your room…"

I knew I couldn't avoid this topic forever. "I was hoping that nickname was just a consequence of you hitting your head."

"Oh no, baby. That name isn't going anywhere." Breaking the tension, he flashes me his trademark grin. "It's totally fine if you don't wanna talk about it. That's part of your past, and—"

"It's okay. What would you like to know?"

Clearly expecting me to shut down, he straightens and considers his question, but he struggles to pick one. "When…? Who…? What…?" He gives up. "I'd like to know as much as you wanna tell me."

I take a deep breath, preparing myself to tell Jessie's story. "My Auntie Nina – not my real auntie, but my mum's best friend – had Jessie when I was eleven, and suddenly I had the little sister I always wanted. I was *obsessed* with her. I got to look after her while Mum and Nina did 'mum things', and I honestly counted down the days until I was old enough to babysit her for real. And then, not long after she turned five, she was diagnosed with Leukaemia. It was…" I shake my head, welling up. "Awful. She spent so much time in hospital, and we all did what we could to make it better for her, but it never felt like enough. Then one day, we all decided to dress up as fairy-tale characters when we visited her, for fun, and I will never forget how happy it made her."

Tom smiles, a tear falling down his cheek as he blinks, but he wipes it away, finding a napkin to give to me to dry my eyes.

"I visited her as much as I could, sometimes dressed up, sometimes as plain old me. She was meant to be one of the lucky ones…" I shake my head. The pain is too much to bear, but Jessie deserves to be remembered. "The last time I got to hug her goodbye was as a princess, and she said, 'Don't worry, I know it's you.'" I let out a little laugh. "Turns out she'd been playing along the whole time, as if the dressing up was for me, not her." I shake my head, the laughter easing the strain in my chest and letting the tears flow freely. I allow myself to smile at the happy memories. "In all the times I went to visit her, I got to meet her friends too, and it didn't feel right not to go back to see them. I hated knowing they didn't have the same escape Jessie had. So I spoke to the hospital, and the next thing I know, Mum and I are setting up a charity and gradually hiring a whole team of performers to help us visit more kids in hospitals all over Sussex."

"You're incredible," Tom whispers.

I tell myself off for the state I've worked myself up into. "I swear I don't always cry this much."

Tom wraps me in a hug and doesn't let go. "Yeah, you're the person I wanna grow old with."

I giggle, feeling his tears drop on my shoulder as I'm sure he can feel mine. I think he's that person for me too. "I've never been on a real date before, but I'm pretty sure you're not supposed to cry on one."

He chuckles. "Nah, it's good luck, I think."

"I hope so." I smile.

"Thank you for sharing."

I excuse myself to freshen up in the bathroom, and once my sinuses are clear and my eyes are de-panda-fied, I check myself once more in the mirror, examining my hair in case I missed a spot when touching up my roots the other day.

A surprised gasp leaves the girl washing her hands in the sink beside me. "It's you!"

Our eyes catch in the mirror and my heart rate skyrockets. I'm too fear-stricken to reply.

She goes on. "Gemma from 'Love Lodge', right?"

Fuck.

"Who's that, babe?" I ask in a spontaneous accent, taking on the caricature of a person I've never met. Scouse. *Okay, we can work with that.*

135

Her excitement falters, awkwardness marring her features. "Oh, sorry. Never mind. Hang on – you mean you didn't watch 'Love Lodge'?"

I shake my head, feigning confusion. "No, never heard of it." I swallow the bile burning the back of my throat.

"It's a new dating show. You *have* to watch it! You look *exactly* like a brunette version of that girl."

Nod like you care.

"Don't worry, it's a compliment. She's like a model or something. But also, good thing you're not her – she's a *psychopath*. No one's seen her in months. I honestly wouldn't be surprised if she was currently locked up in a padded cell."

I can't respond, can't stick up for myself, but I have to say *something*. "It's easy to show the dragon burning down a village and not the teenager with a sword who tried to slay it."

With her being thick enough to believe everything she sees on reality TV, I'm not surprised when the penny doesn't drop. She leaves the bathroom thinking she's given a compliment to some tipsy, rambling Liverpudlian, and my peripheral vision blurs. I keep blinking, but I can no longer make out my hands in front of me. All my limbs feel like jelly in an earthquake while my lungs feel both too empty and too full.

Shit, shit, SHIT!

She believed me. Didn't she? No, she did. She had to have believed me, or else…this little safe haven I've built for myself here, with my crush, whom I promised minutes ago I'd grow old with, will disappear in an instant.

Tom. I have to get back to Tom.

I pull myself together as best as I can and find my way to him.

"Hey, whoa, are you okay?" His concerned voice breaks through the fog in my brain like a beacon of hope, and the relief hits me like a captain spotting a lighthouse in a storm. His comforting hands take hold of me. I must look as unsteady on my feet as I feel.

"Can you take me home, please?"

"Yeah, okay. Just let me pay the bill." He whips his head around, trying to find a member of staff. "I'm so sorry, I shouldn't have asked about—"

I shake my head. "It's not that."

"What happened?"

Dammit, why didn't I go along with it? I can't tell him who I am. It will ruin everything.

"I don't feel too good," I lie. "There's money in my purse."

We fumble with our things for a second – me trying to get my cash out with shaky fingers; him trying to stop me as he flags down a waiter. I feel *everything*. I don't have supersonic hearing, but it's as if I'm tuned in to every frequency around me. Though this place was a serene spot a few minutes ago, in a matter of seconds it's become my own version of hell. Every conversation happening around us is amplified, every cackle of laughter from other guests going through me like a shock of electricity. *Are they laughing at me? Have they recognised me too?*

Tom settles up and asks the hotel staff to call us a cab while I put on my sundress and hide behind my sunglasses and a large sunhat. My bikini straps are too tight, digging into my shoulders, and my new flip-flops rub between my toes. There's a menacing mosquito buzzing around us, sizing me up for its next meal, which I don't even bother to swat away. *Even bugs want to use me for something.*

Tom grabs my bag with our things in it, takes my hand, and guides me out to the waiting taxi. We don't talk on the way home, but he leaves his open hand on the middle seat between us in case I want to hold it – which I do, because I can feel the opportunities I have left to hold him slipping away from me with every minute that passes. We pull up by the ship, the need to be incognito like we were this morning having fallen off Tom's priority list.

"Can I take you to the medbay?" he offers. You should get a sick note."

"It's all right, I'll head there in a sec. I need to find Oscar first."

"Oh, okay." He wants to know what's wrong and why it's my brother who can fix it, not a doctor, but he doesn't ask.

"Sorry I ruined our date."

"No, you didn't ruin it. I'm sorry you don't feel good." I can tell he wants to reach for me.

"Thank you for organising everything. It was perfect."

Was.

I move quickly in the direction of Oscar's office, hoping he's there so I won't have to go on a wild-goose chase around the ship looking for him. I wish I could be honest and tell Tom everything so I wouldn't have to hide from him anymore, but the second he finds out who the world thinks I am and why I'm here, he'll run for the hills. And he'd be right to. It feels like it's only a matter of time before that happens now.

Despite my urgency, I knock on the door with Oscar's nameplate on, and relief hurries through me when I hear him call out. I fly through the door and shut it behind me, leaning against it, my lungs finally able to receive the air they've been deprived of.

"You have to get me off this ship. *Now.*"

TWELVE

TOM

We went from one hundred to zero in the space of five minutes. It's been almost a week since our date, and I've barely had the opportunity to ask if she's feeling better, let alone to see it for myself. I might believe I had something to do with it if she wasn't also avoiding everyone else. At first, I wanted to give her space, but now I'm aching with the fear I'm being shut out again. I've been given the silent treatment before, by Eliza, and it all could have been prevented if we'd just talked, so I'm not going to let today end without a conversation.

I finish hosting the trivia in time to catch the last few minutes of Eliza's performance in the cocktail lounge. Harvey's got one of the best seats in the house, dead centre at the back of the room. I'm sure he'd be sitting in the front row if it wasn't for him being an employee and not a paying guest. I'm surprised to see Megan out, but I'm glad she's facing her agoraphobia to show up for Eliza.

Damn, I love formal nights. Megan's in a tight black dress, which is probably knee-length, but while she's sitting down it ends halfway up her thigh, and the slit in the side fills my head with all kinds of dirty thoughts.

At the end of the song I sneak in, taking the open spot next to Megan on the blue crushed velvet loveseat. It's a snug fit, and she pretends to adjust, but I swear she shuffles up a tiny bit closer to me. I place my hand by my side and test the water by letting my knuckles brush her bare thigh. She doesn't shrink away. Instead, she wraps her left arm around her waist, letting her wrist drop to her side, and she finds my fingers, tangles hers in them, and squeezes tightly.

Oh, thank God. She still wants me. Despite hiding from me, she still wants me. I'll take mixed messages over no messages at all. I steal a glance at Harvey, but he's too transfixed on his girlfriend to notice. No surprises there.

Eventually, we have to pull away to applaud Eliza, and when her performance comes to an end, the three of us slip away, leaving her to work the room.

There was never any question we'd be going all out for Eliza's birthday. I think she was nervous no one would make a fuss, though, so she started trying to organise something herself, and we quickly realised the only way we were going to pull off a surprise party was if we threw it three weeks early.

By the time Eliza arrives, we've transformed hers and Harvey's room into the ultimate slumber-party hideout. Mattresses line the floor – everyone dragged them down the hall earlier – the "Mean Girls" soundtrack is playing on a speaker, and the three of us, plus Jack, Cora, Finn, and our relatively new entertainment friend, Imka, are all wearing our cutest PJ sets and the silliest slippers we could find online. We've got a nail bar, a face-mask station, a friendship-bracelet kit, a Victoria sponge cake, shiny balloons, and a huge banner. My idea to set off confetti cannons as she arrived was shut down the second I suggested it, but I think Eliza would have loved to walk into a glittery reception. *Maybe* Harvey had a point that the tidy up afterwards wouldn't have been much of a gift…

Eventually, Eliza works through her shock. "You know it's not today, though, right?"

Harvey wraps his arm around her and promises we know, and Megan hands her a gift straight away – a new pyjama set patterned with stars and moons – so she can go change and relax into her party.

"What? It's my favourite."

I'm floored – not only by Jack's confession, but also by the new meaning behind the tattoo on his chest that reads "Tomorrow", which he's currently baring for me.

"Your favourite movie is about *singing orphans*. Is that irony? I don't even know."

He smirks. "Call it a dark sense of humour."

"Yeah, no kidding."

"Annie" won the vote for the movie tonight, but it was rigged from the start. I'm the only one in attendance who couldn't give a damn about people singing and dancing their every thought and feeling. The only reason I don't demand a recount is because my favour can be bought very easily with candy and popcorn.

Harvey and Eliza are cuddled up on one side of their bed, Cora and Imka on the other, and the rest of us are on our mattresses on the floor. There was meant to be a sleeping plan. I was going to be by the wall, with Jack next to me, and Megan should've been *all* the way on the other side of the room. Except Jack came along and ruined it by pulling

Megan's bed over beside his earlier in the evening so she could braid his hair more comfortably.

Which was all part of the plan...

Instead of the movie, I focus on finishing off my friendship bracelet for Jack. It's going to spell "brothers". It's already hard to make a bracelet when you're not creatively inclined, and even harder still in the dark, but nevertheless, I persist. It's not only serving as a distraction from the film, but also from the fact Harvey made Eliza a bracelet with iridescent beads that read "cricket", whatever that means.

I lose my grip on the string while trying to thread the last letter through it, and I don't miss the snicker that comes from my left, on the other side of Jack, as half the beads fall into the kit on my lap. Megan's not as focused on the movie as the others either, finding more entertainment in watching me struggle. I pick out what I think are my letters and rebuild the lost half of the bracelet.

While some bald guy sings about New York City I fasten the bracelet around Jack's wrist, pleased with my handiwork. Then I pull out my phone and type a message to Megan on the Notes app, keeping the promise I made to myself.

What's been going on?

I'm not messing about with open questions. Something's up, and I think I deserve at least a little bit of an explanation. I summon the courage to pass my phone to her and anxiously wait to see what she'll reply, or if she'll decide to reply at all.

To my relief, she types something out and hands the phone back over.

Something happened in the bathroom at the hotel. I thought I might have to leave.

I type fast, refusing to prioritise my feelings over the possibility of her leaving abruptly, because my pain means nothing if she's in pain too.

Me: **Did someone hurt you?**

Megan: **No. But it scared me.**

Me: **Why did you stay?**

I peer over, spying the first word of her next sentence: **Oscar**… Then her thumb hits delete a few times.

Megan: **It's safer for me here. And I didn't want to leave you.**

Safer? There are questions I want to ask, but they'll break the rule about me digging into her past. I consider ending the conversation there, but I owe it to myself to speak up, because those last few words don't make me feel as comforted as they should.

Me: **I spent all week thinking I did something wrong.**

I watch as she reacts to my message, her head dipping with guilt. She types and hands back my phone, an apology written all over her face.

Megan: **I'm really sorry.**

I give her a half-smile, turn my phone off, and throw it on top of the sheets by my feet. I shuffle closer to Jack and weave my hand through the gap between his back and the bed to find Megan's hand. We don't let go of each other for the rest of the movie.

After an anarchic sequence involving Tim Curry chasing the redheaded kid up some kind of ladder into the sky, and her being saved by the unwound turban of a man in a helicopter – *where do I even fucking begin?* – the movie thankfully ends, and people start getting ready for bed.

Jack takes a moment to admire his bracelet. "Aw, thanks, buddy. But tell me why it says 'broobies'." He raises a curious eyebrow.

Ah, fuck it. It's the thought that counts.

The last time I spent the night with Megan, I learnt she sticks her tongue out just a little while she brushes her teeth, and it's cute as hell. Jack, on the other hand, is an animal. I've never seen someone so violently dedicated to oral hygiene.

"Elizabeth, sitting through that movie and not complaining was my birthday gift to you," I tell her while puffing up my pillow and settling in. I got her a real gift, of course: a basket filled to the brim with American candy, snacks, sodas, and cereals, which I can't wait to see her open on her *real* birthday.

She gasps and brings her clasped hands to her face sarcastically, like a cartoon. "It's what I've always wanted. How did you know?"

"Did you have a good night?" I ask with more care.

"I did. Thank you for helping organise it all."

We share a smile as I remember all the effort she went to when putting together my party last year.

"We should do something soon. Feels like ages since we've hung out properly," she says.

"Yeah, absolutely. Wanna hit the arcade while everyone's out tomorrow?"

Her smile widens. "I'd love that."

Once the lights go out for good, it's time to initiate phase two of the sleeping plan. Jack complains that he's too hot and asks for the desk fan to be put on. The white noise is then loud enough to cover him swapping beds with Gem. Our covers overlap to make one, and she snuggles up against me as if it's the most natural thing in the world. The knot that's been in my stomach all week finally loosens. I place a hand on the crook of her neck, my thumb brushing over her cheek, and feel her smile. There she is, *my Princess.*

She goes to kiss me, but I pull away in the nick of time. I place a finger against her lips as if to say "shh", and then she puts her finger against my lips too in understanding. Her hands skate over my bare chest, and I stroke her hair, so relieved to have her back in my arms. Needing more, I lean closer, brushing my nose against hers, and she nudges me back. I grip her tightly, the realisation dawning that I almost lost her. I wish I knew what happened. I want to understand so I can stop whatever it was from happening again. My fingers trail up her silk shirt and trace her skin. *So warm. So soft.* But it's not enough – not after being starved of her touch all week. I remove my hands from under her shirt and find her collar, where the fabric dips, then slide down to the top button, tugging at it gently until it slips through the hole.

She makes no move to stop me, her hands taking their own liberties with the growing ache in my boxers. My fingers slip to the next button, then the next one, and the next one, until her shirt opens fully for me. Before I can stop her, she's on top of me. I still, waiting for someone to question the sound of the movement, but no one does.

Her breasts brush against my chest as she settles against me, and warmth smothers my dick. If it wasn't obvious before, it is now: it's going to be some kind of torture to not take this any further. Maybe we could… *No.* There's no way to do anything quietly, no way to clean up afterwards without waking the entire room, and all it would take is something as simple as someone checking their phone and busting us with the light of the screen. *Not tonight.* I shake my head, and I know she feels it as her hand is cradling it.

She buries her face in my neck and breathes me in as I do the same, and for a while we lie there together, until we eventually grow too tired and fall asleep next to each other.

I don't know what time it is when I'm rudely awakened by a flick on the forehead, but I open my eyes to find Jack glaring at me with meaning. The fact I can see him at all should be enough for me to know we're on the brink of being caught, but it's the light spilling out from under the bathroom door that solidifies it.

I give Megan a gentler wake-up call than Jack gave me, and she stirs the same way I imagine a baby bunny would, all wrinkly-nosed and bleary-eyed. Before she can start moving, I find a piece of her open shirt and then try to find the other side, stopping her from going anywhere barely conscious and uncovered. She does up whatever buttons she can find and crawls over to Jack's bed, and he takes care of swapping over their sheets and pillows.

All three of us flop and pretend to be asleep the second the latch on the bathroom door unlocks, as if someone shouted, "Andy's coming!" It's only Imka, though, and she probably wouldn't have even spotted Megan in my bed without her glasses on, but better safe than sorry.

We wait for her to settle back down, and then something soft appears next to me, put there by Megan. Jack reaches it before I do, and the fact he doesn't hand anything over confirms it's his toy pig. He's never told me why he can't sleep without it, but I've never felt the need to ask.

Rule number one of our roommate agreement: Respect the pig.

Closely followed by rule number two: Always be honest, even if it's ugly.

"Suck it, Thomas! I win again!" Eliza has both fists in the air as she celebrates getting more basketballs in the hoop than I did.

"Yeah, by two shots! And you got lucky with those."

"Mm, sounds like loser-talk to me."

"Just wait. You're gonna be sorry when I annihilate you at air hockey."

"Not today. I'm on a winning streak – *I can feel it.*"

I've missed this. Goofing around, just the two of us. As per the bet, I go get her candy from the vending machine in the corner of the room.

"So, Megan's still helping you out with content?" she asks while the machine retrieves the Jolly Ranchers.

Damn, I knew her name was gonna come up sooner or later, but I was hoping I could get away with not having to lie to Eliza any more than I already am.

"Mm-hmm, I know I should have got the hang of it by now, but my ideas are never as good as hers. She's a pro."

"Yeah, it's such a shame she had to give it up."

Huh… Up until now, I assumed whatever brought Megan here was a Harvey family secret, but suddenly I'm realising Eliza knows more than she's let on in the past. The messages Megan "sent" me yesterday have been playing on my mind all night. If I could just find out a little more, maybe I can protect her from any repeats of whatever happened in that resort bathroom that was so bad she thought she had to leave. I can keep her safe.

"What do you mean?" I ask, studying every inch of Eliza's face.

She shoves a piece of candy in her mouth with urgency and then offers one to me, but I ignore it. After a moment she turns away and heads to the ice-hockey machine. She swipes her key card against the sensor to release the puck, but with her hands full, she drops it immediately.

Butterfingers.

We both kneel down to get it, but I reach it first and I don't hand it over. Instead I wait for her to shift her attention off the puck and onto me. Slowly, she lifts her head, and we stare at each other in silence.

"You know something, don't you?" I finally challenge her.

"Know what?"

The indent in her cheek from the Jolly Rancher she's nervously tucked in there reminds me of a hamster, but that's not what's caught my attention – it's how red her cheeks have turned. Shit, I hate myself for trying to dig into Megan's past, especially when I promised her I wouldn't. If I think I know already, does getting Eliza's confirmation – against her will, no less – really matter? Well, Megan's safety does, but she seems to have a handle on whatever the situation is now.

"Never mind." I stand up and offer out my hand. "Are you ready to get your ass kicked?"

She rises to her full height too. "As if you're gonna win."

THIRTEEN

GEMMA

Day 156 of trying to seduce Tom.

All right, fine. It's only been two weeks since Eliza's sleepover, but there has been *zero* sex. We almost did it, but then Jack walked in *just* as I reached for the condom. We should have been in my room. We should have pulled the curtain across the bunk for privacy. But we got caught up in the moment and it was all happening without much logic or thought. I appreciate that no one has brought it up since. Though it's not as if Jack hasn't witnessed us fooling around before.

Jesus Christ, what is this boat doing to me?

Then my period struck me down, taking me out of action for what felt like the longest five days of my life. There was a moment I thought we might do it anyway, but even though Tom defines himself as a feminist and said he isn't scared of a little blood, and even though I *know* I shouldn't have hang-ups about period sex, for my first time, I didn't want *anything* getting in the way of our fun. That said, we're *really* good at dry-humping now.

Tom's one condition of us seeing each other is that Jack

doesn't get left out, so we've been (very carefully) alternating rooms and inviting him along to whatever we're up to – which also helps alleviate my brother's concerns that anything more is going on. I don't think we have him entirely fooled, but he hasn't dished out any more warnings.

I'm glad Oscar got me to stay, because leaving would put me back at square one. Right now, one person in the Caribbean thinks they saw a lookalike. That's nothing on the amount of people who would *actually* recognise me back home. And if I went home, I wouldn't have the hundreds of scrapbook-worthy photos Tom's captured of the two of us.

Jack's trapped in the kids' club, so Tom and I are going out to "film content" today, and I've managed to track down the *perfect* spot for us. It's a bit of a trek to get to, but it'll be *so* worth it.

"Whoa."

Tom's mesmerised as he takes in what looks like the moon pool out of "H2O" – a TV show about mermaids I watched (and forced Oscar to watch) as a kid. Despite us being in a cave, there's nothing dark and gloomy about the space. Light pours in from a circular hole above us and reflects off the teal pool, making it look like it's littered with diamonds. It's as though we're inside a volcano of water.

"Yeah," I agree in awe. "Okay, so go stand by the water and take your shirt off, then you're gonna go to unbutton your shorts, notice me, hit me with that cute little smile of yours, and swipe the camera away."

Tom laughs. "Straight down to business, huh?"

"And what comes after business?" I cock a meaningful eyebrow at him. The word "pleasure" floats around in the air unspoken.

He gets into position comically fast. "Is right here okay?"

"Absolutely."

We get it on the first try because we're basically a professional team now. He even survived doing the upload alone this week while I was on port-manning duty. Of course, I prepped what I could and talked him through everything beforehand, but that's a pretty big deal for Tom.

He looks over my shoulder as we review the footage, and I inhale his chocolatey scent. "We good?"

"I'd say so."

"Great!" He wraps his arms around my waist and kisses my neck before turning me around to steal my lips. His fingers skim the hem of my dress before lifting it up and over my head. "Fair is fair." He loses himself for a moment but then pulls back with confusion. "Why aren't you wearing a swimsuit?"

"I had a better idea." I smirk and step away, reaching my fingers behind me to undo my bra.

"Gem!" He casts a glance over his shoulder as I throw it onto one of the large rocks beside us.

"Chill. Our ship doesn't do excursions out here." Though they really should. Lucky for us, we have this little pocket of paradise completely to ourselves. "I checked."

His shoulders drop, relaxing enough to admire me. I'm still waiting for the novelty to wear off, but I hope it never does, because each time I strip for him, he reacts like it's the first time he's ever seen a naked woman. Completely starstruck.

I hook my thumbs into my knickers, tug them down my legs, and throw them onto the rock too. "Have you ever been skinny-dipping?" I ask.

He shakes his head. "Have *you*?"

"I grew up by the sea – what do you think?" I walk away with a smile, heading down the short sandbank until the surprisingly warm water laps against my feet. I turn back to him. "Are you just going to stand there all day?"

He kicks off his flip-flops, removes his shorts, and stands there in his boxers watching me wade in until I let the water take me. It's shallow enough to stand in, but I choose to tread water while waiting for him to make a decision. He looks back the way we came once more, sucks in a sharp breath, and removes his boxers, chucking everything somewhere in the vague vicinity of my things. He holds his hand over himself as he walks towards me – not because he's gone shy, but because otherwise a specific part of him would be pointing right at me.

We circle one another, grinning like teenagers in love, because maybe we are. In love, I mean. Or maybe I am, at least. How can I expect him to be in love when he doesn't even know who I am? This feeling has an expiry date, I just know it. But right now, I'm going to make the most of it before it's too late.

We quietly enjoy the liberation of the moment, slowly gravitating closer and closer until we can't hold off any longer. Tom reaches for me and pulls me against his naked body for a kiss. We find the ground with the tips of our toes, the water coming up to our shoulders, and lose ourselves in each other.

"*Jesus, Gem,*" he sighs against my lips.

I beam up at him, enjoying how the fractured light shines on his face. "I want it to be here. Now. With you."

Meaning changes his features, a quiet smile on his mouth. "You brought a condom?"

I nod, and my teeth sink into my bottom lip as nerves take over me suddenly.

"Okay," he says, and he doesn't try to talk me out of it

this time, because I think he knows I'm sure now. "We can't do it in the water though."

I frown. That's kind of the romantic bit.

"Unfortunately, water is the opposite of a lubricant. But we can lay a towel down up there." He looks back towards the sandbank. "Make a comfy little spot."

I feel stupid for not knowing that, but I don't let it ruin the moment. I take a second to reimagine the fantasy I've been playing over and over in my head for the past few weeks. Yeah, that still makes my heart do all kinds of things. I still want it.

"Okay."

"You wanna swim a little longer?"

I shake my head. "I don't think I can wait." My voice cracks with the admission.

He rubs his nose against mine and kisses me deeply, then he takes my hand and walks us out of the water. He gets our towels out of the bag I packed, and we both dry off in weighted silence.

He keeps checking the entrance. "Are you *positive* this is safe?"

"I'm positive."

A bird chooses that exact moment to scream in the distance, raising both of our alarms, but no one who could have spooked it appears, so we relax again. He takes his towel and lays it down on the firm sand, then he takes mine and lays it on top of his to pad out our makeshift bed, while I retrieve the condom from the small, zipped pocket inside my bag.

Giving his spot an approving nod, he beckons me over and lays me down, leaning over me as he kisses me softly. He strokes my hair and looks into my eyes. "You're so special to me, Princess. And so goddamn beautiful."

My heart feels like it's being squeezed, but deep down, guilt tampers with this moment. Right then I decide I'm going to toughen up and tell him who I am after this. No more secrets – he deserves to know the truth. And while I might have doubted it in my lower moments, part of me is confident he'll stick beside me.

He takes the condom packet out of my fingers and slips it between the towels before kissing his way down my body.

"I'm covered in saltwater," I protest, letting him know I don't expect him to be subjected to that.

He looks up at me seriously. "You could be covered in that awful smoothie and I'd still want to taste you."

He kisses my stomach, continuing his trail down my body, and when his mouth seals my core I succumb to the feeling, threading my fingers into his curls. He laps me gently, like he's making out with my pussy, and all the tension and unwanted thoughts float away. Once I'm wet enough, he slips a finger inside of me, dragging it in and out slowly. I sigh and squirm with pleasure as his tongue flickers on my clit and his fingertips touch me exactly where I need him. I cry out with my release, my hands tugging at his hair, because I'm scared if I let go, he'll disappear. When the rush subsides, he kisses the inside of my thigh with the most satisfied smile I've ever seen.

"I want you so bad, Tom." I paw for him to come back up to me, and he does.

"Me too, baby." He plants a long kiss on my lips.

He looks back at the entrance to the cave as if he's expecting something to appear.

"If you're worried—" I begin.

"Sorry. This al fresco situation is new to me, that's all. And I want you to be comfortable."

"I'm comfortable with you."

154

He smiles, and I notice the moment he makes the decision he's been mulling over. He gets the condom and sits back on his knees to put it on. My breaths become shallow with excitement as I try to take in this moment before it turns into a memory. A really, really special one.

He wets his fingers and rubs them over the condom, then once again to ensure it's slick enough, and then he leans back over me. "Have you used toys before?"

I shake my head.

"Tampons?"

I raise an eyebrow. "Are we really going to talk about tampons right now?"

"Sorry, sorry. It's because if you haven't, I read that breathing out should help you relax."

He did research. Of course he did – he's Tom.

I smile. "Okay, I can do that."

He rubs the tip down my wet folds, making my body quiver with anticipation, then he ever so gently presses in the slightest bit. Oh. Oh. *Ow. Breathe out.* That's…not. *Ow!*

Tom hasn't moved an inch, and he's watching me like a hawk. "Talk to me, Gem."

"It stings. Should it sting?"

"Um, I don't know. I've never been someone's first before." He pulls back, wetting the condom some more. "Want to try again?"

I nod quickly. "Yes."

He comes in close, and I breathe out again, but the sharp stinging makes me hiss in a breath.

"Baby," he sighs, with worry on his brow. "I think the water won't have helped."

"But I'm wet."

"You might just not be wet enough. I don't suppose you've got some lube in that magic bag of yours?"

I shake my head. Oh no. I'm doing it wrong. We haven't even done it and I'm doing it wrong. I got into that stupid water not knowing what would happen, and I've ruined it. I've ruined everything. My eyes join in on the stinging party and I blink hard, not letting my stress show. I want him. I want us to do it so badly.

"Gem, I promise you this will happen. But not today. Not like this. I really don't want to make you wait longer, but I want you to be relaxed, and we can't do that here."

"But I really want this. I want *you*."

"Me too, but I'm so scared of hurting you. And if I'm totally honest, I can't relax here either. I'm tense too."

Sadness and relief hit me all at once. A tear falls down my cheek, and I wipe it away quickly, hoping he didn't see it, but I know he did. Guilt swallows me again. I didn't think about him having an issue with this before I brought him here. I didn't check in properly, because he's the pro out of the two of us, but I should have done.

"I'm so sorr—"

"Don't you dare say that word. You're allowed to change your mind."

I kiss him hard. "Maybe we'll go back and I can suck you off or something?"

He blinks slowly as he processes my offer. "Why would you do that?"

"Because you're all…" I point to his still hard appendage. "And you'll get blue balls."

He giggles and shakes his head. "That's a very kind offer, Princess, but I'm pretty sure blue balls are a myth invented by the patriarchy. And even if they aren't, that'd be my problem to deal with. Consider this my contribution to levelling out the orgasm gap."

We sit up, waiting for one of us to decide what's

happening now, and, unsurprisingly, it's Tom who comes up with a plan.

"So we could get back in the water, have a swim, or we could go find somewhere to get ice cream."

This boy has changed so much about me, because the thought of walking down the beach, with one hand in his and the other holding an ice-cream cone, fills me with pure joy.

"Ice cream."

We get dressed, pack up, and take one last glance around the cave. At what this place almost meant for us. What if the opportunity never comes up again?

"I still fancy you." Tom interrupts my thoughts. "In case you were overthinking it. I still want you. This doesn't set us back. It just wasn't the right time."

I pull him in for a kiss, his words meaning so much to me, then I take his hand tightly and we head out. "Told you I'd make you cave," I mumble smugly. You've got to take the little wins when you can.

He snickers and then groans. "I don't know what's worse – the fact you made a cave pun or that I *like* a woman who makes puns."

We laugh, and he tucks me under his arm, both of us carrying on like we didn't try and fail epically at having sex today. Yeah, nothing could ruin us. I'm certain of it.

Not even my secret.

FOURTEEN

TOM

My TikTok account is *flourishing*, and it's all thanks to Megan and her breadcrumbs. Aside from playing up to the hot, maybe-single guy thing, I'm actually inspiring people to look into a new career – be that onstage or on a cruise ship – and I'm making them laugh with my commentary. And without Megan there to help last week, I added a link in my bio to donate to two charities – cancer research and her princess charity – because what's the point in having a platform if you're not gonna make a difference?

Maybe I should have asked her first. But I also don't want Megan thinking I did it to win some kind of favour with her. I sneakily asked Harvey what his mom does and got the name of the charity that way, and I only searched as much as I needed to get a donation link, because even though I could have used the name of the charity to find out more about Megan, I can't betray her like that.

Jeez, I'm obsessed with her. To the point I wanna call Mom and tell her I'm falling for the sweetest girl in the whole world. I'm in deep with *a Harvey*. *Holy shit.* There's a portal at the entrance of this ship. There's gotta be. Because there's no way I would have willingly fallen for a Harvey before I came back here. No way.

Wait – would marrying Megan make Eliza my sister-in-law when she gets married to Harvey? We could even have a double wedding...

Okay, okay, slow down, Parks. We need to work on something else before we start planning the wedding.

I haven't rushed to find our moment since our trip to the cave. It's gotta be organic. I know Megan likes to plan everything, but maybe being spontaneous is the way to go. I'm aware that with each day that passes, she's probably worrying it's never gonna happen, though, so if she's free tonight, I might *spontaneously* go for a sleepover in her private cabin.

I'm partway through this morning's breakfast rave, adjudicating the cereal-box challenge, when Harvey enters the room. His gaze sweeps across the dance floor as if he's on the hunt for something. Then his eyes land on me and he strides over. *Ohhhh shit. He knows.* Took him long enough. I prepared myself for this fight, but now it's happening, I'm not ready for it.

His eyes burn into me as he gets closer. *Not the face. Anywhere but the face.* I steel my spine even though all my instincts are telling me to cower, and I stare up at him, tall fucker that he is.

"You need to take that video down. *Now*," he demands, his face stern, jaw ticking.

"What video?"

"Which one do you think?"

Could I have...? *No.* I didn't. *Please* tell me I didn't. There's the content I created to post, and then there's the private montage I made with all the pictures and quick clips I've taken of me and Megan, and that was *never* meant to see the light of day until our wedding. From the daggers in

Harvey's eyes right now, I'm guessing I must've selected it by accident. *Shit.*

"I really like her, okay? We're taking things slow. She's allowed to make her own decisions."

"That's the least of my concerns right now."

So what's he this mad about?

"I didn't mean to post it. I'll take it down, okay? I get that you're pissed, man, but it's not that big of a deal."

He shakes his head and takes a deep breath, choosing his next words carefully. "The fact you still don't know why it's a big deal is the exact reason I told you to stay away from her."

"Stop talking in riddles."

"She came here for a break from the trolls, and you led them right to her."

My heart thumps impossibly hard, but it feels like it's in my stomach, not my chest. "What do you mean? What—?"

Fuck, fuck, fuck, *fuck!* I frantically search my pockets for my phone.

"Not here. Go!" Harvey barks.

I waste no time and head out, knowing he's taking over my shift. I rush below deck, and as I fumble to buy a Wi-Fi package along the way, I crash into Eliza.

"Tom!" There's an urgency to her voice, like she was sent to track me down too.

"How bad?"

"Bad."

FUCK!

I hurry to my room and load up TikTok. *Holy shit*, I've not had a video blow up quite like this. I don't bother to look – I archive it immediately. Then I take a deep breath to calm myself down.

Okay, it can't do any more damage than it's already done.

What are you running from, Princess?

160

I promised I wouldn't dig, but I'm buried six feet under now, so I have to at least claw my way out of the shit pile I've landed us in. Needing to face how badly I've hurt Megan head-on, I take a look at the comments:

> Yesss, girlfriend reveal! FINALLY!
>
> I swear she looks like Gemma from Love Lodge.
>
> It is! It's her! The link in his bio is for the same charity she supports. Looks like she dyed her hair and ran away to work on a cruise ship. That tracks after what she did.
>
> Why is he dating that psycho slut?
>
> Tom, RUN. Get out while you still can.
>
> Ugh, it's always the crazy bitches with no personality that get the nice guy.

So that really is her name. She wasn't jumbling her words, she slipped up. Regardless, how can people be so cruel? What could she possibly have done to upset this many people?

The search bar at the top of the comments reads "Gemma Harvey Love Lodge", and I don't waste a second before clicking it.

What is all this? Because that's not Megan. But it looks and sounds like her... Except she's blonde in these videos. I scroll and scroll through what feels like thousands of clips of her in a ski lodge with a bunch of other people. *Is this some kind of game show?* One minute she's fighting with some guy; the next she's...*fucking him?* Then she's in bed with some other dude, and then crying over the first guy. She's *screaming* about junk food and sugar but is then shown eating that same stuff a few seconds later. Yet somehow she looks gaunt, like she's wasting away, and there's no life behind her eyes. The next videos show her sabotaging others' relation-ships, shouting and crying, storming off, and rolling her eyes.

I thought I knew her, but she's...*horrible*.

I swipe up again, needing to find proof this isn't her, that it's just someone who looks like her, but I don't find it. *What on earth was she doing on a dating show?*

"Gemma's nothing but another bogus fitness influencer trying to promote a healthy lifestyle for show, while stuffing her face with crap and then sticking her fingers down her throat when you aren't looking," some girl says in her video with tens of thousands of likes and comments.

What? She doesn't have a problem with food, does she? I think back to the day she went out with her team. There's some kind of hang-up there, for sure. I'd put it down to anxiety rather than an eating disorder though. And she's so into her fitness...which is how a lot of people control their weight when their eating is being monitored... But she got ice cream with me the other day. I guess I don't know if she kept it down. I ache to think of what she might be doing to herself and wonder how many more secrets she's been able to hide from me.

I can't find her actual profile on TikTok, so I Google her, only to be confronted by some of the most horrendous head-lines. I should stop. I *know* I should stop. But then I find a link to an Instagram account – which I click – and confirm the woman I know as Megan is actually this Gemma person.

1.5 *million* people know who she is. And I was kept in the dark. Hurt cuts me like a knife.

"You would hate me if you knew me. Because everybody does."

She tried to warn me, and I ignored her.

So have I met the new version of her or some fake so-

and-so she's impersonating until the noise dies down and she can go back to her normal life? I'm all for self-improvement, but a leopard never changes its spots. How long does she think she can keep up this new act? And what will it take for her real colours to show one day?

My head is spinning. I don't know what to believe anymore, but I know what I have to do. She may be in the wrong for letting me get so close to someone she isn't, but I fucked up by not checking my content before leaving that cafe – though I'm almost glad I didn't now, because who knows how much longer she would have strung me along for? – and I owe her an apology.

I head to her room with my tail between my legs and my guard all the way up. She opens the door a crack, sees it's me, and then closes it. I glimpse enough of her to notice the redness in her eyes, and my heart breaks for her. The version of her I knew anyway.

"Meg—" *Nope.* "*Gemma.* I think we should talk." When there's no reply, I continue to plead my case. "I didn't mean to post it. It was an accident. I've taken it down. I'm so sorry. Please, just tell me how I can handle this."

The door opens, and I step inside. My nerves prickle with unease. I should sit, but I'm almost scared to, so I stand awkwardly in the corner of the room while she sits on the edge of her bed.

"How do I fix this? I can do my best to put out the fire, but I'm scared I'll only stoke it more."

"You say nothing. This is it. *This* is the ultimate engagement opportunity for you. You posted a mysterious video with the most hated woman in the UK and deleted it. Everything we've been working towards was for one big video to kick it all off, and it's finally happening. Now you have to stand back and watch the dominoes fall."

"I can't do nothing."

She shrugs. "Yes, you can. Let them talk, let them feel sorry for you, and let them debate how on earth someone like you ended up with someone like me. People are going to make it their mission to analyse every single one of your videos now – in addition to whatever tales the scum who stalked me before I left decided to weave – and they're going to tell their versions of the story despite having no involvement in it whatsoever. And then the next bunch of people will listen to all those theories and come up with even more. We're not in charge of what's next. They've lit their torches – you've just got to run with them now."

"But at the cost of your *safety*? No. I want to make this right."

"I promise you, defending me will only make it worse. So the two options you have are to give up and disappear or to keep going and let them get bored of asking," she says, matter-of-fact.

Neither of those options feel like enough to repair the damage I've done.

"I'm so sorry," I say, meaning it, but I'm not able to bring myself to comfort her with more than words.

Our eyes lock onto one another's as the seconds drag on, and then something in her expression hardens.

"You believe it, don't you?" she asks quietly, and I can't tell if she's amused or distraught. "What did you see?"

I don't know where to start. I haven't taken a second to process what I saw, nor to decide how I feel about it. I saw enough to see she's not the person I thought she was, but I'm pretty sure I don't need to state the obvious.

I sigh, completely defeated. "I didn't even know your name."

"So that's that then." There's an edge to her voice as if her barriers have gone up too.

"I just need a second to take everything in. Is that allowed?"

She stays where she is but stretches out her arm, presenting the door to me, her expression completely flat.

"Are you offering me time or demanding I leave?"

She lowers her hand and turns her gaze on me, and it's so empty it's as if she's turned to stone. "I don't think it matters."

FIFTEEN

GEMMA

Five months earlier

"Are you sure you want to do this? You've seen what can happen to these people afterwards."

I chuck my phone into the basket of warm laundry from the dryer and carry it up to my room, ready to organise it all into packing cubes. "Harassed by trolls, ugly pictures from before their glow-up leaked by school friends, people rating their bodies on podcasts. It's nothing I haven't already coped with in the past three years."

Oscar stays quiet, agreeing but clearly working out what else he could say to deter me. He hasn't had very long to sit with the announcement I'm going on what's set to be the next big dating show, but then again, neither have I. It was only two weeks ago that a casting researcher slid into my DMs, and everything's moved so fast since then.

"I think you need to take some time to think about it."

"I'm being picked up for my flight at 5 a.m. tomorrow. I can't exactly back out now."

I mull over which pieces from my extensive bikini collection to take with me. I would take them all, but we're going to be in ski gear, thick coats, and bobble hats most of the time. The info pack said we don't need many, but some dates might involve a hot tub.

When Oscar doesn't reply, I continue my reassurance campaign. "I've worked so hard to get to where I am, and to build my platform to what it is. I've always made my own opportunities, and I've toughed it out in spite of everything in the hope that one day it'll pay off and work will come to me. This could be *huge*." I didn't even apply; I got recruited via Instagram. *I was noticed.*

"I know. But it's… I'm…scared for you. That's all. Not because I don't think you're tough enough to handle it, but because I'm not sure I'm tough enough to watch people tear you apart. Because they will, no matter who you are. You're the type of person people envy, and envy has a way of bringing out the worst in someone. It'll be everything you've experienced but a thousand times over."

I take a second to centre myself. "I know. But things have changed in the wake of… There are duty-of-care procedures in place. I've already seen a psych, been given the talk of doom—"

"Talk of *doom*? Because *that's* not a red flag."

"It sounds scarier than it is. They walk you through the worst-case scenario, and again, it's stuff I face on the daily and I'm still standing." I pull up Instagram. "I'm going to unfollow you and archive anything with you in it. You should set your socials to private before your internet runs out too."

They can come for me, but not for my family.

"Promise me you'll be careful. Think before you speak. Prioritise yourself, because no one else will. So long as you stay true to who you are, you'll be fine."

Part of me wonders if he's saying that last bit to comfort me or himself. "Thank you."

"And don't trust anyone. The guys they put on these shows—"

"It's a career move, nothing more," I say, but I don't fully mean it. I'm not going to get my hopes up, but it would be nice to meet someone who likes me for me, and not for my looks or my follower count.

He sighs, and silence stretches between us. "You're really going to do it, aren't you?"

I take a second to consider pulling out. "Yeah, I am."

"Okay." He breathes out, and with that one noise I know he's done playing "man of the house". "Do me a favour?"

"What's that?"

"Don't feed the plant."

I smile. It's the finale song and overall moral of Oscar's favourite musical, "Little Shop of Horrors". Some cute, nerdy guy gets tricked into killing people and feeding them to a singing Venus flytrap to get enough notoriety to win over the love of his life. Who, depending on which version you watch, ultimately gets eaten by the plant too, leaving him with nothing. Oscar's obsessed with the movie, but it always gave me nightmares. What he's saying in his own special way is, "Don't sell my soul for fame and success."

"I won't."

The call came in a few hours ago. After being held captive in a hotel room somewhere in Canada for eleven days – *eleven. Days. Without my phone.* – it's finally time. I've been brought in as an "Avalanche", chosen by the public to go on a date with Gavin, a property broker to London's elite. I say "date"… He could have easily been set up with the producer, because I don't think I said anything she didn't feed to me line by line. It was honestly like a naff comedy spy film where someone's hiding behind a menu on the next table over, telling you what to say. It's overwhelming, and it's going to take some getting used to, but loss of autonomy aside, I think it went well.

The crew pack up their equipment and head out of the remote cabin we've been filming in, but we're told to stay behind while they bring the 4x4 around to pick us up. I breathe a quiet sigh of relief when the door closes behind the last runner to leave, looking over at Gavin, sure he'll have the same reaction as me. But his finger is pressed against his lips as he shakes his head, soundlessly shushing me. Then he taps the top of his chest, signalling the mics we're both wearing around our necks like collars.

But we aren't filming anymore… I guess someone could still listen in though.

My gaze sweeps the ceiling, checking for cameras rigged in the corners like they are on other reality shows – and back at the main lodge too, I suspect – but there's nothing. The ongoing silence isn't awkward, but there's a tension in the room, thick like smoke.

What the hell have I signed myself up for?

The sky was clear when I first skied down the mountain to Gavin, but it began to snow when we arrived at the cabin. Wind whistles down the chimney and in through the fire-place, and now the adrenaline of filming has begun to wear off, I'm struck by a chill. The longer we wait, the worse the wind gets, and I can no longer see through the windows by the front door. They'd better come get us soon, or else we'll get snowed in.

The sound of a radio crackling on the kitchen counter

startles us both. "Gavin, Gemma, can you hear me?" It's the producer's voice. She talked enough for the past hour – or was it longer? – for me to recognise her easily.

Gavin and I stare at each other nervously for a moment, and then he moves to pick up the radio and reply.

"There's a blizzard passing over – it's not safe to come and get you."

No. It can't be that bad, can it?

"You're going to have to sit tight and ride it out until it clears up."

What? Refusing to believe it, I head over to the door and try to open it while Gavin asks more questions. The door doesn't budge, and the windows are already a wall of white, but I can't tell if it's from the snow that's settled or the mist of snow falling thick and fast.

Oh no.

Gavin sets the radio back down on the counter, then he reaches into his pocket and removes the mic's battery pack, turning it off before loosening the wire around his neck and lifting it over his head. Without questioning it, I do the same. Then we just stare at each other, the reality of our situation settling in.

He's clean-shaven and has mousey-brown hair. I wouldn't say he's my type, but he's definitely handsome, no question. He's a posh boy, though from what I gleaned from the words being fed to him, he's also relatively down-to-earth.

"Hi," he says with a sweet smile.

"Hi," I reply, less sure of myself.

It's clear that even though I've been on a date with him already, I haven't actually *met* him yet. *This* is him, the real him, and despite being told he's trapped here for the next few hours or days – *how bad is it out there?* – he's keeping his cool.

"Apparently, there are some tins of things the owner keeps stocked here that we can help ourselves to. Let's get dinner sorted, and then I'll answer all the questions I imagine you have."

Yes. Please.

"So you don't think you guys will last?"

We lost power very shortly after Gavin finished cooking a surprisingly edible bean chilli, and with no sign of the weather easing up anytime soon, we reluctantly accepted that this is where we're spending the night. The biggest issue with that, though, is there's only one bed. I guess I knew I'd be sharing a bed with someone when I came on the show – that's all part of it – but sharing a bed in a room full of other people doing the same thing is very different from being alone. I've not done that before.

"Not a chance, but it's about keeping up appearances."

It's *freezing*-cold and the wind is howling, not to mention my mind is racing a mile a minute, so I doubt I'll get any sleep tonight. We're wrapped up under the covers, both of us staring up at the ceiling, close enough to keep warm, but neither of us has initiated spooning, and I can't tell if I'd want that. Maybe I would and that's why I want to know if he's serious about who he's currently paired up with or not. *Christ*, I can't think straight at all.

"I'm scared," I whisper.

He turns his head towards me, and I turn mine to him. So much passes between us in just a look.

"It'll be over soon."

Does he mean the storm or the show? Because I know I wasn't talking about the storm.

His hand reaches up to the side of my face and I sink into the comfort of it. He leans in, and my heart rate picks up as he kisses me softly. And for no other reason than it feels good and will distract me from the panic overwhelming me, I kiss him back.

We're rescued sometime in the morning and blindfolded for the journey home as we were on the way in. It's a bit overkill considering the NDAs they had us sign, but I comply none-theless.

I didn't realise how disorientating it would be not knowing the time. It could be 6 a.m. or 12 p.m. The only thing I have to go off is my hunger, and right now, I'd say I'm at least 8 a.m. hungry. But surely it's later than that? The sun couldn't have melted all the snow so fast, could it? Perhaps that chilli was more filling than I thought.

My pulse hammers in my ears as we pull up to the lodge, and we're told we can remove our blindfolds. Every-thing about the place screams "big budget". It's a ginor-mous chalet, all wood and glass. I was envisioning something like where we were yesterday on a slightly larger scale, rustic and homey, but this is *glamour*. If someone told me it was owned by the Kardashians, I'd believe them, no question.

We stand outside for a while, until we're instructed to hold hands and enter quietly. I try not to react as I'm met with a panoramic view of the snow-tipped mountains through the window running the entire length of the outside wall, but it's stunning, untouched by the bad weather. Everyone's sitting on plush sofas adorned with (hopefully fake) fur throws, staring at a huge TV – not that there's anything on it. The roaring fireplace on the far wall taunts me while we wait for the other contestants to notice us.

And we wait.

Finally, heads turn, but no one stands up to greet us. Have they been told not to say anything? Are the producers about to jump in and film our arrival again from three different angles? I already know I'd hate that, but I'd prefer it way more than whatever's going on now. Silence has never felt so loud.

At long last, someone gets up. A girl with long auburn hair. As she heads our way, I notice the mascara running down her cheeks.

Gavin lets go of my hand and reaches out for her. "Jazz, what's wrong?"

"Fuck off, Gav." She flinches away and continues walking past us, running up the staircase.

A warm sinking feeling overwhelms me. *Why were they all crowded around the TV?*

The rest of the girls follow Jazz upstairs. Most of them don't spare me a glance, but the ones who do look at me as if I killed their childhood pets.

Why were they all crowded around the TV?

Gavin tries to go after Jazz, but one of the guys gets up to stop him. "Not a good idea, man. Give her a minute."

I'm glad Gavin looks as confused as I do, but he's welcomed onto the sofas by the guys while I'm left standing there, not knowing what to do or say. Gavin wipes a hand down his face as he tips his head back and groans.

I pray for someone to emerge from a room down the corridor and clue me in on what the *hell* is going on, but no one does. No one's coming to save me.

I've never felt so uncomfortable in all my life. I could be naked in a street and have my hate comments written in

Sharpie across my body and I'd still feel more comfortable than I do here. This has to be some kind of nightmare I can wake up from. *It has to be.*

When pinching myself doesn't work, I head in the direction of the corridor in search of a toilet or a coat cupboard I can curl up in and cry. The first door I try is locked, so I try the next one, and then the next, until I find one that gives. There's a small corridor and then another door, which goes through to a toilet. I walk through it, lock the door, close the lid, and sit on it, finally letting out the sob I've been holding in.

What am I doing here? Were we filmed last night? Were there cameras hidden in that room? I realise now that no one said we *weren't* being filmed, but there were no obvious signs we *were* being filmed either. Someone went to great lengths to ensure that was the case.

I give myself a minute to panic before setting myself straight again, and when I go to blow my nose, I look up, paranoia crawling over my skin. Yep – there's a camera in here too. *Seriously? What about when I* actually *need to use the bathroom?* I can't even think about that right now. If we were filmed and the other contestants saw something, that means the whole world saw it too. Obviously, I know what I signed up for – or at least I thought I did – but I assumed I'd at least *know* when the cameras were rolling and when they weren't.

I'm so bloody stupid!

There's a knock on the door. Someone must have tracked me down. Though that's not exactly hard in a place under better surveillance than Buckingham Palace.

"Just a second!" I call out, standing up to preen myself in the mirror. *God*, I'm a right state.

I plaster on a smile, even though it's pointless because it's more than obvious I've been crying, and then open the door. I'm greeted by a man – another contestant, I think. Gentle. He has tight brown curls on top of his head with blonde tips. Worry is etched on every part of his face.

"Was there a storm last night?" I blurt out, because the question is burning me alive.

"Huh?"

"A blizzard. Were you trapped here last night?"

"No. Why?"

Anger rages inside of me. They're playing poker while I thought we were playing gin rummy. Oscar's warning sinks in now, a few hours too late. *Don't. Trust. Anyone.*

"What's going on?" I ask urgently, not giving him a chance to ask me the same thing.

"Those guys were, like, *the* couple, and everyone saw you break them up."

Yep. We were set up. "I didn't break them up. I didn't… mean to. He said… What did you see?"

He looks up, raising his brow as if he's working out how to say it best. "You guys were in bed, and you said, 'I don't think you guys will last. Forget about her right now.' And then you kissed him, and the duvet moved a lot."

"What? I didn't say that… I…" I was fed lines on our date, but none of them were that. I would have questioned it. "*He* said he wasn't into her. *He* kissed *me*. It was one tiny kiss. I'm not even sure why, but that was *it*! The duvet moved because we were doing the cold bed dance from 'Miranda' to try to stay warm." Knowing now that there was no blizzard and therefore no power cut, it hits me just how much control the people who make this show have over us. All my fingers and toes had felt like ice.

The door behind him whips open, and someone dressed in all-black with a headset on glares at us. "Can we get you both in the lounge, please?" It's phrased as a question, but it's an order. To both of us.

With his back to the crew member, my only ally gives me some kind of reassuring look, like he believes me. Then he heads out, and I follow suit. This place is like "The Truman Show" but worse, because at least Truman got to go about his day thinking everything was perfect, while I've just found out this place is everything *but*.

I'm still single four days later – *shocker* – but there'll be a ceremony soon, and with there being too many girls, the boys are likely going to choose, and the last woman standing will get her freedom back. I haven't made any effort to flirt or win favours, because I want out. There's no other way to leave. I tried playing the mental-health card, but we get an extortionate fine if we walk out. Plus, they've already aired my arrival – leaving of my own accord would only make the backlash worse when I got home. They don't tell us anything around here, but the psychiatrist, whose motives are frankly dubious, implied I shouldn't expect a warm welcome.

Gavin crawled back into bed with Jazz after grovelling enough, saying he was tested and failed, but he's realised what he was giving up and he won't make that mistake again. I should be mad at him, but I know he's doing what he has to do to keep up appearances. It's not like our kiss meant anything anyway. It was just nice. Comforting. Something that felt real in this manufactured fishbowl, but nothing more. I've barely been here for as long as he has, and already, I'd kill for a touch of reality again. How poetic.

No one talks about it, but I can tell I'm not the only one whose expectations haven't been met when it comes to taking part in this stupid programme. It's not a dating show like we were told; it's a survival show about sex.

We're heading off to today's challenge. Something to do with a slalom where you're asked questions and then you have to choose either blue (true) or red (false) flags in a split second. I'm excited to ski and to be outside, but I'm going to be set up to look bad and given tough questions they can turn into tonight's argument, exactly like yesterday's challenge. I'm exhausted already and it hasn't even started.

We queue up to get on the ski lift, everyone else standing in their couples while I stand alone. Even though it'll only be five minutes, I'm looking forward to having a moment to myself on the way up. Pete, the only person who's been on my side from day one, is ahead of me with his partner. But as they go to stand in position for the chair coming around on the conveyor belt, he struggles with his skis, and his partner gets on without him before realising he isn't with her. He doesn't panic like she did though. Instead, he quietly gets into position beside me and waits for the next chair. He pulls the lap bar down and then immediately fumbles inside his coat before reaching over to me, unzipping my coat too and turning my mic pack off.

"Are you crazy? They'll kill us!" I turn back, looking for the producers, who missed a few chairs and are only now getting onto the ski lift themselves.

"Doesn't matter. My days are numbered anyway."

"What do you mean?"

"I know I'm getting zero airtime. Hilary and I barely talk, let alone fight or do anything worth filming, and everyone else is playing the 'deeply in love' angle, so I'm not gonna get a look in. My producer's completely given up on me."

"You say that like it's a bad thing. You don't want this to be over?"

"Oh, absolutely, but I need to be someone when I leave here more. And before you say it, I'm not on some ego trip. I need the opportunities that come after this. My mum…" He looks away, considering his words. "She lost her job last year after getting badly hurt in a car accident, and she'll lose her house soon too because she doesn't have anything left to pay the mortgage with. Benefits only get her so far. I barely have enough to make a dent, but I've given every penny I can. I've taken on two more shitty jobs around my other one, and I'm living on potatoes and beans at this point. I've got a following online, but I was never smart enough to monetise it properly, and I don't have the time to keep up with it anymore. But with this show, landing a decent manager, that could change our lives. I need this. I need to stay."

Oh, Pete. My heart aches for him, and for his mum. "What can I do to help?"

"I wanted to see if you'd like to form an alliance. Fake this with me, and when we get out of here, we'll fizzle out. No drama. Just go back to our own lives."

He can't be serious. "Why me? Why not Hilary?"

"Because you deserve a chance. They set you up because they needed a villain, and it was never going to be one of the OGs."

I realise he's right, but he might be the only one who sees it that way.

"Frankenbites. That's what they call them, by the way, when they stick different audio clips together to make it sound like one sentence. You can always tell, because they'll either cut to something or someone else or there'll be the slightest shift in pitch or tone. They can edit a lot, but not everything."

I *knew* I didn't say those things! But over the past few days I've doubted myself, assuming I must have said them at some point during our date and not paid it any mind because of everything going on.

"How do you know that?"

"I did a lot of research before I came in. So when you said you didn't say that, I thought back to the clip and remembered I never saw the words leaving your mouth."

How many people out there are sharp enough to come to that conclusion on their own or savvy enough to know the industry tricks? Because I sure as hell didn't know they could do that before now.

I deliberate over his offer for a moment. I want to go home. But I also don't want to be known as the bitch they've already portrayed me as. And now I want to help Pete and his mum. I can't let him go home and struggle knowing I could have at least tried to help.

"I'm in."

Relief and gratitude wash over him. We're halfway up the mountain, and I'm aware we don't have long left to talk privately.

"So what's the plan?"

He huffs out a short breath, getting to work. "Depending on what other shit they've got up their sleeve for the next couple of days, I'll either pull you for a chat and lay on the old charm, or if there's some kind of challenge, I'll make a move."

"What if there's a ceremony? They won't let you pick me – why would they? They can easily get rid of me now they've used me to stir up some drama."

"Then I'll tell them I'm picking Hilary, and when the cameras roll, I'll pick you. They won't want to pass up the footage of everyone losing their minds, which they will."

"And if it works?"

"Then we keep looking at each other like we love each

other and roll with the punches. And there'll be plenty. The closer we seem, the harder they'll try to split us up, and we have to give them what they want, let them think they're winning. All the while we've got the ace up our sleeve."

Looks like I'm going to play poker after all.

It worked. It's been two weeks, and we have everyone fooled. We've snuck around pretending we're trying not to get caught, we've fought and I've cried, the girls pretending they care when I know they only want to share the airtime. We've put the covers over our heads in bed and kissed our hands and sighed. We spent our date in the hot tub making it look like we were doing exactly what someone would expect two people in love to do in a hot tub. Pete's a good kisser, and he's attractive or else he wouldn't be here, but there are no fireworks. It might seem like I'm always grinding on him, but we don't even let our laps touch, and I doubt his body would respond if they did. He's never tried anything on, and neither have I with him. We hold hands in bed sometimes to check in after having a row for show, but he's the perfect gentleman. It's honestly a shame I don't like him as more than a friend.

Even though that's all going to plan, the producers are still toying with all of us. The games are a head-fuck. They're making up our sleep schedules to suit the shoot needs, and to use our delirium to make us more erratic and vulnerable. (Fun fact: sleep deprivation is the most effective form of torture. It's not always quick, but it gets everyone in the end.) But the thing that's really getting to me? They're messing with the food.

My food.

I'm not fussy. I'm not picky. I'm not even vegan. But they

seem to struggle to provide anything vaguely healthy. I'm all up for the occasional cheat day, but I need fresh food, a salad, some fruit – *anything* that isn't hot dogs or pizza or deep-fried chicken. Even the eggs we can have at breakfast come pre-beaten in some kind of milk carton.

I've asked so many times, but nothing's being done about it, and I'm hungry more often than I'm not, especially with all the long days and skiing we're doing. I know I'm not eating enough, but I've worked so hard to get myself in shape, sort out my gut health, regulate my hormones, and keep my skin clear – not to mention how sick the crap they're either cooking for us or providing for us to cook ourselves makes me feel – and I can't force myself to eat any more than I have to.

Desperate and hopeful, I head into the pantry for breakfast to see if my requests have finally been granted. No changes on the shelves, but the fridge is where I'll find what I'm looking for if it's there. I open it up and disappointment finally breaks me. I close the fridge and collapse against it in silent tears.

One rogue carrot, one slice of apple, a wilting bag of spinach. That's all I want at this point, and they can't even provide that. *I'm so hungry.*

My sobs are interrupted by a voice in the wall. "Everything all right, Gemma?"

"There's nothing to eat." My words sound as weak as I feel.

"Sorry, we seem to be having some issues with your mic. Can you speak up so we can hear you?"

I repeat my words louder. "There's nothing to eat."

"What's wrong with the food?"

"It's all processed junk."

"Yeah, sorry, we can't hear you over here. Hang on…

Okay, can you say that again? Maybe shout a bit so we can hear you through the room mics. Yours has stopped working."

"It's all processed junk!" I project my voice.

"What do you mean?"

"There's nothing—"

"Louder, please. Maybe stand up – we'll be able to hear you a bit better then."

I get up with a glimmer of hope that maybe *this time* they'll listen to me. "There's nothing here that isn't in a packet or hasn't been pumped with sugar, or all of the above! I've asked so many times. I don't understand why you're denying us fresh food. It's not fair!"

"And what would you like to eat?"

They're listening. My brain whirrs with hope. *Don't ask for too much, or else it won't happen.* "Vegetables. I just want vegetables, please." I panic. What if they only give me spring onions and garlic to screw with me even more like the pedants they are? "Peppers, carrots, corn. Things like that," I specify.

"Is that all?"

I nod. "Yes, please."

"We'll see what we can do."

Do I have "kidnap me" stamped on my forehead or something? Because I seem to be making a habit of getting held captive in ski chalets.

Us girls have been separated from the boys for the past three days and forced to socialise with a new batch of poor souls who fell for the same schtick we all did about this being a life-changing opportunity. We've just been played a montage of the antics each of our partners back at the main lodge have been up to, and while real me doesn't give a damn that Pete's been speaking to other girls in my absence, fake me needs to make this my entire personality.

Cue the waterworks.

My game plan has been to stay true to Pete while I'm here in this new lodge, but I've decided what my heartbroken alter ego would do is get even.

Three days later, the powers that be tell us we're finally heading back tonight. *About bloody time.* The catch, because there always is one, is that we're at risk of being sent home if we're left single. People keep asking me if I'm going to pick one of the new guys to go back with, and though I've pretended to hum and haw about it, I'm obviously going to return on my own, because I know Pete will stick to our plan. And that's what I tell my two-faced bitch of a producer, Bethany, when she asks me later that day. I make up some rubbish about "forgiving him" and "having hope", and I assume that'll be the end of it. But later that night, I discover it's not.

We're all dressed up and ready to get taken to the bottom of the mountain. Once there, we'll be put into a gondola either alone or with our new man, and we'll ride it to the top, where the boys will be waiting to reveal if they've done the same.

Before we leave, Bethany pulls me to one side.

"Babe."

I hate it when she calls me "babe".

She checks over her shoulder and then turns back to me, talking low. "You have to pick someone to go up with."

"But I don't want to. Pete—"

"Pete's picked someone." She whips her head behind her again. "Shit, I didn't tell you that. But you need to pick someone."

Why would he do that? Is he giving me an out? Maybe letting me go home single and scorned to get public sympathy? But why would he want to be seen as the bad guy? Unless he's managed to form a real connection with somebody and that reputation is worth it… But we're not in the final yet. That was the goal: get to the final. Or maybe he's hoping I'll pick someone too, give us some drama to work with, and then we'll reconnect by the end of the week and get to the final together. *Who knows* what he's thinking? But I trust him to have thought this through.

"Fine. I'll take Jim."

I've gotten to know him a little this week. Nothing going on there, but he's nice enough and seems genuinely pleased to be here, so I'll bring him back with me and give him a chance to find someone else.

We're the last ones to go up. Jim, ecstatic to have been picked, thanks me as the doors close on us. My heart thumps as we ride up, and I brace myself for the fake fallout Pete and I are about to have. The radio they left in the gondola for us tells us to get ready as we approach the top, so we stand beside one another, and I slip my hand inside the crook of Jim's arm.

Here we go.

The doors open, and it takes me a second to get my bearings. I scan the row of couples behind the smarmy host – some new, some reunited – then my eyes spot Pete. Standing alone.

You've got to be kidding me.

I let go of Jim and rush over to Pete. *No, no, no.* I've

ruined his whole plan. Everything he was going to do for his mum. His *life*. Because I was stupid enough to believe *Bethany. Again.*

"Cut!" one of the directors shouts into a megaphone from the gazebo they've set up to the side, with screens and chairs for the crew. He picks up a radio to speak into, and the host presses a finger to his ears.

"Gemma, go stand back with Jim, please. Don't run over to Pete. There's a good girl," the host orders.

I bloody hate this guy.

I look over to where he is, noticing Bethany standing by his side. *Smirking.* I want to scream and shout and tell them I was tricked, but I know making Bethany look bad will only worsen my situation when I get back to the main lodge. And the cameras are still rolling – they could capture my melt-down and use it however they please.

I take a few breaths, short and sharp, as I stare her down. Then I set my jaw, lift my head, and stride back over to Jim, carefully wiping away the tear that rolled down my cheek. They force me to play out the scene as if I'm unaffected, but rage radiates from every fibre of my being, and I know it shows.

Later, once the ceremony is over, they allow me a moment alone with Pete in the bedroom as he packs his bags – only because Pete seems to have some kind of dirt on his producer, who hasn't been able to say no to him since week three. I wrap my arms around his neck and sob into his chest. "I'm so sorry," I say over and over, but he reassures me he'll be okay.

He pulls away to look at me, cradling my face. "Thank you – for everything." He kisses me on the head and then pulls me back into his arms. "I'll see you on the outside."

A few days later, due to mental exhaustion, malnourishment, and aggressive period cramps, I pass out while on a date. Halfway down a ski run. And it's going to be used as tomorrow's episode's big drama. And how do I know that? Because the first thing I see when I come to is a camera in my face. Not a doctor. Not one of the ski instructors. A camera.

They eventually get a doctor to me, making sure to film the panic on the faces of the crew crowding around me, asking deliberately pointed questions about my eating habits and my refusal to eat what they're giving us. I'm sent home on medical grounds, my entire reputation as a health-and-fitness content creator ruined.

But I'm free.

Or so I thought. Little did I know, life outside the lodge would be so much worse.

SIXTEEN

GEMMA

"It's. Not. Safe." Oscar spells it out for me as if I'm five, resting his hands on his desk and leaning forward like a stern boss.

"Don't you get it? He's just dropped a pin on my location. It's not going to *be* safe after the next embarkation day."

He sighs. "We'll take it one week at a time."

"*You* can do that, but *I'm* going home!" I stride to the door.

"Gemma…" There's a warning in his tone. "You're going to stay here and keep your head down."

"Until when! The paps could literally turn up on Monday, and if not then, it'll be the week after. And even if it's not some creep with a camera, the crew could start selling stories about me, or guests will hear the news and look for me. Either way, I'm going to be hunted down like a bloody Pokémon."

He doesn't have a comeback for that.

"I'm screwed, and you know it. So send me to another ship or send me home." I grab the door and fling it open.

"For God's sake, Gemma!" he shouts and bangs his fist on the desk.

I freeze, my heart hammering in my chest. He's never raised his voice at me before.

"Shut the door, please," he asks softly, and I do, but I can't look at him.

"Why won't you just let me leave?"

"Because I can't look out for you if you go." His voice breaks, and I face him again, noticing his eyes have turned a little red. "I tried to tell you not to go on the show, and you didn't listen. I tried to tell you not to mess around with Tom, and you didn't listen. And now I'm telling you not to leave, and I *need* you to listen."

I step away from the door.

"I'm all for you making your own mistakes and learning things the hard way, but you've made some *big* mistakes."

"Oh, have I? Thanks, I hadn't noticed," I snap, then I regret it, bowing my head. "Sorry."

He goes quiet. Both of us are aware the wave's about to come crashing down, but neither of us know how to protect ourselves from it.

"I wish they'd left me to die on that mountain," I murmur. My lip trembles and tears spill down my cheeks.

"Take that back."

I glance up, finding tears threatening to fall from Oscar's eyes too, so full of pain. Guilt stabs me in the chest, but I can't take back something I meant.

"I ruined *everything*."

He steps out from behind his desk and rushes to wrap his arms around me. I put down my sword, unable to fight anymore. I break down and sob into his chest as he holds me tight.

"I'm so tired."

"I know. But I'm here this time. We'll work it out together, okay? You're not alone."

SEVENTEEN

TOM

For the first time in my life, I show up early to the pool deck for the Sail Away Party, knowing this is where I'm most likely to find Eliza. I love every part of my job, but Sail Away Parties are literally my worst nightmare. I can't line dance for shit. Sure, I know the moves now, but dancing in front of a crowd still makes me uncomfortable.

With no sign of Eliza yet, I find a spot along the railings that I can look over to see the port we're about to leave. I feel sick to my stomach thinking through everything that's happened since "Megan" and I met. Nothing adds up. She's gentle and sweet. *But she isn't.* She's a virgin. *But she's not.* She opened up to me. *But she didn't.* I've picked apart all our interactions, trying to pinpoint the moments when the cracks in her perfect exterior began to show, but somehow, I keep coming up empty.

I don't understand how someone can lie for as long as she did. I thought I knew her – *I thought I'd fallen for her* – but it seems I was so desperate to find love that I was willing to give it to someone I didn't even know.

Regardless of how she may have deceived me, I still feel awful for accidentally outing her.

And I miss her.

"I've been looking for you everywhere." Eliza, punctual as I knew she would be, brings my mind back from wherever it had drifted off to. Worry pours out of her, and I immediately feel even worse for ignoring her knocks on my door throughout the day. I wasn't up for talking then. I mean, I'm not exactly jumping at the chance now either, but I live on a ship, where life goes on whether you're ready to accept it or not.

"You okay?"

I take a deep breath before shaking my head, and she wraps her arms around me in a tight hug. "I'm so sorry," I say into her shoulder.

"I know. It'll be okay. She'll—"

"No, I'm sorry to *you*."

Eliza pulls away, looking confused.

I tip my head to the side a little. "Come on. We both know I've been the worst friend to you lately."

I put sneaking around with Gem over my friendship with Eliza. It was all fun and games while I was hiding in closets when Harvey paid Gem a visit, but it came at the cost of shutting Eliza out, because I couldn't keep track of the little web of white lies I was spinning.

"I'm sorry I couldn't tell you. I was between a rock and a hard place, and I promised them I wouldn't."

Even though part of me wants to be mad, a bigger part of me understands the position she was put in.

"And when I slipped up when you first started going out, I felt so—"

"Wait. You knew we were seeing each other? Before today?"

She nods her head sheepishly.

Before I can even begin to process what that means, the DJ starts the party by playing "Wobble" by V.I.C., so now I have to shake my ass with a smile on my face.

As if I haven't suffered enough.

I should be concentrating on the moves, but my brain is a million miles away. "And Harvey?"

She nods again while rolling her arms to the right.

I throw my head back and silently curse into the sky, two-stepping back and forth before slowly turning to face a new direction, putting Eliza behind me.

"How?" I lean back and wobble.

"You weren't subtle, Thomas." We lean forward and wobble again. "Why do you think I never pressed for answers about the two of you?"

All this time, I thought we were being so convincing.

"Also, if anyone knows what sneaking around looks like, it's me and him."

I two-step again. "Why didn't you say? And why hasn't Harvey ripped my head off?"

"Because it would have made us hypocrites considering how he and I got together."

We both move to face the crowd in front of us. I opt to keep my mouth shut, or I'll risk saying a lot of things I'd end up regretting – and with an audience, no less.

Eliza must realise she's touched a nerve, so she lets me stew for a few rounds of the dance before continuing. "We both knew we couldn't stop you. Once you get an idea in your head, Tom, you're doing it. And you were happy – you both were – and that's all Oscar wants for Gemma after everything she's gone through."

With a whole stampede of thoughts messing with my head, I end up turning the wrong way, which puts me face-to-face with Eliza. I quickly jump and spin 180 degrees to correct myself.

"What was that look for?"

"I didn't do a look." It's so hard to be serious when I'm wiggling my butt at her. I guess I'm not doing as good of a job at hiding my disdain as I think I am.

"Yes, you did. Hold on – *do you believe it*?"

"Why does everyone keep asking me that? Why wouldn't I? What's there to question? It's there, as clear as day."

The track finally fades out, but my relief is short-lived, because the next song to play is Tag Team's "Whoomp! (There It Is)". I try not to groan too loud. For fuck's sake, I can barely get this damn routine right on a good day, let alone while my thoughts are somewhere else entirely. There's too much footwork to remember without concentrating.

"So I guess you think Ryan Reynolds really is Deadpool."

"Huh?"

We tap our feet in front of us before shuffling forward and doing the same with the other foot.

"And that Hugh Jackman can actually pop claws out from his knuckles."

"What?" I regret introducing her to the Marvel Cinematic Universe. "You've spent too much time with Harvey. Talk in real sentences, woman." We body roll and clap, restarting the choreography in a new direction.

"The whole show was rigged. They set her up to be the bad guy. She played along to survive because they wouldn't let her leave."

What? I trip over my feet and hurry to correct myself, apologising to the guests who were copying me. So what I saw… She was… And I thought…

Oh fuck.

I made her biggest fear come true.

"So that was…a performance?"

I'm such an idiot. I need to get out of here. I need to get on my knees and beg her to forgive me for jumping to conclusions. She didn't tell me her name, but she let me in when she was keeping everybody else out. She had no reason to open up to me, but in her own way, she did.

And I doubted her.

Who am I kidding? What good will admitting I was wrong do? I don't deserve her time, let alone her forgiveness. I'm no better than the mob leaving her hate comments. It's only dawning on me now just how *colossal* of a fuck-up this is. No one knew who she was until I accidentally posted that video. Why would she ever forgive me when I will never forgive myself?

The sound of the guests singing the chorus at full volume snaps me out of my thoughts.

"Whoomp! There it is," indeed.

There it *fucking* is.

EIGHTEEN

GEMMA

I bump into Jack on the crew stairway as we both head below deck. There's a familiarity when we notice each other that shifts to formality a second later. I hate that in losing Tom I've lost Jack too. But in the same way Tom is Oscar and Eliza's friend, Jack is Tom's. Not mine.

Stuff it. If he's not my friend, I don't have to choose my words carefully.

I stop in my tracks, and Jack follows suit. "Why is it that *he* messed up, and yet *I've* spent *a week* trying to get a moment alone with him to explain myself?"

Once I had some time to calm down, I realised that while I might feel powerless, I did have a choice: I could stay upset about him falling for what he saw like everyone else did and stubbornly end it there, or I could clue him in on what really happened and be in with a chance at getting back to how things were.

"Would you like to grab a drink?" Jack asks.

"Yes, I think I would."

We go to the bar. It's a far better option than my plan to wallow in my room. It was either that or go out to some social where I'd only be stared at and excluded from conversations about me, all the while being supervised by my brother. For once, I ask for vodka in my soda and lime. I need a little courage if we're going to have this conversation. We find ourselves a table, and I choose the seat that faces the wall. Less people to see, less people to *see me*.

"How long is he going to keep avoiding me? If he seriously thinks *that* was the real me, I *swear to God…*"

"Of course he doesn't."

"No, not 'of course'. He won't even look at me!" I don't mean to snap, but the frustration has reached boiling point, and I've had enough of being ignored. "Why—?"

"He won't go near you because he thinks he ruined your life."

His words put me in my place, but to lighten the mood, I tut. "Men. Always trying to take credit for a woman's work."

Jack chuckles, and the tension in the air eases.

"Is he mad that I hid it from him?"

He shakes his head. "Not anymore. He said he would have done the same."

"I was going to tell him. I was just trying to find the right time." I study the ice cubes floating in my glass. "I've never felt like this about someone before," I admit quietly, unable to bring myself to look up and find pity in his eyes.

"You two look like you could use a distraction." Tiegan places three drinks on the table and then sits down on the chair next to Jack.

He smiles and takes his. "What should we toast to?"

We look between one another, waiting for an excuse to drink.

"My virginity. Long may it stay intact."

I think I might be entering my shameless era. I've decided that if other people can discuss my fake sex life, I can talk about my real one. Even though I doubt my admission will leave this table, if it does, it'll be the only true rumour in circulation.

They smirk with me as we clink our glasses together before taking a sip.

"Wait. I thought you had sex in a hot tub."

Jack and I both stare at Tiegan, stunned by her bluntness. Though I'm honestly relieved to have someone talk about their assumptions of me to my face, because the things I've overheard…

Enough crew members follow Tom that when the video of us got posted, everyone saw the aftermath too. Gossip spreads like wildfire in a place like this. Some pervert even went so far as to find and slowly circulate a montage of all my "sexcapades". It's one thing knowing the faceless population has watched those moments, but to have my work colleagues – people I have to see every day; people I'm *trapped* on here with – watch them too, it's beyond humiliating. My brother made it his mission to track the creep down and took great pleasure in being the one to give him the "6 a.m. knock", which saw him kicked off the ship that very hour without so much as an explanation or a discussion.

I shrug. "Faked it. All of it. Couldn't even tell you how big his todger was."

Tiegan and Jack titter at my word choice.

"Never felt it, never saw it." I know I have to be careful with what I say now everyone seems to have a vested interest in my life. Hell would rain down on me if that admission got out – more so than it already is. Though I reckon fans of the show would discredit it immediately if the news ever hit the tabloids.

All Tiegan does is stare at me for a second as she takes in

the new information, but she quickly moves on, not doubting me or questioning it further. "Shit. Well-played."

"Thanks." I sip my drink.

"Hold on – so you and Tom never…?"

"Nope." I let the word pop on my lips.

The conversation moves on, and it's refreshing to be spoken to like a person, not an alien. It's the first dose of normality I've had in a while.

Tiegan can be quite an intimidating presence, but it's only because of how she carries herself. She's so confident and self-assured – or, in other words, *sexy*. But I've gotten to know her over the past three months, and she's someone I hope I could call a friend even without Tom or Jack by my side.

In the middle of a sentence, Jack stops talking, both him and Tiegan tensing at something behind me. I turn around and goose bumps spread across my skin. Tom's standing frozen in the middle of the bar, looking as downtrodden as he has been since he found out the news. Being this close to him finally makes my stomach drop.

I watch as a mumbled "sorry" leaves his lips before he dips his head and walks out. My leg shakes under the table, and tears well in my eyes as I look anywhere except at the others.

"Ah-ah. We're not gonna do tears, honey." Tiegan places her hand over mine.

Jack shakes his head and rolls his eyes. "He's so fucking stupid."

I shoot Tiegan a quick glance. I've never seen Jack in this mood or heard him speak about anyone like that before, let alone Tom.

He lets out a short huff. "He has it in his head that you're better off without him, and worse than that, he thinks he can cope without you. And he can't. I have never seen a more hopeless boy in all my life, and let me tell you, that is *really* saying something."

As much as I want to be pleased with Jack's opinion, I'm infuriated to discover Tom really has given up on us. And for *what*? To save me from himself?

"Let me tell you a story about my baby brother," Tiegan begins. "My parents figured out early on that he had celiac disease. Absolute curse to put on a person, if you ask me, but anyway. One day, we went to a party, and he was beside himself that he couldn't have cake. I mean, you try explaining to a three-year-old what gluten is. He caused a big old scene but eventually got over it and weirdly didn't ask again. Flash-forward to that evening, when he's puking his little guts out because he snuck a piece while no one was looking… All of us paid for it that night, but he learnt very quickly that when we say he can't have something, *he can't have it*."

"I'm lost. How's that relevant?" Jack asks.

"Because sometimes people need to suffer the consequences of their choices before they can admit they made a mistake."

I can't get the hurt on Tom's face out of my head. "I think we're both suffering."

"No – *you're* suffering. Tom's just commiserating."

Jack and I are quiet for a moment as we process this. The fact he doesn't have anything to counter with means she's actually right.

I don't want his pity. I want *him*.

"You know what I think would really make him suffer?" Jack looks between the two of us, his cunning eyes so blue they're almost grey.

Tiegan smirks. "That's a bold move, my friend."

"What?" I ask, not catching their drift.

"He needs a wake-up call," Jack states, ignoring me, full of vengeance.

Tiegan looks my way. "What do you say we throw a little party…and tell Tom his favourite kind of cake is on the menu?"

Oh… *Oh…*

He thinks he's the only one being tortured by distancing himself, but he turned my life upside down and walked right out of it, leaving me up shit creek without a paddle. And yet *I* have been the one trying to get a *morsel* of his time to *grovel* for his acceptance and *prove* who I am and why he should still want me. Well, screw that. And screw him.

"What have I got to lose?" I hear my words out loud and realise the innuendo I unintentionally made. My confidence suddenly dwindles. "Wait, I'm not going to—"

Both of them are shaking their heads.

"It won't get that far," Jack reassures me. "He'll make sure of it."

"What if he doesn't turn up?" I ask Tiegan, noticing we're only a few minutes away from the cut-off time.

"Don't worry. He will."

We stay perched on the end of the bed as others chat around us. I shouldn't be here – and I still think I might leave – but I'm tired of getting attention from everyone except the one person I want it from. I'm tired of being ignored. So I remain patient, focusing on the chilled music in the background as the seconds drag on. I'm putting all my faith in Tiegan and Jack that this will work.

There's a knock at the door as the digital clock on the nightstand strikes 11 p.m., and Tiegan gets up to open it.

Please say it's them. Jack's tall form enters the room, and as despair threatens to crush me, Tom steps out from behind him, his hair damp and slicked back, his cheeks still flushed from what I assume was a hot shower. Tiegan locks the door behind them and heads back to me while I study Tom. He's breathing so hard it's impossible not to see his chest heaving, and from the look in his eye as he glares at me, it's not from rushing here.

Good luck ignoring me now, American boy.

"You still up for this?" Tiegan checks in, sitting beside me once again.

"Yeah-huh." I nod and let out a shaky breath.

"Try to relax, okay?" She leans in close, placing a hand on my thigh. Her breath is warm against my neck, making all the little hairs there stand on end. "You're a free woman. You don't need his permission to have a little fun."

Anticipation flurries through my veins, and she places a kiss on my skin. I ripple as a shiver passes over me, my nipples hardening beneath my lace bra.

She purrs in response. "So sensitive." Her kisses move higher, closer to my ear, and she trails her fingers slowly up my bare thigh and under my tight dress before skimming back down again. I've never kissed a woman before, but every now and then I've found myself daydreaming about what it would be like. The idea has always interested me – I've just never acted on it.

Feeling braver, I turn my face towards hers, but I let her take the lead. Her lips touch mine, and energy courses through me as I kiss her back. My hands roam her body, squeezing the curve of her hips as the kiss grows deeper. As I enjoy it. I find the hem of her dress and lift it up and over her head, and then she feels for the bottom of mine and does the same. I thought all I'd want to know was Tom's reaction to seeing me in my underwear, but I want to take in Tiegan's reaction too. I chew my bottom lip as I admire her body. Her dark green underwear complements her emerald eyes, while long, fiery-red hair cascades over her shoulders. I wish I could be confident like her.

I think she's waiting for me to make the next move, but I can't bring myself to initiate it. I want more, but I don't know how to get it.

"Do you want to kiss me here?" She points to her collarbone, and I nod.

She takes my hand and pulls me closer until I can cautiously place my lips on her. *So soft.* And sweet like shea butter. "Another one," she requests. "That's so nice. Keep doing that."

I appreciate her encouragement. I'm so nervous that I have no idea how to process what's happening. I do know, however, that I'm enjoying it. *A lot.*

We didn't plan much past making out and feeling each other up a bit. I honestly thought Tom would have stormed over here and claimed me as his by now. But he isn't a caveman – he's complicated. Maybe he's not even watching. Maybe he's decided to play me at my own game by playing with someone else.

No.

"Tell me what he's doing," I ask Tiegan urgently while my back is to him.

"He's sitting in a chair by the door. Watching us."

"Alone?"

"Alone," she confirms, and she squeezes my bottom.

Thank goodness. I know how hypocritical it is of me to be upset at the thought of him with someone else, but this is all about him.

"He's not the only one watching us."

Self-consciousness swarms me, and I glance around, real-ising we've got an audience. Other couples are working each other up through their clothes. One girl on the chair by the window rolls her hips on her partner's lap underneath her. All of them keep curious eyes on us.

"Do you like that?"

I get lost in my thoughts for a moment. *I*... Yes, I think I do. But—

"You're allowed to. It doesn't make you dirty if you do," she reassures me.

"Yes. I like it."

A smile grows at the corner of her lips. "Your consent is your power. You're in control here. They'll only watch if you let them."

My eyes begin to prickle, but I blink the sensation away. I feel so safe in this room. So liberated. Millions of people thought they saw me have sex with more than one person on multiple occasions. It doesn't matter that we were faking it or that the editing implied something that wasn't happening. I thought I was in the driver's seat then, but the wheel was never in my hands. Deep down, I think I knew that, but I couldn't let myself accept the truth. Denial was the only thing keeping me sane.

"What would you like to do next?" she asks.

I place my lips next to her ear, ensuring no one else can hear. "Make him fight for me."

She smiles and then kisses me hungrily while laying me down on the bed and placing her thigh between mine. We let ourselves get carried away, our hips rolling and my body chasing the need building between my legs. Before long, the bed dips beside us, and my heart trills. *Finally.* But when I look up, my relief falters as I discover a grey pair of eyes looking down at me, not brown.

"Mind if I join you?" Jack looks from Tiegan and then to me.

This wasn't part of the plan.

I finally give in and glance over at Tom, still in the chair Tiegan said he was in. Still alone. He's staring over at the three of us with heat in his eyes.

I turn my attention back to Jack. "Is this a test?"

"Not for you."

He's punishing Tom. I don't know what I did to earn his loyalty, but I'm not going to take it for granted. I grab his T-shirt and pull him into me, determination and Tiegan's words giving me the confidence to kiss him like the world will end if I don't.

I'm a free woman. And I know how to fake it.

Kissing Jack feels like getting off a train after a long day. I'm near, but I'm not home yet. That feeling, plus the slight sharpness of his beard against my lips, only serves to further remind me that nothing can compare to Tom. I ease off and look at Tiegan, who's been nibbling my neck while I've been occupied. Then I turn back to Jack. They kiss, and my heart skips with it happening so close to me. *With me.* I sit up and brush my lips over Tiegan's skin, sliding her bra strap off her shoulder. She eases her arm out and then breaks the kiss with Jack, coming back to me. Jack does the same to her, removing the strap off her other shoulder before unclasping her bra. Her breasts fall free and I stop to appreciate her. She's so beautiful. And I'm so turned on right now, knowing Tom's watching this unfold. I want to taste her, but I hesitate.

"The answer's yes, honey." She sweeps a strand of hair behind my ear, and I can't stop my tongue from darting out over my lips. Then I dive in, sucking her nipple into my mouth, my face pressed into her full breast as she moans.

Jack's quick to join me, taking her other breast as Tiegan writhes on top of me.

How is this happening? Am I actually having a threesome right now? I have to be one of the most advanced virgins out there. This is…*so hot*.

Jack grazes his teeth on Tiegan's nipple, then he kisses her there once more, soothing her. And suddenly both their eyes are on me.

I release my lips from Tiegan.

"Do you want us to do that to you?" Jack asks, his voice rough like sandpaper.

Yes. But…

I look back at Tom. Why isn't this working? Have we got this completely wrong? Am I making everything worse? Have I crossed a line I won't be able to come back from?

Tiegan leans closer, she and Jack now shielding me from Tom's view. Noticing the war I'm at with myself she says, "Until he tells you you're his, you don't need to feel guilty. Jack knows what Tom can handle. And he knows how to make a woman feel good." A devilish grin plays on her lips, while Jack remains stoic, letting me make the decision on my own.

I nod, then Tiegan snatches up my lips again while Jack places kisses on my neck, and the overstimulation makes me squirm with need.

"I promise I'm going to take care of you," he whispers as Tiegan's lips make their way down my body. "You're as much mine as he is, and I'm angry too. I know why he backed off, but I don't agree with it. I love him, but I want to make him hurt for hurting you."

I hadn't considered Jack was caught in the middle of this. I didn't think I really meant anything to him – I just thought he accepted me in when Tom and I started hanging out. But he's proven that's not the case tonight. *I'm his too.*

"I need you to trust me." He pulls back and looks into my eyes.

"I do."

"Thank you." He claims me with his mouth, kissing me fiercely, and my clit pulses immensely – both because of him and because Tiegan's fingers are incredibly close to where I ache for them to be.

I open my eyes and pull away from Jack to give her a quick "yes" before going back to him for more. I bend my knee and Tiegan's fingertips brush over my knickers so lightly I think I might die if I don't get more from her.

Despite eventually begging her to, she doesn't apply any more pressure.

"The teasing's all part of the fun," Jack mumbles as Tiegan watches me with a smirk.

I sink my head back with a groan while they giggle. Tiegan works me up, and Jack's lips hover over my nipples, still woefully covered by my bra, but through the lace I can feel the warmth from his mouth, and it drives me wild. I arch my back, searching for real contact, but they keep themselves distant.

Impatient, I glare up at both of them. "*Please*," I implore.

Jack looks up to Tiegan with the devil on his shoulder. "What do you think, Tiegs?"

"Seeing as she asked so nicely, why don't we give her exactly what she wants?"

"We might just have to."

Before I can even process what's happening, Tiegan's by my side and Jack's head is between my legs. His lips trail over the inside of my thigh as Tiegan helps me out of my bra.

Her eyes wander over me, my nipples so desperate for attention it's almost painful.

"Such a pretty thing, and he still thinks he can live without you." She pushes my buttons and I give in again, glancing over at Tom, who I hope to see in distress – but there's an expression on his face I can't read instead.

My body melts and explodes like popping candy as Jack pulls my knickers to one side and covers my core with his mouth at the same time as Tiegan sucks my breast while squeezing the other. A smile spreads on Tom's lips, and I almost come at the sight of it. *Jeeeesus.* Tiegan was right: Jack knows exactly what he's doing. But Jack was wrong to think this would hurt Tom.

I dig my fingers into Jack's long, dirty-blond hair and hold him against me, scared he'll decide to ease off any second and I'll be left high and dry.

"Does that feel good?" Tiegan asks, lying down beside me, skimming her fingertips over my bare skin.

"*So good*," I answer deliriously.

"Do you know what would feel even better?"

She lifts Jack's hand to her mouth and sucks on his middle and ring fingers, causing anticipation to rock through me. Jack gauges my reaction and grins when he sees the smile I'm biting back. Tiegan watches him with me, but he doesn't slip inside; he strokes me again and again, like an animal playing with its food.

Unable to bear it any longer, I reach for his wrist and guide him to my entrance. "I'm begging you, *please*—"

Ohhhh my God. He glides his fingers in and out, and I'm so sensitive it almost tickles. Though, before I can get close to a climax, Tiegan stops him, and I'm so exhausted from being wound up I nearly scream. But I stop myself from complaining when Tiegan sucks on his fingers again, closing her eyes and moaning softly as she tastes me on them while I stare at her, slack-jawed. *Jesus.*

Jack kneels over me, and I follow his gaze to Tom, who's the only one watching now, the others in the room seemingly lost in their own plans. "Keep your eyes on him," he tells me.

He eases both his fingers back inside of me, and it is *incredible.* As he pulses them with a come-here motion, his thumb taps against my clit, and I lose any shred of composure I had left. I'm facing Tom, but I can't keep my eyes from shutting tight as a long-awaited orgasm crashes through me. Jack doesn't let up while I wriggle with pleasure; he keeps me floating for I don't even know how long. But when my feet find the ground again and I open my eyes, Tom's there, standing beside the bed. Taking a second to catch my breath, I notice the apology written on his face.

I'm aware of Jack and Tiegan beside me, but no one moves until I reach for him. And then he's mine, and the world fades away.

Tom kisses me as if I'm the air he breathes, and like a fire, my oxygen only makes the flames burn brighter. I tug at his clothes, needing to feel his skin against mine, and he moves quickly to strip down to his underwear. We hold each other, moving and feeling, getting everything and not getting enough at the same time.

"I'm so sorry, Princess," he says between kisses.

"I know." I pull away slightly. "But I'm not sorry for tonight." I study his face. I need him to be okay with this, because it was messy and spontaneous, but I don't regret it. Because it was for him.

"You shouldn't be." His expression is so easy, so gentle, so happy.

And I'm…*shameless.*

I reach for him through his boxers. "I need you," I say, making my meaning clear.

"Yeah?" He grins. "Here?"

I smile, no longer nervous, just excited. "Yeah."

Tom shuffles up the bed, trying not to disturb Jack and Tiegan next to us, and rearranges the pillows so he can sit up and lean against the wall.

I straddle him, a little unsure. "Like this?"

"I read…uh, I heard it won't go as deep."

I still can't get over the fact he's done research for me.

When I don't reply, he counteroffers, "Or if there's another position you wanna try, we can—"

"I'm good. My heart just feels like it's glowing."

His concern disappears and he beams a smile at me. "Come here then, firefly." He pulls me in for another kiss and my hips roll against his, craving more of him.

I slip my fingers inside the waistband of his boxers. "Please take these off."

He giggles, and we both rid ourselves of our underwear.

Tom caresses my pussy and groans. "*Fuck*, Gem. I was gonna ask if you feel ready, but I think I know the answer."

I've never been so wet in all my life, and I'm confident we'll be successful this time.

"Did my best friend make you wet, Princess?" A sly grin brushes his lips.

I fight the urge to crumble at his touch and nod.

Tom exchanges a look with Jack, who reaches over to the bedside table and passes us a condom and a small bottle of lube, barely breaking his rhythm with Tiegan. Tom puts the condom on and then squeezes some lube into his hand before stroking himself. "I don't think we need this, but I wanna be extra careful."

We both hold him as he strokes himself against me, and

then we line ourselves up, and my heart races as I realise this is it.

"Don't rush – we have all the time in the world." He holds me close, and I start lowering myself onto him, but even though I'm so ready for him, there's still resistance. "Breathe out, baby. Let your body get used to it. And if it hurts, we don't have to—"

Oh, wow.

The second I relax, he enters me in one mind-altering motion. *Ohhh* my goodness. I feel…full. I try to move, but I stop when I realise I'm not quite ready yet. It's a strange sensation, but not a bad one.

"Are you doing okay, Princess?"

I was looking at where we're joined, but at this, I turn my attention back to him. *"Yeah."* A huge smile breaks out on my face. "I'm doing great!"

He smiles back, but then another emotion crosses his face.

"What's wrong?"

"I fucked up, Gem. And then I went about it so wrong and I—"

I push a wave of his hair behind his ear and gently lift his head to look at me. "I forgive you. Which you'd know if—" I cut myself off and kiss him instead. "We'll talk about it tomorrow, but right now…*I want you.*"

"Thank you."

We steal each other's lips, and as I get used to the feeling, I begin to move my hips until I'm able to slowly rise and fall a bit at a time.

"You feel amazing."

Delight swarms me. "I do?"

"Mm-hmm. And you're doing so well." He sweeps back the strands of my hair that fell over my face while finding a good rhythm. "I'm so proud of you."

Tingles shiver up my spine. I like making him proud. "I want to try…" I stop, realising I don't quite know what it is that I want.

"Deeper, faster, a new position?"

"Faster."

His grin matches mine. "Yeah? Okay, can you put your knees up so you're kinda crouching over me?"

I wriggle around and do what I think he means. "Like… froggy-style?"

He laughs. "Yeah, that's it. You got it." He puts his hands under me, making it much easier for me to ride him. He lifts me up and down slowly at first, then he picks up the pace, and my eyes roll to the back of my head as I land back down against him again and again. "Holy shit, Gem."

The sensation of him hitting the spot deep inside me, not to mention the way my clit knocks against his skin with every movement, is both too much to handle and not enough. Every muscle of mine tightens. I feel as though I'm driving a hundred miles an hour and can't find the brakes. "I think— *Tom*— I think…"

My hands dig into the back of his neck so hard I'm sure I'll leave a mark, and I press my forehead against his. *So close.*

"That's it, baby. Let go. I got you."

I fall, and warmth flushes through me, everything relaxing as Tom takes my full weight and continues moving me exactly right. I whimper and groan, neither caring nor having any restraint about how loud I am. *Why have I never done this before?*

Tom slows his pace, and the haze eventually clears enough for me to see him. Kiss him. Melt into him. We huff and puff as I lean on his shoulder.

"I get what all the fuss is about now."

He giggles softly. "Look how far my little wallflower has come."

Awareness itches my skin as I recentre myself, remembering where we are. There are so many people around us, but I like it. Does that make me kinky? *I hope so.*

"Tom."

"Mm." He brushes his thumb over my cheek.

"It's happening."

He smiles. "Yeah, it's happening."

"I'm so glad it's you," I confess.

Something deepens in his gaze and his dimples become more pronounced. "Me too."

I press my mouth against his, starving for another taste of him, and he slowly moves to lie me down on my back, staying connected with me as he does.

Oh, that's nice. That's *really* nice.

He slowly moves on top of me, sinking so much deeper than before.

"Ohh fuck!"

He stops completely still, and I frown in confusion.

"You okay?" he asks.

I reassure him with a drowsy, bliss-filled nod of my head.

"That was a good 'fuck'?"

"That was a *very* good 'fuck'."

He relaxes again and beams. "Did I make Little Miss Perfect cuss?"

I sink my teeth into my bottom lip. I've never suited swearing. I rarely have big enough feelings to warrant it, but doing this – experiencing sensations *like this* – I can't help myself. Placing my hands on his hips, I guide him slowly, gasping with every inch of him that I take. He gradually speeds up, and I crumble with every mind-blowing thrust, but there's tension in his brow that isn't entirely from pleasure, and I worry.

"Is it still good?" I ask. "Should I be doing something…else?"

He shakes his head before kissing my forehead. "No, baby. I'm just trying to keep it together. It's been too long. You feel too good."

The tingle returns, and I love knowing I'm undoing him. "Don't hold back."

"You sure?"

"So sure."

"But you'll tell me if—"

"I promise I'll tell you if it hurts. But until I do, please act like it doesn't."

There's a rumble in his chest, almost like a growl, as a devious smile tugs on his lips. "*Jeez*, Gem. I'm having a hard enough time as it is."

I bite my lip, enjoying how he's coming apart. *Because of me.* He pulls back and thrusts into me hard, stopping to cast me a glance.

My mouth drops open with pleasure. *"Do that again."*

He leans in closer, his skin pressed against mine, and he does, driving me wild as sounds of his ecstasy pour into my ear, so needy and masculine. The feeling from before builds again, so much quicker this time, and I spiral fast. He pants and moans as I sense myself squeezing around him, taking everything he's giving me.

"Tom…I'm— *Shit!*"

He grunts as he loses his restraint too.

Seeing him like this, being here, where it all began for us, is beautiful and meaningful and everything I wanted my first time to be. We collapse together, lying side by side, unable to do anything other than smile and breathe each other in.

"I missed you," he says, stroking my cheek.

There goes my firefly heart, shining away again at seeing how much he cares for me. I know there's so much more he's not saying, but it's not needed tonight.

"I missed you too."

When the night wraps up, Jack, Tom, and I stick around to help tidy Tiegan's room and change the sheets, and then we say our good nights and head down the hall. So many thoughts are running through my mind, but the loudest one of all is: *I just had sex with Tom bloody Parks!*

My room is en route to Tom and Jack's room, and as we approach it, I prepare myself to part ways and pretend I'm fine with going in alone. I could always invite Tom in to stay with me, but the idea of Jack being left on his own doesn't sit right. Without him, I wouldn't have Tom back.

I come to a stop outside my door, and the boys carry on for only two steps before they both turn back to me. Tom grabs my hand and drags me with them.

"If you think I'm going to let you leave my side after tonight, you're so wrong."

There's my caveman.

NINETEEN

TOM

"Get your head out of your arse and open your eyes! You've got this so wrong! Own your mistakes and stop running."

"She's better off without me. I should have listened to Harvey. She should have too. I'm not good for her. Or anyone."

"Can you hear yourself right now? You're agreeing with Harvey?"

I can't believe it either, but that's exactly what I'm doing.

"Do you have any idea how much I would kill for my ex to forgive me? What I wouldn't do for her to be here so I could stand a chance at making things up to her."

"Nothing I do will ever be enough."

"It was an accident. She knows it. I know it. Everyone else knows it. Take it from me – walking away will rot you from the inside. I'm not going to let you fuck up the same way I did, because you will spend the rest of your life paying for it."

"Then that's what I have to do."

"Oh, stop with the self-pity! It doesn't make you a martyr. It makes you an idiot."

I don't want to be a martyr; I just want her to be free of me and any more damage I can possibly do.

"She's going to Tiegan's tonight."

"What?"

"But that's fine, right? Because she's not yours."

"Why would she—? Who—?"

"Me. I'm taking her. I'm going to be everything to her that you refuse to be."

"Jack."

"And if you can sit there and watch without stepping in, I'll believe you can let her go."

I wake up with a start, Jack's voice sounding as real now as it did last night. Catching my breath, I loosen my grip on whatever I'm grabbing onto like a life ring. *Gem.* She's…?

Memories of last night flash through my mind, and I'm struck by a wave of relief and happiness.

She's mine again.

She stirs in my arms, and I kick myself for waking her. "You okay?" she asks, her voice soft and fragmented.

I relax back into my pillow, pulling her in closer against me. "Better now."

Jack has to get up to open the kids' club, but she and I luckily have a lazier start to our days. We wake up slowly and enjoy being close for a while, but I have a lot of apologising to do, and I'm determined to start today as I mean to go on.

"I shouldn't have expected a secret like that not to blow up in my face," she says before I can make the first of a million speeches.

"I should have been more careful. I'm so sorry for the hell

I put you through, and I'm sorry I believed the internet over you."

She doesn't say it's okay and I don't expect her to, but she's willing to forgive me all the same.

"I don't know why I did. It didn't make sense. The version of you I knew with…some of those things I saw you doing…" I tamp down the rising jealousy.

"I'm guessing Eliza filled you in."

I nod shamefully. "It shouldn't have taken that, but yeah. Once she pointed out how wrong I was, I started with the first thing I knew to be true and went from there."

"I want to tell you what happened. I don't want there to be any more secrets between us from now on, but you have to promise me you won't share any of it publicly, because you're going to want to. And if you think what you did already put me in danger, sharing *any* of this will make it so much worse."

There's a way to make it *worse*? I'm already worked up, worried I'm not ready to handle whatever I'm about to hear if it comes with a warning, but she's strong enough to cope with it, so I need to be too.

"I promise."

She talks me through it – everything, from the beginning – and suddenly I get why Harvey looked so exhausted when I got here. Why he was so worried I'd hurt her. Why she was so terrified of everyone.

"I knew there could be potential downsides to it. I wasn't naïve enough to think I would escape some kind of hate. But I knew in myself that I'm not capable of being toxic, unkind, or evil enough to warrant coming across that badly. But they decided I could be edited that way, and that's the story they ran with."

"So they covered you in blood and fed you to the sharks."

"That's showbiz." She shrugs as if that's the end of it – the end of her story. She's completely defeated, with no hope of being able to redeem herself, and it breaks my heart.

I'm so *angry*. Angry at the creators of that show for inciting a mob; angry at the world for going after her with their pitchforks; angry at myself for believing a second of what I saw. And if I wasn't feeling enough guilt for the part I played in this new wave of hate crashing down on her, I sure am now.

Something she said when we first started hanging out comes to the forefront of my mind, and it makes nausea roll in my stomach. *"I'd honestly rather not exist, but I do, so I have to endure all this nonsense."* I blink back the emotions suddenly taking over.

"Are you...? Before I... Well, especially since I..."

"Tom?" she grounds me.

"Are you doing okay? Have they offered you any kind of help?"

"I can speak to a psychiatrist who claims to be independent from the show, but they're loyal to whoever pays the bill. None of what's discussed is private – it all gets fed back to the production team, emailed around and discussed in meetings, and then they pretend to care for a day or so. But their offer of speaking up for you comes alongside their warnings of even more repercussions following that, so their best advice is to hunker down and wait for it all to blow over."

"I mean, I'm no lawyer, but there's a defamation lawsuit in there somewhere. They can't—"

She shakes her head. "The contract is...ironclad. I waived my rights to 'an accurate representation of self', and I agreed they could 'use my image to reveal information about me that's unfavourable' and 'could expose me to public ridicule'." She exhales a deep breath like she's silently berating herself. "Everything happened so quickly, and I was so excited to be a part of it I didn't think any of those clauses would apply to me, because like I said, I know who I am. I'm not looking for solutions though. I got myself into this mess. This is the bed I made, and now I have to lie in it."

She might want to accept it, but I want to make people *pay*.

"You can always talk to me. I know I maybe need to earn your trust again, but…I'm gonna be here for you, always."

"Thank you." She gives me a kiss, and I pull her into me, the T-shirt of mine she's wearing feeling so damn good on her body. "How's your account anyway? I'm sorry if—"

"You have nothing to be sorry for. We don't have to talk about it. I'm not… I don't want it anymore."

I didn't pause the scheduled content like I now know I should have done. I was dumb enough to think no one would care about hating on Gem in the videos that came next, and that people would forget all about it soon enough. But I was wrong. *So wrong.* I couldn't keep up with deleting comments, so I just took the new videos down. Everything Gem told me would happen *did* happen, and it's probably still happening on my older videos now. I wouldn't know – I had to stop checking, because not responding to the awful things people were saying became impossible even though I knew it wouldn't solve anything. It goes without saying that I haven't been in the mood to film anything more. Why the hell would I want to entertain these jerk-offs?

Worry crosses her brow. "But you worked so hard on it. You made so many people happy."

"But it came at the cost of making the one person I care about *un*happy."

For a second, I think she's disappointed in me, but then I realise it's guilt. "I'll figure something out so you can get it back. You don't deserve to be dragged down with me."

"I do."

"No, you don't. If I were any other person, it wouldn't have mattered. If I'd told you *why* I couldn't be in your videos, I know you would have triple-checked your content. Avoiding me when I needed you the most was…" She shakes her head.

"I'm sorry," I interrupt before she can remember the pain I caused her and decide to un-forgive me.

"I know. And I'm sorry again for not coming clean when things started to get more serious between us. But I'd like to draw a line in the sand, or we're never going to be able to move on, and I'd like at least *one* thing in my life to get back to normal at some point."

"Done."

I've created a monster. A beautiful, sex-crazed monster. And I'm the happiest guy alive.

Our first time together opened the floodgates to some kind of horny paradise. I tell her I've gotta be someplace in ten minutes, and she tells me to make it fast. There's not a moment alone that hasn't started with her tearing my clothes off or ended without protest from her, nor a night we've spent apart. And you can bet there's a new colour in her schedule solely for me. That's right. I'm Mr Bubblegum now.

It's not only sex though. It's a connection deeper than I've ever had with anyone. I didn't know it was possible to feel so wanted and…*loved*. We've not said it yet, but I can feel it, and it's getting stronger every day.

It's finally my turn.

She's currently trying to catch her breath on top of me, having instigated another quickie while Jack was in the shower.

"Is it safe to come out now?" he calls from the bathroom.

"Just a second!" I reply as we giggle.

All I want to do is lie in a sweaty heap on my bed, but instead, I hurry to tidy up as Gem throws on her clothes. She gives me a kiss and tries to rush off to the Zumba class she's about to be late for, but I keep a hold of her.

"You can come out now," I tell Jack, and he emerges with a playful smirk.

Gem tries to tug her arm out of my grasp. "Tom, I'm going to be late!"

"Go pee."

"I'll be fine."

"*Go pee,*" both Jack and I say in unison.

She huffs but does as we say. "This is so silly."

"You wouldn't be saying that if your pee felt like hot, broken glass." I remember Maddison once telling me what a UTI was, and I have *never* been able to unhear it.

"I'm surprised you've still got a dick at this point." Jack pokes fun at me.

"Me too, man. Me too."

He titters to himself. "You ever seen 'Twilight'?"

"Of course. Team Edward or Team Jacob?"

"Team Edward but Team Taylor."

I perk up. "*Yes*, okay, glad we're on the same page. Continue."

"She's like a newborn, all that energy and no ability to contain it yet. Not like us old-timers."

I laugh, seeing the parallels instantly.

"I heard that!" Gem shouts through the door.

Once she's gone, I freshen up and head back to my bed to collapse. My post-orgasm high gradually fades and the thought I've tried to push away so many times, like a balloon on a windy day at Navy Pier, bounces back to bother me.

"Uh-oh… What's that look for?" Jack asks.

Goddamn this boy and his hypersensitivity to mood shifts.

"Come on – get it all out so I can tell you you're being stupid and you can put that loved-up, shit-eating grin back on your face."

I lie back down with a sigh, staring at the bunk above me. "I have all this experience when it comes to sex. I've ticked off bucket-list items and I've had more than my fair share of what were meant to be once-in-a-lifetime opportunities, so I can say with confidence that committing myself to her – and only her – for the rest of my life is all I will ever want and need. But for Gem…the journey only started last week. What if I'm just the first stop? She could think this is it, but then she could wake up one day and realise she missed out on so much and feel like I'm holding her back. I can't shake this fear that any minute now she'll want more, and she won't want it from me."

"And what are the things she might want that you can't give her? You didn't seem to have a problem with letting her explore the other night."

I've never got off on watching before, but I like to watch *her*. There's something about seeing her with other people – people I care about – and having her choose me still that drives me wild.

"I… It could be… What about…?" Okay, maybe he's onto something.

"The way I see it, she's decided to be with you even after everything, so don't doubt her unless she gives you a reason to."

"And what if she gives me a reason to?"

He smiles. "You're an open-minded guy. I'm sure you'll figure something out."

"Morning."

From the way all the hairs on the back of my neck stand on end – all right, from the accent – I realise it's Harvey coming up next to me at the coffee machine as I fill a hot water bottle that looks like a dog. Gem sent me to fetch it after she woke up in my room with stomach cramps.

"Morning," I reply, terrified of him noticing what's in my hand and realising it's his sister's. Harvey might have tolerated our relationship before, but in his eyes, I had my chance and blew it, and he's paid the price for it alongside Gem. I try to stand in such a way that I'll block his view of the dog, but it's not exactly easy to hide.

Damn, this thing takes so long to fill up.

He reaches for two mugs and two different types of teabag, and before he can even begin to wait for his turn, his eyes land on the dog. If the gates of hell were a person, I'm looking right at him.

"I know, I know. I swear, I tried to stay away, but—"

"Try harder." His jaw ticks as he glares at me.

"I can't."

"Yes, you can."

"I won't." I stand my ground, and a weird wave of calm washes over me. For once in my life, I don't want to argue with him; I want to win him over. I screw the cap on the hot water bottle and set it down. "I know I'm the *last* person you ever want your sister to be with, but I'm crazy about her. I know that my mistake cost both of you a lot, but I will *never*

let something like that happen again. She's told me every-thing, and I've promised her I won't get involved no matter how badly I want to. I don't have a hero complex. She's not some damsel in distress that needs saving. But I want to look after her. She deserves to have something that makes her happy, and unfortunately for you, that thing is me. So you can either get in our way and force her to suffer for the rest of her life, or you can step aside and let her forge a new path."

That was either my victory speech or my swan song, and I can't tell which. Harvey gives nothing away. Seconds pass by, and I discern he's not going to say anything, so I pick up the dog and step aside to let him make his teas.

"Do you know what a Mars bar is?" he asks out of the blue.

You can always rely on a Brit to come up with small talk even in the most uncomfortable of situations.

"Never had one. It's chocolate, right?"

He nods. "They sell them in the crew shop." Commissary. "She loves the first bite of them – not that she'll admit it or let on that she wants any at all. But she always feels better after chocolate."

Oh. That's...kind of him to share. I'm sure it's for his sister's comfort more than as a favour to me, but it's an olive branch I'll accept all the same.

"Thanks."

As quickly as I can, I swing by the commissary and head back to my room.

Jack's perched on the bed beside Gem when I return. She's lying on her front with her T-shirt lifted up, and he's rubbing her back. I give myself a second to really take in the scene, because I want to start throwing hands. The strong smell of Tiger balm is in the air, and Gem sniffles. Jack leans back to look at me, revealing the agony on Gem's face – red, with tears streaming down it, her lips pursed like she's concentrating on pushing out her breath.

I drop every thought I shouldn't have had and rush to her side. It wasn't this bad when I left. *Fuck*, why did I waste time placating her brother or getting her chocolate when she needed me?

"Baby." I kneel on the floor and hand her the soft dog, which she tucks under her stomach. I stroke her hair, hoping it soothes her, because I suddenly feel powerless. I can never be the one who gets her pregnant; if *this* is soul-destroying, seeing her in labour would be a thousand times worse. Though not being the one she starts a family with one day would be…unthinkable.

Toughen up, Thomas.

Jack finishes rubbing in the Tiger balm and steps away. I thank him with a half-smile, pushing aside my questions about why I felt jealous over that, but not about seeing his head between her legs.

I've heard cramps suck, but I've never seen them wipe out a person like this.

"I thought the painkillers woulda kicked in by now?"

"Sometimes they don't."

I cast a helpless look at Jack. He has to go for his shift, but I need him to stay. He's done the boyfriend thing before – a long time ago, but still. He already seems to know all the tricks, and I know nothing.

"Is there anything else I can do?"

If she said having me roll around on a pile of razor blades would make her pain go away, I'd do it in a heartbeat.

She shakes her head and thanks me for the dog. I keep stroking her hair and wait for however long it takes for her pain to ease slightly, then I reach into my pocket and casually examine the candy bar in my hand before tearing it open.

"Tom, what are you doing? You've not even had breakfast yet."

I roll my eyes like a kid being told he has to finish his homework before playing video games. "This *is* my breakfast."

She looks at me perplexed.

"I've never had one of these before." I attempt to bring her focus back to the bar.

"They're really good."

"I'm not sure. Looks kinda sus. Can you take the first bite, make sure it's not poisonous?" I move it towards her, hoping she'll take the bait.

She doesn't.

"What are you up to?" She narrows her eyes at me.

Game over. "Your brother caught me filling up your hot dog. Said these made you feel better."

She's briefly lost in thought, either worrying about her brother having confirmation we're back together or that he shared her secret craving. "Fuck it. A bit of chocolate isn't going to be my biggest issue today." And with that, she takes the bar from my hands. But she doesn't bite off the end in a hurry like I thought she would, as if the quicker she does it, the quicker she can pretend she didn't. Instead, she sucks it so slowly it's sensual.

My jealousy was misplaced with Jack just now; it's this chocolate bar I want to beat up for getting… Actually, I think my dick's pleased for the break – not that I'm able to stop it from straining in my boxers.

She takes her time, sucking all the chocolate off a small piece of the end, and then she bites it off and enjoys it. Satisfied, she hands it over to me, and I'm desperate for a taste, because if it can make her *that* happy, it must be good.

I take a bite, expecting something completely new, but it's familiar. "Oh, this tastes exactly like a Milky Way."

"No, Milky Way's a different thing. It's all fluffy inside."

"Like a 3 Musketeers bar?"

She looks at me strangely. "A *what* bar?"

I smile. "Never mind."

I just had to fall in love with a British girl.

TWENTY

GEMMA

As much as I hate leaving Tom to wake up alone in my bed, I love teaching Boxfit. I always come away feeling energised, and with what's been going on lately, that's not a feeling I take for granted. I contemplate knocking on Oscar's door and bringing him along to help alleviate the anguish I'm causing him on a daily basis, but I decide against it. He'd be better off belting a musical theatre ballad with Eliza than throwing punches with me and the guests.

I pass the crew noticeboard and try to ignore the newest letter warning all crew members not to engage with journalists or speak to any of the guests about other crew members, and to report anyone acting suspiciously to senior management. It's presented as a blanket statement reminding everyone about the rules of GDPR or whatever, but everyone knows why the reminder needs to be shared and who these guests want dirt on.

The UK gossip rags are running a story about me. That's all Mum and Oscar are letting me know, and I'm not stupid or brave enough to look it up for myself. It'd be a lie anyway. I haven't accessed any news or social media apps since I left home, and I'm better off for it.

It's always assumed that as an influencer I crave attention, but I craved the connection I got with people who were actually interested in my content – either because they were fitness freaks like me or they simply wanted to get healthier and needed a helping hand. It wasn't until Oscar worked on his first ship that I realised how daunting a gym could be for a woman on her own, and not just because of gym creeps. After finding a girl crying in the changing room, ready to quit straight after joining because it was too overwhelming – and because the PT who gave her the orientation was too busy promoting his side hustle of home-based sports massages to teach her what to do – I took it upon myself to show her around. I'm pleased to say I saw her in the gym regularly after that. It inspired me to make new content on how to use every weird and wonderful piece of equipment I could find, with suggestions for sets for different difficulty levels. Like how Tom's content makes people smile, mine helped people feel confident.

As I kick off the class, through the window I spot Jack outside, a few decks down, sitting on a bench looking out to sea. *What's he doing up so early?*

Half an hour passes, and he's still there when my class wraps up. Unease settles over me. I make quick work of packing up so I can go check on him. Even as I approach, he remains undisturbed, not looking back at where I know he hears my footsteps.

"Hey. Everything okay?"

He doesn't turn to face me straight away, but when he does, I can't miss the pain in his eyes. He isn't crying, but he looks so small and lost, and I ache for him.

"Bad day," he says, not bothering to lie or pretend, but he doesn't share any more than that.

Bad day and it's only 7 a.m.? There's more going on here, but I don't think he'd appreciate me prying.

"Come get breakfast with me."

It was my idea to spend the past few nights in my room. Once shark week came to an end, I was very keen to resume mine and Tom's mission to complete the Kama Sutra (turns out what I thought was froggy-style is something completely different, *and I like it*), and now I feel tremendous guilt for putting my sex life ahead of Tom's promise to not let his friendship with Jack fall by the wayside. Jack's been there for me through this whole shit show, and for no reason other than because he cares, he's become one of the handful of people who are fiercely protective of me. So now it's time for me to be protective of him.

Without a fight, he straightens up and follows me. He doesn't join me in the serving area but goes to the coffee machine and makes two teas – green for me, Yorkshire for him – and a coffee when he spots Tom coming up behind me and kissing my cheek.

"Something's not right," I tell Tom as we head over to the table where Jack's waiting for us. I've never seen him not interested in food.

Jack and Tom have some unagi thing going on, so I let Tom steer the conversation about highlights from yesterday and what's on the schedule for today. I hate seeing anyone sad, but Jack? It breaks my heart. After breakfast, I go back to my room and let the boys have some privacy in the hope Jack will release whatever's on his chest. With too much time to do nothing, and not enough time to do anything vaguely interesting, I tidy my cabin before I have to man the climbing wall.

As I straighten out the freshly changed bedding, knuckles rap on my door in a way only Tom's do. I've barely opened it before he's inside kissing me, but not in a take-off-your-clothes-we've-got-five-minutes kind of way; it's one single, desperate kiss, as though twenty *years* have gone by, not twenty minutes. I pull back and scan his face. Whatever's bothering Jack is now bothering Tom, and I wish there was something I could do to save them both from hurting.

"Can you tell me?" I ask, running my fingers through his hair.

He furrows his brow and looks down, unsure. "We are *all* he has." When he looks up again, it's clear he's holding back tears.

"What do you mean?"

"I thought fighting with your brother over you was bad, but Jack lost *everything* fighting for the girl he loves. *Including* her."

It takes me a second to process what Tom's saying. Understandably, Jack isn't much of an open book, so when a page reveals itself, I'm never quite expecting it.

"He's in love?"

Tom nods. "With a girl called Sadie. He's mentioned her to me before, but never…" He shakes his head, distressed, seemingly lost in his previous conversation. "Today's the anniversary of when he was forced to leave her and never go back."

Injustice and sorrow hit me all at once. "Who would…? Why would…?" I stop myself, realising those questions aren't important right now. "Is he going to be okay?"

"He said he would be. It's not the first anniversary, so he's…learnt how to get through it. One big day of feelings, then 364 days in denial."

I sense the quiet fury rising in Tom. I love how fiercely he cares about the people around him.

"He's called in sick, and I just wanna be with him, but I have the *busiest* day today, and the thought of him sitting alone in our room—"

"I'll pop by when I can. If that's not…intrusive."

"No, I think that's a good idea. It'd make me feel better at the very least. Even if he tells you to go away, at least he knows we're here."

I've always considered Jack introverted, but today I'm realising it's more like he's isolated. Alone, and not by choice.

Well, not anymore.

Once climbing's over, I shower, grab the book I'm currently borrowing from the onboard library, and hurry over to Tom and Jack's room, ready to be rejected but hopeful that I won't be.

He answers the door so suddenly I lose the words I came here ready to say.

"Hey! How…? Uh…" It's pointless asking someone who's obviously not okay if they're okay. "I…" *Think of an excuse, dummy! You've not said any words yet. Say words.* "You—" Giving up, I sigh and admit what I'm really here for. "I would like to be here with you."

Jack smiles softly and welcomes me in. "Come on, Bella."

Any other day, I'd continue to protest his new nickname for me, but I'll let him get away with it this once. I follow him inside the dark room, illuminated only by the TV at the foot of his bed.

"And you call *me* a vampire," I say as a joke, hoping it lands.

"Because you are." I spot the smirk on the corner of his lips before he scales the ladder up to his bunk, looking comfy in his mismatched hoodie and jogging bottoms. "I hope you like 'Shrek'."

"Who doesn't?"

I settle on Tom's bottom bunk and get back to the book I've been using to escape reality, letting a Scottish ogre and Jack's soft huffs of laughter fill the room.

It's late when Tom finally finishes work. He's been able to dip in and out, but with it being a sea day, his schedule's far busier than on a port day. He managed to get Jack to eat something while I was running Clubbercise earlier, and that was a relief to us both.

With only the lamps on, Jack and I are sitting on Tom's bunk playing cards, using the desk chair as a table, and Tom's standing in the middle of the room with his wrist in the air, studying his watch. He counts down from three.

"*Andddd* it's tomorrow. Deep breath, everyone."

We put the cards down and humour him. Aside from the occasional sniff and a shaky breath, I'm relieved to say Jack survived his purge. But though emotions like that can come on like a tap, they can't be turned off quite so easily.

"Jack-O'-Lantern, what do you need?" Tom asks.

Jack shrugs one shoulder. "I'm okay. I'll sleep it off."

"Are you tired?"

"Not really."

"Cool. Come here then." Tom grabs Jack's arm and pulls him to his feet, then he drags him towards the bathroom. I stay seated, not prepared to get in the middle of whatever Tom's up to.

"What are you doing, funny boy?" Jack resists a little, making Tom work to pull him further.

"Cold shower. I let you cope how you wanted to, and now you have to do things my way."

"Tom!" I scold, but he ignores me, continuing to tug Jack into the bathroom.

"Clothes on or off, buddy – now's your chance."

"I'm okay, I swear!" Jack insists, amusement in his tone.

Tom turns the tap on. "Sure, but we've gotta reset you. Cold water cures depression."

Jack giggles. "I'm not depressed!"

"Mm-hmm. Last chance to save Pig."

Pig? There's a moment of silence, and then Tom calls my name, holding his small toy pig out the doorway for me to rescue. *How did it get in there?* I take it from him and put it up on Jack's bunk. As I do, the steady flow of water gets interrupted and I assume Jack's caught under the stream.

"Fucker," Jack mutters.

Tom complains, and I head back to watch the show. They're both simultaneously trying to get out of the shower while also holding the other under it. They erupt with laughter, and so do I.

They're a strange pair, but they understand one another.

A few more seconds pass before they give up, both stripping and then giggling to themselves as they twist the water out of their clothes. Any hopes of Jack's clothing drying on its own are futile, and Tom doesn't seem as bothered as he probably should be about his smart evening uniform suffering the same fate. Still in his wet underwear, Tom takes his towel, wraps it around his waist, and leaves Jack in the bathroom. I swoon as he comes over to me. I don't want to flaunt our closeness in front of Jack though – not today – so I keep our kiss short and my hands to myself. Mostly. Tom steps away from me and changes into dry boxers. Jack joins us, and I turn away so he can redress too.

"You're safe," Jack says, sitting on the edge of the desk, now in a different pair of jogging bottoms that he usually wears to bed.

He certainly seems brighter, but there's still a raw ache in his chest, and I can feel it. I know he hasn't been starved of human contact all this time, but to know his heart belongs to someone else, someone he can't have, and what that's doing to him… It's soul-destroying.

I lock eyes with Tom where he's sitting on the chair, having pulled it away from the bed and over to the wall. I'm so grateful to have found him. I have to refrain from considering how much it would hurt to lose him for good, but I continue to sense his worry for his friend. He won't feel better until Jack does, or until he's done what he can to make him feel better, so now it's my turn to try.

I approach Jack on the desk and place my hand on his cheek, his stubble just long enough not to be sharp against my palm. Though a little confused, he smiles.

"Close your eyes," I instruct him.

He does, but his back remains straight. He takes a few slow breaths, and as sudden as a flash of lightning, he sinks into my touch, needing it. I brush my nails along the side of his head softly to comfort him, his wet hair scraped back in a bun.

"You're so loved, Jack."

He reaches for me, and I hold him tightly, hoping it helps to lessen his despair. A moment passes and we drift apart. I study him. His eyes glisten, but they don't stay on me – they flick to Tom behind me briefly. He shifts his gaze back to me, and the next thing I know, his lips are on mine, gentle but definitely there. I tense on instinct, pulling away.

"It's okay, Gem," Tom reassures me, and I turn back to look at him. Helplessness is written on his face. He's hurting for his friend, not for himself. He wants to comfort Jack, but he knows he isn't able to give him what he needs.

But I am.

No one speaks, both of them making their consent clear and waiting for mine. I put my hand out for Tom, who gets up to take it, stepping closer and covering my back. Then I turn back to Jack and let our lips meet again. Tom sweeps my hair to one side before burying his head in the crook of my neck, planting kisses lightly there. Shivers tingle all over my skin, my nipples hardening under my silky nightshirt.

I want to ask what we're doing, but tonight isn't the night to think about it. I stroke Jack's bare chest, sighing against his lips as Tom's erection presses into me.

"Do you want this, Bella?" Jack asks softly.

"Do you want to be shared?" Tom echoes, and I get flashbacks to the night we met. The nights I've been bold.

"You're allowed to. It doesn't make you dirty if you do."

"You're safe in here. No one is judging you."

"Yes," I admit with confidence.

The boys sigh collectively, and Jack spins me around to face Tom, who kisses me urgently. Jack traces my waist with his large hands.

"Show me where you want to be touched."

I place my hands on top of his and slowly guide him to my breasts. He squeezes me, and I grind back against him, his warm breath of relief landing on my neck. I slither my hand inside Tom's boxers, gripping him where he's hard, and remove any of the doubt in my mind that I shouldn't be doing this. As Tom gasps, I lean back to kiss Jack again. Tom unbuttons my shirt until I'm exposed for them both, and Jack repositions his hands, pinching my nipples, which sends a rush of heat between my legs.

"We're so lucky to have you," Jack says. "Do you know that?"

I hum, feeling adored, as Tom slides his hand down my shorts and inside my knickers. He drops his head and sighs in the way he does when he's turned on. The way I love. Then he slips a finger inside of me, instantly finding my weak spot and flickering there. I'm on the edge in seconds, and Jack has to adjust his hold to keep me steady.

"So easily pleased, aren't you?"

I shake my head. "He's just that good," I pant.

There's a rumble in Jack's chest behind me. "I can *hear* how wet you are." His voice now has an edge to it that sounds almost sinister, and my cheeks heat with a tinge of embarrassment.

"Don't hide. Let us fucking hear it."

My knees buckle from the way Tom's touching me.

"Is that for us, Princess?"

"Mm-hmm." I nod feebly.

Jack chuckles. "I got it wrong. Maybe you're the lucky one to have us."

In the blink of an eye, I remember Jack's lips on me and his fingers where Tom's are now.

"You going to let us have some fun with you?"

"Yes." Tom's touch could satisfy me, but he's toying with me, and it's agony. "Please don't tease me," I beg, looking desperately between them both. "I can't handle it. I can't wait."

"You heard her, Thomas."

Tom leaves me in Jack's arms unsatisfied, and Jack

snatches my lips with his. His tongue glides against mine and it feels like being charged with electricity.

"I need to come," I say earnestly.

"You will, I promise."

Tom returns, passing Jack a condom and our bottle of lube and throwing another condom on the bed, presumably for himself later. He pulls me into a kiss, my want for him stronger than ever, but too soon he breaks away and directs my attention behind me. I sense his eyes on me as I look at our friend, now naked. I've been in the same room – the same *bed* – as him while having sex before, but I've never taken the time to really look at him. Jack's beautiful. Tall and slim, with intricate tattoos scattered over his body. My gaze is drawn to one part of him in particular. One *very large* part of him. When I try to meet his eye again, I notice the desire in his as he appreciates my body.

Tom guides my shirt off my shoulders and down my arms, his gentle touch leaving goose bumps on my skin. He kisses my neck, hooking his thumbs in my shorts and knickers, before slowly pulling them down, once again exposing me to Jack. He returns behind me, pride radiating off him as if I'm a prized possession he wants to show off.

Jack's eyes darken, our mutual attraction new and foreign but innocuous.

Tom places his hand on my waist. "Go to him. It's okay," he says again.

I didn't realise how much I needed to hear it.

I close the distance between me and Jack, and he kisses me hungrily.

"You still want to come?"

"Yes." The word sounds broken as it comes out of my mouth.

He spins me around so fast I gasp, but Tom is there to catch me. "Like this?"

Where Tom can hold me. Watch me.

"Yes."

Jack moves his hand between my legs and strokes me gently as I throb. I reach back and try to line myself up with him, grumbling when I can't get the angle right because he's too tall.

Tom laughs playfully. "I think she wants you to fuck her."

On the balls of my feet, I move my hips, rubbing myself over Jack's tip.

"Is she always this needy?" They're gossiping as if I'm not here.

"Always."

"Little vampire."

"Please." I moan like it's my last breath. I don't have patience when I'm horny. I spent too much time not having sex, and now waiting even a minute for it feels like a lifetime.

"Breathe out, baby."

"Why? I'll be— *Holyyy…*" My grip on Tom tightens as Jack presses himself inside me. Jack leans forward slightly so his lips are by my ear.

"I'm not even all the way in yet," he purrs.

Warmth rises in my cheeks. *Oh God.*

"Bet you miss my boyfriend dick now." Tom smirks.

I nod, biting into my bottom lip so hard I'm sure it's turned white.

"Want him to stop?"

I shake my head sternly. I'm determined to take it. I made such a thing about needing him that I'm not going to back out now. Plus, as much as he's a lot to take, he feels *unbelievable*.

Jack doesn't move while I acclimatise to his size, slowly

building up until he's rocking back and forth. But it still feels like asking someone to scratch an itch and they keep missing, so I take him deeper, thriving on the way they both tell me what a good job I'm doing. The three of us lose ourselves to the moment, and before long, I don't know whose hands are whose or which of their tongues is tracing the sensitive spots on my neck, our mouths and fingers seeking, feeling, wanting, *needing*.

"Fuck, it's so hot watching you two together," Tom mumbles, a tortured lilt to his tone.

When I focus on him, it's as if fireworks have been set off in my belly. Not so long ago, I thought I was merely a girl with a crush on my brother's friend, and now he's mine.

Jack's been gentle with me, but all this time I've felt something simmering beneath the surface – something wild, waiting to be unleashed.

"The chair. Here. Sit," I instruct Tom breathlessly.

He steps away and pulls the chair closer to me and Jack. Tom takes a seat and fists himself as he watches us. Jack slows his rhythm as I bend forward and lower my mouth over Tom. His sigh of relief causes a surge of lust to race through me. I push back into Jack a few times, giving him permission to let loose, and the spot he hits, the speed with which he hits it, makes me feral.

Each of his thrusts sink Tom deeper into my mouth, and I love how overwhelmed I am with the two of them and the frenzy we're all working ourselves up into.

"Not a virgin anymore, are you, Bella?" Jack notes.

Smugness fills my chest. *No. No, I'm not.*

TOM

This isn't a competition, but I'm still winning.

Gem is it for me. The one. My person. My world. Even with Jack inside of her, she's mine and she's perfect. *So fucking perfect.*

Watching Jack come apart with her sets the fire in my heart ablaze. I understand now what my parents meant when they said that if we were going to experiment with drinking or other teenage antics, they'd rather we did it in the house where we were safe. Jack is my safe place. Even while he kneels behind her and talks dirty in her ear as she rides me. Even while he squeezes her breasts with one hand and strums her clit with the other. Jack gets off on the pleasure of his partners – I mean, who doesn't? – but he *really* fucking gets off on it. So while Gem gets all our attention, this is for him. Our pleasure is his tonight.

"Look what you do to him. Look how desperate he is for you."

Gem glances down at me with a devilish grin, rolling her hips slowly as she conspires with my best friend.

"I reckon if you go any faster, he'll break. What do you think?"

She smiles and leans on me, picking up her pace, rising and dropping herself onto me. *Fuck.* I wish I could prove them wrong. I wish I were unbreakable so this moment could last forever. But I'm a china shop, and they're the bulls charging around it.

"That's it. You're doing such a good job." He nibbles her earlobe. "You love him, don't you?"

My heart squeezes tight, and the fear she could say no threatens to take over.

"Yes," she admits with a sigh, not missing a beat. "So much."

The sensations rushing through me are insane. I could

combust at any second. Relief. Elation. So much damn euphoria. *She loves me.*

I grab her hips and take control, my thrusts meeting her again and again, as fast as I can manage. "Fuck, I love you, baby."

Gem cries out, another orgasm cresting as her pussy tightens around me, and not a moment later mine comes crashing down, hard and unrelenting. Jack pours praise into her ear as we let the ecstasy wash over us.

Once we've caught our breaths, I pull her down to me, needing a taste of the girl who just said she loves me.

My Princess.

While Gem brushes her teeth, Jack makes sure there's no tension or worry or regret lingering, and I assure him there isn't now and there never will be. He wraps me in a tight hug, and I can tell the burden of his day has been eased.

I get into bed, and when Gem emerges, she goes to Jack, who's waiting to check in with her. She smiles up at him, reassuring him with her answers that she's okay – that we're all okay – alleviating his concerns that he might have come between us. He leans down to plant a kiss on her forehead, and she closes her eyes.

Their gazes meet again.

"Look after him."

"I will," she promises.

"Come on, girlfriend," I call. "Bedtime."

A grin spreads across her lips. "Girlfriend?" she challenges, coming over to me as Jack climbs up to his bunk.

"You heard me. You said you loved me. Pretty sure that means we're a done deal now."

She nestles up next to me and kisses me.

"I'll look up how to get ordained tomorrow," Jack muses above us, turning off his light.

My breath hitches with an idea. "We could get the captain to—"

"Easy now, Thomas. You'll scare her off. Plus, you have to buy her a ring first."

"Minor details." Tom dismisses him.

"And get her brother's permission."

I can hear his playful smile. He knows exactly how to unleash the feminist rage in us both, but most importantly, how to knock me off my perch.

"Gem, you know how we like to keep secrets from him…"

"Good night, boys," she sings and turns off my light.

One day.

TWENTY-ONE

GEMMA

Two months later

"So I'll go sign off at the office, meet you back at yours, and then you'll give my crew card to your magic friend and let them do some sleight of hand stuff at the exit so the system thinks I've gone, and I'll just hide out in your room for a few weeks. Easy."

"Gem." Tom gives me that same forlorn look he's given me every time I've tried to plot my escape from the flight home.

Tears well in my eyes because he still isn't taking me seriously, but I've never been more serious about anything in my life.

"It's only my room for one more week. Then what will you do?"

"Befriend whoever's moving in and live off rations like a little cabin mouse."

"You'll get rickets."

I shrug. "If that's the price I have to pay…"

Silence falls between us. We've been over this conversation a million times before. I want to extend my contract so I can give the general public even longer to forget me before I go back, but it would throw mine and Tom's future contracts out of sync. We've been lucky enough to both secure this ship again for our next contract, and he doesn't want to extend his because it would mean leaving his mum for longer than six months, which he doesn't want to spring on her, and that's completely fair. Not to mention Jack's currently staying with Tom's mum in Chicago, and they've got all sorts of plans I don't want to ruin. I want to see my mum more than anything, but I know wherever I go, drama follows, and she doesn't need that. *No one* needs that.

But we've got everything under wraps here now. What if someone spots me on the way home? What if I'm cornered by camera-happy lunatics who hate me? What if…?

Oh no.

I hurry to the bathroom and dry-heave over the toilet bowl for the second time this morning. I've not been able to keep my food down for the past week. I *wish* it was something I ate. I'd even take a surprise pregnancy at this point, because that would be far more manageable than my current situation.

I'm barely able to keep my hair away from my face, but Tom catches up quickly and holds it for me, rubbing my back until this latest wave of nausea dies down. He allows me a second alone to freshen up, then I go back into my room, where he looks as powerless as I feel.

"Please don't make me go," I beg with a sore throat.

"Baby."

He wraps his arms around me, and I don't bother to hold back my tears anymore. My watch vibrates with the reminder of the inevitable. I have to leave. And I have to leave *now*.

Accepting my fate, I take Tom's hand while he wheels my suitcase in the other, and we head to the office together.

It's hard not to notice how excited everyone around me is to go home, whereas on my journey to the gangway, I feel more like a prisoner on death row being taken to the electric chair.

I say my goodbyes to Eliza and Oscar, who won't go home until a few days before Christmas, and then they head off to give me and Tom some privacy. Tom fusses over the straps of my backpack while I find the nerve to walk away from him knowing this will be the longest six weeks of my life.

"Have you got your disguise?"

I nod firmly as my bottom lip trembles. In an easily accessible compartment of my bag, I have my large sunglasses and Tom's beloved Chicago Cubs baseball team cap. I also have a hoodie ready to put on if I really need to hide. Hopefully, no one will recognise me, but I've come to learn "hope" is simply another word for "delusion".

"I'm a narcissist, aren't I?"

"No, Princess, you just have trauma. I'll let you know if you ever cross that threshold." He gives me one last kiss, and I cling to him harder than Rose clung to that door at the end of "Titanic". "Bye, Gem." He takes a step back, encouraging me to do the same.

"Bye." The word barely makes a sound.

"Keep messaging me. I'm staying signed on till you get home."

I've already told him not to spend this month's salary on a week of Wi-Fi usage. I can handle a few days without constant communication. It'll feel like going cold turkey after having 24/7 access to one another since we met, but there are still internet cafes he can get to every few days. Today, though, I need to know I can reach him.

"I will."

"And I want pictures! I need proof you actually get your flight and don't sneak onto one of the lifeboats."

I giggle. I love that even with this dark cloud looming over me, he can still bring out the sunshine. "Love you."

"Love you more, Cabin Mouse."

It's not until the front door shuts behind us that I let myself breathe. Tilly's always interested in whoever comes through the door, but when she enters the hallway, there's a moment of stillness as she processes my arrival before she bounds over to me, knocking me over. I sit on the floor and let her attack me with kisses and the whipping of her happy tail. Immediately, all the anxiety from the trip diminishes. I coo over her and tell her how much I missed her, suddenly feeling bad, because a few hours ago I was prepared not to come back to her for a few more months.

Once she's tired herself out, I get to my feet and throw my arms around Mum, sinking into her. I was too on edge to appreciate her half-hug in the car. Against my chest, I feel her uneven breath, and I squeeze her even tighter.

"I'm so pleased to have you home."

When I eventually pull away, emotion clouds my vision. There's too much to say to know where to begin, but there's plenty of time for a catch-up now I'm home.

She cups my face. "Do you need a lie down?"

I shake my head. "I'll be okay for a bit." It's early, and I've been awake for almost twenty-four hours, but I'm not ready to leave Mum's side yet.

"Why don't you go freshen up, and I'll let Nan know you're back? She's been so excited to see you."

My heart warms at the mention of her. With a smile, I

head upstairs, and it's not long until I remember that while I don't feel safe outside these walls, inside of them, I do.

"Oh, Princess, you're so cute! Jack! Doesn't she look cute!"

Jack comes into frame and smiles. "Ohh yes, very cute. Good afternoon, Bella."

"Morning!"

Tom wanted to see me in my full princess get-up before I put my lazy clothes back on. Just a few days of hiding in my house was enough for me to hit my limit of doom and gloom. I decided I could sit around and feel scared and anxious and worry about my problems, or I could actually get out and help people with real problems worth being scared and anxious about. So I put myself back on the rota and have been spending my mornings in a local children's ward while Tom sleeps. My paranoia dissipates there because the last person I'm thinking about is myself. No one recognises me – especially not in costume – and no one would care even if they did. "Gemma" is insignificant there, and I love it.

Jack says something about going to take a shower, and Tom's smile widens when he's got me to himself.

"Hey."

His bedhead is insanely cute while also being sexy as hell, and it makes me hurt with how much I miss him already. We're not even halfway into our break yet.

"Hi." I grin back.

He's always so excited to see me even though we've pretty much lived on FaceTime since he got home over a week ago. We don't actively talk to each other most of the time, but it's nice to have the other there when we do want to say something. It's as if we've got our own personal livestreams of our favourite YouTubers. It's not like we use our phones to do anything else. Ship life conditions you out of the habit of scrolling mindlessly. Occasionally, I've dipped out to let him and Jack enjoy their time off-ship together, but I usually get a call from Tom halfway through their adventure to show me something cool, or when they go to grab food and he can get a table near a plug socket. For once, I get to be the third wheel while the two of them enjoy some time together.

"Seemed like a great crowd last night. Well done!" He was nervous about trying to get stand-up gigs before he left, but I'm so glad he reached out to his contacts. He easily managed to get something lined up for nearly every night he's back.

"Yeah, it was a fun one. Wish you coulda been there."

"Me too."

We've spoken at great length about him posting on TikTok again. He wants to, for all the good things it brings to other people and himself, but he's terrified of spotlighting attention back on me, and that's where the conversation ends every time. I've convinced him to keep filming his sets at least, then he has the option to post it later down the line should he change his mind.

"How are the girls?"

Though I see all the kids on the ward, there are two girls in particular who make my day, hopefully as much as I make theirs. They're as thick as thieves and giggle non-stop at the silly stories I make up.

"Cheeky as ever. They tried to prank me today." I begin taking my makeup off.

Tom's eyes light up. "Oh yeah?"

"Mm-hmm. They'd switched beds and dressed up in each other's clothes. The nurses said they'd been scheming all night. They looked ready to burst with excitement when I turned up and lost their *minds* when I called them each other's names. Honestly, they laughed for about ten minutes straight."

Tom giggles with me. "Oh man, I wish I could meet them. They sound perfect."

"They really are." My smile fades as I worry about the possibility of the girls not getting better, but I don't allow my emotions to take up the space they're trying to.

Tom never lets me struggle alone though. "Are you doing okay?"

I straighten my spine and take a deep breath. "I'm out of practice." I shrug, pretending I'm handling it well. "But it's not about me."

"No, I know, but you're allowed to feel things."

I thank him with a tight-lipped smile but move to change the subject as I step out of frame and get changed. "What are you guys up to today?"

"The weather's *diabolical*, so we're thinking it might be the day for our 'Twilight' marathon."

"Oh, you were serious about that?"

"Absolutely! We don't mess around when it comes to 'Twilight'. You wanna watch along or watch me?"

These two are like teenage girls on a sleepover, and I can't get enough of them. "Can't I do both?" I pick my phone back up now I'm decent to find him smirking.

"I like the way you think, Princess."

We don't watch "Twilight"; we heckle at it. Every famous quote and every overly-memed moment gets us shouting at our screens like the best kind of pantomime. We sync our timing perfectly so we're both watching it on our own TVs, and we set up our phones so Tom and I can watch each other watch the TV. There's a "Black Mirror" episode in there somewhere.

We're on the second film now, and at the same moment Edward tries to reveal his sparkly skin to a bunch of Italians, a WhatsApp notification comes up on my phone telling me I've been invited to a group chat named "Torture Lodge".

Weird.

Panic swims in my stomach as I study the participants, all of which are people I hope I'll never have to see again. Excluding Pete. He actively defended me when he was sent home, and though it didn't have much of an impact on anyone's opinion of me, it meant a lot. Plus, he was there for me the second I finally got released from the show, and he's checked in a few times since I've been away.

Messages trickle in, and a horrible sinking feeling overwhelms me.

> WTF.
>
> ARE YOU FUCKING KIDDING ME!?!?!
>
> This has to be some kind of joke.
>
> No amount of money is worth this.

The next few minutes pass in a blur. One second, I'm typing out a hurried message asking what's going on, and the next, I've accidentally accepted a call.

From one of the "Love Lodge" producers.

My phone buzzes in my hand as the room spins. I'm not sure how long I've been sitting here since the call ended. There are so many thoughts swirling around my head that I've been sucked into a void of nothingness.

This can't be happening.

Seeing Tom's name on the screen, I answer the FaceTime call.

"Hey, baby, where'd you go?"

I try to respond to his cheery face, but words don't form.

"Gem…you okay?"

Tears fall silently down my cheek, and I swipe them away with shaky fingers. Then I look up, hearing Mum come down the stairs.

"Oh no, poppet. What's the matter?"

I said I wouldn't be in the country. I said I was struggling with my mental health. *I said no.* But they reminded me of the clause in my contract that gives me no choice.

"Gem?"

I force the words out. "There's going to be a reunion episode."

My phone slips from my hands as I leg it to the kitchen sink, barely making it there in time to bring my lunch back up.

TWENTY-TWO

TOM

"Are you sure I'm not crazy for wanting to go?" Gem blinks against the brush of her mascara.

"No, I think it's a great idea!"

Charlotte, the girl from the winning couple on "Love Lodge", made a separate group chat for the ladies. They're anticipating being pitted against one another during the reunion, so they wanted to have a good-vibes-only dinner of their own beforehand, which Gem's currently getting ready for. It's the first time in the two weeks since the news came in that I've seen her actually excited about something that isn't my stand-up gigs. Maybe "excited" is a bit of a stretch. She's terrified, but she's interested, and I'll celebrate that.

Not once has she let us work out a strategy to keep her off the show or find a way for her to come out on top if she really has no choice. That's what I'm hoping tonight will be good for. I know there's a contract, but contracts always have loopholes. *Don't they?* I wish I understood why she's lying down and letting it happen when I know she's got a fight in her.

She gives her all to the kids, even extending her reach to do home visits after her favourite pair of girls were discharged due to their conditions improving significantly, but once that tiara comes off, she disappears into herself, spending the rest of her day and night playing "The Sims". I saw a TikTok recently about how playing that game is a trauma response, and I wholeheartedly believe it now. But if that's her escape, I'm gonna keep hyping up her creations and asking her to show me all the little quirks of the world she's making.

"I know I've not exactly sung their praises, but I'm starting to think we were all so caught up in our own things, both during and after filming, that we never really got to know each other, and they're the only people who actually get it, you know? Not that you—"

"I know what you mean."

"And if they're all brave enough to go out, then I should be too, right?"

"I think you're brave to even consider it. And if you change your mind at the last second, no one's gonna hold it against you."

She goes quiet, and I know she's disagreeing with me. It was hard enough for her to voice her fears of going to London and ask them to go somewhere more low-key. It took no convincing at all for them to decide to go to Brighton. Partly because they're probably not as bad as we thought they were, but I think mostly because Gem's the one they all want to see. Until the reunion announcement, they'd had no contact with her since the show, and by now, they've seen the number the editing team did on her. They know who she really is, and I'm hoping they'll confirm what I've been reminding her of all this time: they've got her back.

"Did anyone reply about giving you a ride?" Gem's mom was meant to be driving her, but her car broke down a few days ago and has to stay in the shop over the weekend.

"Yeah. Luckily, there's a spare seat in the posh people carrier they've hired."

"Great. Remember, I haven't got a gig tonight, so Jack and I are here to keep you company if you do decide to stay in."

"Thanks." She packs her makeup away and then goes to stand in front of her mirror, taking a deep breath as she looks herself over. "I'm going. I'm definitely going."

"Good job, Princess. Proud of you."

8 P.M.

Having a good time x

No one hates me :)

9 P.M.

Told them all about you xx

11 P.M.

Wrapping up, will call you when I'm home x

The call comes in a few minutes after her last message.

"That was quick." My smile drops instantly and panic floods my senses as she appears on my screen. She looks terrified, and she's crying her eyes out. "Baby, what happened? Where are you?"

"There were paps waiting for us outside. They must have followed Charlotte here. Or someone saw us and posted about it. I don't know." Her bottom lip trembles, and she sniffs. From the slight echo, I work out she must be hiding in the bathroom.

"Are the girls still with you?"

She shakes her head. "They all rushed to the car, but I panicked and ran back inside. I was too scared we'd be followed to my house if I got in, but now I'm—" She keeps breathing in sharply again and again, and she can't seem to stop to release all the air.

"Deep breaths, Gem. I've got you, okay? Out... In... Good. And another one." She does as I say. "That's great. Keep going. You're so tough, Gem. We'll get through this together, I promise." She finds some tissue and blows her nose. "Is there anyone at the restaurant who can help you? Can they call you a cab?"

"I don't want to..." She looks up, double-checking she's alone, and then lowers her voice. "I can't be sure they're not the ones who..." She takes a jagged breath.

Shit.

"Okay, we'll just wait it out. The paps will get bored eventually. They might not even know you went back inside."

Five minutes later, once she's steadied her breathing, she bravely decides to dial a cab, and I wait nervously until she calls me back.

"They haven't got anything for over an hour. I shouldn't have relied on the girls to give me a lift. I should have been more organised and booked this when Mum's car—" She's spiralling again.

"Then we wait till it arrives, okay? Rather we lose some time and get you back safe than—"

The bathroom door swings open, and Gem tenses as she snaps her head in the direction of whoever's come in.

"Oh, I didn't think anyone was in here. I'm so sorry, but we're closing."

"Are they still out there?" Gem asks.

"Doesn't look like it."

Trepidation is written all over her face as she accepts her fate.

"Wait – how are you getting home?" I ask, trying not to let my fear show. "The cab—"

"It's only a ten-minute walk." She downplays it, and I know it's only because she doesn't want to inconvenience the staff.

"It's late."

"If they've gone, I'll be fine." I wish she were the diva the show made her out to be so she'd demand to stay until she could get a ride home.

"Excuse me, is there a staff entrance she can leave through in case they haven't gone?" I speak up for her.

I don't see the worker, but my voice must confuse her, as she takes a second to answer. "Sure."

"People care way less about me than I think they do," Gem mutters under her breath as she squares her shoulders and follows the girl.

Someone calls out to the person helping her. "Yeah?" she replies. "Coming! It's just through there. Careful – the door's quite heavy. Get home safe."

Gem thanks her and keeps her phone close as she leaves. A door clunks open and slams shut behind her, and she wastes no time in heading down the street. Then I hear someone call out her name, and the next thing I know, Gem's surrounded by flashing lights and the sound of camera shutters clicking. She snaps her head in different directions, taking in what seems like chaos.

"Talk to me." My throat is so tight with emotion it hurts.

"They're everywhere," she whispers.

"Run, Gem!" I cry, because she's frozen in place like a rabbit caught in headlights.

I can't focus on how scared I am for her right now – I have to get her to safety. She pushes through the crowd and hurries away, but the noises don't get any quieter.

"Hey! It's Gemma from 'Love Lodge'!" someone yells so loud I'm sure the whole town hears.

She glances back briefly and then sadness returns to her face. "They're filming me, Tom. I don't know what to do." The fear in her voice is agony.

"Are there any bars around you? Do they have security?"

She doesn't answer, but she keeps walking, only looking forward now.

"Choose whichever path is well-lit. Especially where there's likely to be CCTV." I feel so helpless, but I have to keep it together. "I'm gonna screen-record too, okay?" I want that thought to comfort her, not alert her to the fact this could get worse and she might need the evidence later. I quickly swipe down on my phone and begin recording.

"Fucking slag!" another voice bellows, and then there's jeering and whistling, and suddenly other people start shouting at her too.

She keeps jogging as best as she can in heels, not retaliating to any of the awful things people are screaming at her. To the people laughing at her. It's as if her hate comments have grown legs and become sentient.

"Everyone fucking hates you!"

"Kill yourself, you ugly bitch!"

"Dress up all you want – everyone knows you're scum."

"I love you, baby. Keep looking for someone to help you." *I* should be that person.

"This is for Pete!"

Gem flinches, and glass shatters on the ground nearby. *They didn't.* She stops running as she panics and tries to step over it. Then a sob wracks her body.

"Are you hurt?" I ask, but she doesn't reply.

"Look – it's the psycho from the telly," some asshole who's clearly drunk says as if talking to someone else. His voice is closer than the others.

Gem shields her face. "Please leave me alone," she begs. Then, all of a sudden, she whips around. "Hey! Get off me!"

He grabbed her.

Everything's shaking, so I can't see what's happening clearly, but I can tell she's desperately trying to tug herself out of his grip. *While he films her.*

"Get your hands off her!" I scream, but it makes no difference. "Self-defence, Gem! You can hurt him! Don't stop fighting. Don't give up!" I want to burn the world for her. "*I'm filming you, asshole! Let her fucking go!*"

She yelps in pain, and then there's a new male voice. Deep and threatening.

"If you ever get bored of sticking your fingers down your throat, I've got something else for you to gag on."

Jack and Mom burst into my room, but I don't answer their torrent of questions. I can't take my eyes off the screen. I can't leave Gem even for a second. There's a scuffle, and she shrieks as her phone clatters to the ground, and quickly they both stand beside me to see what's happening for themselves.

There's a thud, and a few wisps of her hair brush her screen. "Gem!"

She's on the ground. *She's on the fucking ground!*

Terror has completely consumed me. My face is wet, and Mom holds me tight to keep me from crumbling as the struggle continues.

"Tire them out. Pull their hair. Dig your nails in for evidence. Aim for the eyes and the crotch," Jack instructs her, but a few seconds later, the men curse and run off.

She grabs her phone and pulls it into her chest as though she's curled up in a ball. "Tom…" My name sounds painful for her to say. Like she's winded.

The snaps of camera shutters become prominent again,

and I'm almost grateful for them. They're likely the only things that stopped those men from torturing her further. She doesn't bother to call out for help. She keeps herself small and still as she cries quietly, lying on the concrete while the paps swarm her.

"I'm here, Gem. I'm here. Tell me you're okay. Please be okay." My voice cracks.

She mumbles to herself, and I can only make out parts of it over the mob. "This is all my fault. I asked for this. I wanted this."

"Don't give up, Gem. Don't let them win. Take off your heels and run if you can. You're faster than all of them."

She either can't hear me or can't find the strength to fight anymore, and it feels like my heart's being ripped out of my chest. I know the only thing I can do now is be with her and wait for this to end.

"Oi! Get back!"

There's shouting as a woman steps in to defend her. Then another voice, this time a man's, as he also attempts to defuse the crowd. It takes a minute or so, but the noise dies down. Gem remains where she is though.

"You okay, love?"

Gem lifts her head, and I catch a glimpse of a black-and-silver uniform looming over her.

"Do you have any injuries?"

"I just want to go home." Her eyes have glossed over, and she's shaking like a leaf.

"Have you had much to drink tonight?"

You can't be serious.

Gem simply stares at the woman a little longer, and there must be a moment of recognition, because her tone changes.

"Are you able to stand up? We can get you back."

I don't relax yet. The paps may have gone, but I can still

hear a rowdy mob of people nearby. I watch Gem follow the officer until they come to a stop by a fluorescent blue, yellow, and white cop car.

"Tom," she whimpers.

"I'm still here, Princess."

She climbs into the back seat and I'm able to breathe a little easier. *She's safe.* But she looks so small and scared.

"You'll be home soon."

The other officer gets into the car and the engine starts up, but then there's a bright light on her face, moving her attention to the window. The way her phone's angled allows me to make out the sea of phones pointing at her from outside.

And dread drowns us both.

I thought bad things were supposed to come in threes, but Gem's about to take her fourth hit with no sign of her luck improving anytime soon. After images of her sitting in the back of a cop car made headlines over the weekend, along with the videos circulating online that made her look like she was having some kind of episode, HR emailed her to set up a meeting for later today.

We haven't ended our call since that night, and I'm never going to. I cancelled the gigs I had lined up for this week and quickly acclimated to UK time, because I can't bear the thought of there being a moment when Gem's awake and I'm not with her, nor am I in the mood to cheer up anyone besides her. I'm not sure what's around the corner, so I'm clinging onto her as tight as I can.

She's currently in her pyjamas, wrapped in blankets, at her computer playing "The Sims", and if the bags under her pink eyes and the almost continuous stream of tears aren't enough of a tell of how bad things are, she's deactivated my favourite mod, so now none of the NPCs start spontaneously sixty-nineing anymore. She's basically playing so she can exist somewhere else. Hell, even *I'm* thinking about downloading the game, because if she's about to be fired, I'll go from seeing her all day every day for six months at a time to a few weeks at a time every six months, and I need a reality where we never have to be apart. And definitely one where there's always a chance to spontaneously sixty-nine. I'm prepared to make long-distance work. In my head, there's no other option. We're it. She's the girl I'm gonna marry someday. But, understandably, Gem's current ability for optimism is non-existent.

She's in the bathroom freshening up for her meeting when her mom comes in to bring her another green tea. "Hi, Tom," she says with a soft smile.

"Hey, Mama Harvs." We both share a look of exhaustion.

"Did you manage to get some sleep last night?"

I shrug and say, "A little," because I know that's what she needs to hear. But the real answer is not a wink. Each time I dozed off, I jolted awake in a panic, remembering everything from Friday night. Then I'd recall the moment Gem got ready for bed and examined herself in the mirror, discovering the finger-shaped bruises forming on her arms from where those creeps grabbed her, and the cuts on her face and down her right side from where she fell on the ground. Anger burns like acid inside me at the memory.

"Do you think it would help if I flew over there?"

The second she was safely home with her mom I started checking flights. Jack left on Sunday, but even if he'd stayed longer, he'd have supported me flying out there too. Hell, he was ready to come with me.

"That's a lovely idea, but I can't encourage that, for your mum's sake. I know how precious these few weeks are."

I nod, accepting her polite refusal and deciding not to mention Mom already approved the idea. She's in a good place now, and no doubt excited to get her house back after having us boys around for so long. Not to mention she'd do anything for her future daughter-in-law.

"Thank you for being here for her."

I smile back, but I don't need to be thanked. Gem needs me. And I need to be hers.

TWENTY-THREE

GEMMA

"We just feel it's best to delay your embarkation date until this all calms down."

Mum and Nan both squeeze my hand from where they're sitting behind my laptop. Tom's on my phone next to me, and Oscar also has his own virtual seat at the kitchen table on Mum's iPad. I knew what was coming, and I couldn't face it alone. Even if everyone else disposes of me once they've had enough, at least I still have my family.

"So what's my new embarkation date? What ship?" I already extended my contract break by two weeks to allow for the show – I can't stay here any longer than that.

"You have the reunion coming up, don't you? That will likely keep you in the headlines for a while, but let's book in a call for a month's time and we can reassess then. How about that?"

"You know I wasn't arrested, though, right?" I keep my tone as polite as possible, but all I want to do is scream at the woman simply doing her job. "I didn't commit a crime. You can do another background check on me and it'll tell you exactly that." I don't even have a name for the protective new alter ego currently defending me. I don't know who she is, but she can take over. I'm done running my life into the ground.

"Of course. We understand your situation is…a complex one, but for that reason, we've agreed that now's not the best time to bring you back on board. There's a risk – not only to your safety, but also to those around you – if this gets out of hand. We also can't have anything happen that would impact the guest experience or risk a bad reflection on the company. I'm sure you can understand from our side of things why this decision has been made."

"I understand." I comply through gritted teeth.

The woman wraps up the call and I close my laptop. Defeat sinks in around the table. I've heard of quiet-quitting, but I'm pretty sure they're quiet-firing me. I'll be in this same spot in a month's time, and they'll say one more month, and it will carry on until I give in and stop asking when.

Tom and I have to break up. We're coping with the long distance now, but soon he'll be busy on the ship with no Wi-Fi, and I'll still be here, slowly crumbling under the consequences of one bad decision I made more than nine months ago and living vicariously through my Sims. Again, why couldn't it have been an unexpected pregnancy?

Because you were a virgin, idiot.

Okay, that's enough of the voices in my head. *Jesus Christ.* Once Tom gets some distance, he'll realise the new heights he can reach without his association with me dragging him down. He'll be better off without me. Everyone would. They should all run while they still can, because the rest of my life is cursed. I will never *not* be the psycho-slut from "Love Lodge". That's my legacy.

"So if we can get you out of doing the show, you might be able to come back sooner."

Despite everything, Tom's refusing to give up on me. I cast a solemn look his way.

"I can't get out of it."

"This isn't 'The Hunger Games', Gem. They can't force you to go back on that show."

"They can. It's in her contract." Oscar speaks for me.

"What if you don't turn up? They can't do anything about that," Tom suggests. I know he's been wanting to say this for a long time, but I haven't entertained the conversation because I already know the answer.

"They can fine me *a lot* of money."

"What about talking to a lawyer?"

Mum looks Tom's way with a kind expression. "We don't have the kind of funds we'd need to go up against a production company and a mainstream channel. Also, they wouldn't have sent out those contracts without having a whole team of lawyers approve them first."

"And even if we did have the money and the lawyer thought she had a case, if she lost…they could probably then sue her for defamation, or for breaking her NDA, or for some other clause in the fine print," Oscar adds.

"Not to mention what they'd say about her in the press." Nan shakes her head at her newfound disdain for the media.

Mum's phone chimes and she glances over at the notification. Oscar and I told her to turn off the news alert she set up for the show and my name, and she said she did, but when her attention doesn't immediately come back to the room, that sinking feeling settles in again.

"What is it?" I ask.

She looks at me as if she's fine, but I know her too well. She's seething. "They're casting for series two."

No one says a word. The anger that's been simmering inside me all this time finally boils over. I was misled. I was too naïve. I made mistakes and I have to live with them, because the damage is done, and nothing can change the past. But to let them set a trap to catch a whole new set of victims is a brand-new level of bullshit. They'll entice them with the supposed glamorous lives the finalists are now living, only to make them pawns in a game they don't know they'll be playing. And I'm not allowed to speak up and warn anyone not to fall for it. It's not fair. There's no way I'm going to let anyone else suffer the same fate – not if there's something I can do.

The others begin to scheme among themselves – something about hiring Oscar's actor friends to be paramedics and Nan taking one for the team in the shopping centre the day of the reunion – but the ringing in my ears is too loud to make sense of it. Ignoring them, I excuse myself from the table and head to the front door. The wind blows it out of my hands, revealing a furious grey sky, which makes my exit way more dramatic than it needs to be. It's pouring with rain, but that doesn't deter me from shoving my feet into Mum's Crocs, stepping outside, and marching to the seafront.

The only people I pass are rushing to get home or under cover – not that it matters anymore. I decide I wouldn't care if it was a perfect day and there were hundreds of people out and about. I've been held hostage in a ski lodge, then captive on a cruise ship, and now I'm trapped in my own home. I'm done. Done with being the victim in this story.

The sea's rougher than usual, but I'm a strong swimmer, and I'm not stupid enough to go in if there's actually a chance of getting swept up in the tide. I continue walking as I shed my layers, pulling my jumper and T-shirt over my head in one movement. I stop briefly to fling the Crocs off and step out of my leggings. The pebbles are rough under my feet, but I welcome the discomfort. It's better than the numbness I felt before. It almost feels good.

Oscar's calling out to me, which means Mum's followed me and brought him and probably Tom, too, to witness my mental breakdown, but I don't stop. I've kept myself quiet and hidden away all this time, and for what? I've still been harassed. Still had lies spread about me. Still brought stress and grief to everyone I love. And now I'm living out some Groundhog Day nightmare I don't ever think I'll wake up from.

The freezing water hits my feet, but I don't even wince. I keep walking until I'm deep enough to bathe in the furious waves. Suddenly, all the noise in my head stops and peace settles in. I tip my head to the sky and smile, letting rain pummel my face as I laugh like an absolute lunatic, because there's an opportunity for something huge here, and I've been too scared to take it. Screw being scared anymore.

Screw. It. All.

There are clauses to prevent me taking the production company and the channel to court, but they said nothing about the court of public opinion. I kept my eyes wide open in that place and I'm not naïve anymore. I've learnt their tricks. It's time someone played them at their own game.

Since the group chat was set up and my dinner with the other girls, I've discovered I'm not the only one whose life took a downward spiral after the show. I'm also not the only one whose name still comes up in the press. Some get raked over the coals more than others. Some have pictures and headlines less flattering than others. It's either that revelation or simply that enough time has passed, but the animosity I feel towards my castmates has begun to wane. We were all in survival mode, all moving in accordance to the strings being pulled above us, and if I don't want to be judged for who I was made out to be in there, I have to offer them the same grace, otherwise I'm no better than the mob.

Up until now, I haven't sent a single message in the main group, because I didn't trust someone wouldn't leak the chat for the right price. But this could be an opportunity to redeem myself, and them too. And I can't do it alone.

Adrenaline courses through me and keeps me strangely warm as I emerge from the sea. Mum and Nan stand there in their raincoats, Mum sharing an umbrella with Nan in one hand and holding Tom in the other, while Nan clutches the iPad with Oscar on it to her chest. As I get closer, I see Tom's grin on my phone screen as he whoops and hollers at me. Not because I'm in my underwear, but because he knows his cold shock technique has worked on me. I gather my clothes as I head back up to them, and Mum whips off her coat to wrap it around me. Everyone wears their anticipation on their sleeves as I cover myself up.

"You okay?" Mum asks.

"Yep." I pull my wet hair out from under the coat. "I'm going on that show."

"But we've got a plan. We can help you—"

I cut Oscar off. "No need. I've got a better one."

"Gemma…" he says in the same worried tone he had when I first told him I was taking part. I know he thinks I'm about to make a big mistake, but it's time to stop letting him tidy up the mess I made.

Everyone before me except Tom is wearing a look of sympathy and concern. Yep, they definitely think I've gone insane, and I can't exactly blame them after I just went full "Moana" on them.

"Why? You don't have to. Let us—" Nan tries to explain.

"Because it's live. And I have something to say."

TWENTY-FOUR

TOM

My girlfriend's leading a rebellion and I've never been more in love with her.

"Will you sit down already!" Eliza grumbles at me after I reconsider my third seat.

"I will once I've figured out what's uncomfortable enough that you won't have fucked on it."

Harvey has the audacity to smirk. "My office gets cleaned regularly."

"The fact you're not denying it is the problem." I share my focus between him and Eliza, who's sitting on his lap. I make sure they're aware I'm judging them, all the while knowing I'd be no better behaved if I were in their shoes.

I eye Jack up and down. He's sitting in the seat next to them. "Do *you* get cleaned regularly?"

"You're welcome to check for yourself," he flirts.

"Shh!" Eliza silences us both, and I plonk myself down on Jack's lap so we can all crowd around Harvey's computer screen in time for the show to start.

Over the sound of a theme tune and the cheering of a live studio audience, cameras pan around the stage set up to look like a ski lodge. All the cast are on couches, staggered around the room in pairs or small groups, and behind them is a projector screen showing ski slopes through a wooden window frame. The host, a young-ish guy with a fancy suit and a smile I don't like, comes into view. He's sitting on a large armchair lined with white fur blankets beside a fake log fireplace. The room looks cosy, but I know the atmosphere inside will be everything *but* that.

He makes some speculative comments about a few of the participants, and the camera catches up to them to gauge their reactions. My breath hitches when I see her. Tonight's the first time it's really sunk in that she's a celebrity. Obviously, I know how big her following is, and I know the level of torment she's received as a consequence, but it's the first time I've seen her like…*this*.

I expected her to be a bag of nerves ahead of today – I sure have been – but she's like a completely different woman from the one I met all those months ago. She's confident and composed. An absolute ball-buster. Not the type of girl who hides behind her brother or a fake name. She's not cowering away from the spotlight like I've seen her do; instead, she holds her head up high and looks the picture of grace. And she's *blonde*.

Apparently, the hype for the show exceeded the expectations of the TV execs. A few weeks ago, that would have terrified us, but today it fills me with joy because it means Gem has every chance of pulling this off. She already is.

It took some convincing, but she managed to get everyone to agree to her plot for redemption. And since then, each of them has laid their reputations on the line and triggered a media frenzy by either announcing huge projects with no ability to see them through or getting caught in their own fake scandals. "Slammed" this. "Blasted" that. "Hits back" at whatever-the-hell. They're "sparking outrage" in every gossip column going, and people are losing their minds online. From the stories I heard before Gem went back to the UK, I wouldn't have thought any of the other contestants had it in them to help her, but I'm pleased to say I was wrong.

By the first ad break, the host looks about ready to lose it with the hoops the cast are making him jump through. One guy announced he's launching his own clothing line with a nonsense slogan and a logo that looks accidentally phallic – though it's no accident. The couple who came in second place have come out as a throuple with the same person they supposedly both had beef with. And apparently, the next part of the show will be opened with a live performance of Gavin's upcoming debut single, which will be a trainwreck because he's tone deaf and wrote the song he claims he "heard in a dream" on some AI software last week, then hired someone else to put it to a tune. His prank is by far the most humiliating, and it'll be the toughest to redeem afterwards, but it's come to light that he's been riddled with guilt over how he handled Gem's arrival, and he knows he owes her this favour at the very least.

"He's bricking it," Jack says about the host, stretching his legs with a smile as I get off him.

"Huh?"

"It means he's shitting the bed," Eliza clarifies, giving Harvey's legs a break too, and I grin. I'd feel sorry for the host if I didn't have it on good authority he's a douchebag when the cameras aren't rolling.

Harvey's quiet and pensive on a good day, but even more so right now.

"You doing okay, big man?"

He nods, but the rest of his body reveals the lie.

"Have some faith. She's got this."

"I know, but…" He sighs. "I'll be fine once it's over."

I reach over to Oscar's phone, which is propped up beside the computer, and unmute us.

"Are you all right, Mama Harvs? Nana Harvs?" They called a few minutes before the show started, not able to cope with the stress on their own.

They both raise their cups of tea with nervous smiles. I wish I could give them the biggest hug. I mute us again, and I swear I catch the corner of Harvey's mouth curling into an approving smile. *Would you look at that?* I'm starting to suspect Gem and her castmates aren't the only ones who've trauma-bonded.

Gavin's one brave motherfucker. How he keeps a straight face through his song and the interview afterwards, I will never know. Serious props to him – he's redeemed as far as I'm concerned. The others all deserve awards for their poker faces too.

The next to be interviewed is Jazz, Gavin's former fling. From what I hear, they split amicably after the show and remain good friends. She steps up to the spare armchair by the fireplace, and it's as if she and Gavin are competing for who can come off worse on this show.

"Oh…my…*God.*" Eliza leans into the screen in awe.

Jazz spent several hours earlier today getting the most convincingly terrible prosthetic nose applied to her face. She's managed to keep out of the press over the past few months, and in the only pictures of her from the pap-attack in Brighton she had her handbag over her face, so a reappearance with a new nose is more than believable. Not that she's publicly commented on it. As if that weren't enough for people to talk about, the state of it has whipped up a storm. It's large and crooked, and the makeup artist even added some slight bruising under her eyes in such a way that it looks like Jazz tried her best to cover it up with foundation.

Like everyone he's interviewed so far, the host forces Jazz to sit through a clip of her best and worst moments. We're silent as we suffer through them too, because Jazz and Gem share the same lowlight: Gem's arrival into the main lodge. I'd never seen it before, and I hope I never have to again. The look on her face as the reality of what's going on hits her destroys me.

"Was that hard to watch?" The host probes Jazz when she remains silent.

She struggles to come out with a reply more than I expected her to. "Yeah, it was. I'm just not that girl anymore, you know. I've changed a lot since the show, and it's hard to recognise myself there."

"It's hard to recognise you *now*." The host attempts a joke at her expense, which makes the four of us audibly wince. You *never* make a joke at someone else's expense. But I'm so glad he did, because he's fallen right into her trap.

"What do you mean by that?" The way her face falls in the blink of an eye makes even *my* blood run cold, so I can't imagine what the host is going through.

He stutters. "Oh, nothing, no, I mean… You've changed since we last saw you." He waves his hand, gesturing to her face.

She continues to stare blankly at him, pretending not to know what he's talking about, and he sputters to fill the dead air, but he can't find the right words. He laughs awkwardly, shuffling in his seat, and his eyes briefly dart around for someone to save him.

"You know…" He does the same thing with his hand again.

"*Jeessuusss.*" Jack cringes behind me.

"No. I don't."

All of a sudden, red and blue lights start flashing as "Sound of da Police" starts playing. The cameras snap onto a blindsided Gem.

They fucking didn't.

"Easy. *Easy.*" Jack restrains me, preventing me from jumping to my feet. "Not in front of Nana."

I could smash something.

Eliza squeezes Harvey's hand so tight her knuckles turn white to keep him from doing the same. We knew they wouldn't be able to resist bringing it up, but like *that*? They deserve everything coming to them.

"That was a low fucking blow," I seethe.

Realisation dawns on Gem, and her brief overstimulation morphs into a confident smirk. *Fuck*, I don't know how she's keeping it together. *Shit*, I love her so fucking much, and if they hurt her again, I swear I'll fly over there and torch the place down myself.

They cut back to the host, whose grin is as sinister as a cartoon villain's. He clearly feels somewhat back in the driver's seat. Unsurprisingly, Jazz is nowhere to be seen. With the promise of a juicy interview happening momentarily, he wraps up this part of the show, and the ads come back on.

You could cut the tension in Harvey's office with a rusty spoon. Though we were stressed out of our minds before, it turns out we were keeping it together pretty well, because right now we're all close to falling apart. We knew it would be bad. We knew they wouldn't go easy on her. Hell, the biggest sign they want to make her suffer is sitting right next to her on the couch. She had another call with an assistant producer earlier this week to discuss the show, and she made a point to lie and say she was dreading seeing Pete again. And guess who they sat her with…

He's one of the lucky few who are actually doing okay after the show. He got a modelling contract straight off the back of it, and though everyone gave him sympathy, he's only ever spoken highly of Gem and his time with her. He could have looked after her in a way that *didn't* involve touching her so much, but still, he took care of her, and for that, I can't not love the guy. Also, after hearing what he was going through before the show, I'm happy for his success.

"I thought she said she was going to be later in the episode. It's too soon. They haven't all gone yet. They're not ready," Eliza frets, giving voice to the same concerns racing through my head.

There are so many more things that have been planned. Gem was supposed to deliver the death blow in the show's final moments, but this changes everything.

"They'll adapt. They've all had plenty of practice coping under pressure. This is no different," Jack reassures us.

When the show comes back on, Gem's sitting in the armchair beside the host with her head held high, looking like the ultimate femme fatale. Like *royalty*. Next to a roaring fire, and in a tight red dress with red lipstick to match, she's pure sin. All the anxiety vibrating in my chest settles down, because there's something in the way she's holding herself that says she wants to own the place. And she's sure as hell about to.

She appears in a small square in the bottom left-hand corner of the screen acting wholly unfazed by the video playing only her lowlights. Everyone so far has had at least a few redeeming clips, but she's given none. It's weird to see an edited version of what happened when I know the truth behind every sentence and camera angle. Her lips remain in a flat line and there's an arch in her brow, almost as if she's bored. She could just as easily be seated upon a throne in her castle judging the evening's unsatisfactory entertainment.

"Give it up for Gemma Harvey, everybody!" The host encourages a round of applause from the room. "So...you made bail then?"

She plasters on a fake smile. "It would appear so."

"I mean, the question on everybody's lips. What were you arrested for?"

Jack steadies me again before I can erupt.

Her brow rises with shock. "Wow, straight out with it."

"See this as a chance to say your piece." His lips break into a sly grin.

"You'd make a terrible lawyer. Has anyone ever told you that?"

He chuckles along with the audience but says nothing more, forcing her to end the silence.

She grins, and a small giggle leaves her lips. "It's a funny story, actually."

"Come on, Gem," I mutter. The others have done what they can – now she has to get through this.

"First of all, I'd like to say for the record..." She shoots her gaze over to the camera, showing two surrendering palms, and then turns back to him. "It wasn't me." She says it in such a way that people laugh with her. "It was the plant."

Harvey hums with amusement.

The host scrunches his brow in confusion. "Sorry, the plant?"

"Mm-hmm." She nods confidently, as if that should explain everything. "There was a total eclipse not too long ago."

Eliza gasps with a smile.

"I don't get it." I look back at Jack, who seems as lost as I

277

do. She rehearsed a few different explanations with me before today, but none of them went like this.

"And I found this *strange* and *interesting* plant in my local florist. I knew immediately that I had to have it, but ever since then…things have been getting *wildly* out of hand." Her expression turns serious, as if she's seen some dark things.

"Can someone please explain what's going on?" I look across at the others.

"It's the plot of 'Little Shop of Horrors'," Harvey says with a smirk.

The host chooses his words carefully. "That's almost…*impossible* to believe." He bares his teeth with a fake smile.

"Oh, he's *pissed*," Jack sings behind me.

Gem throws her head back with the sexiest laugh I've ever heard. "I know, but you can't make this stuff up."

Strike one.

"But I do have the CCTV footage to explain everything, which I'm more than happy to share on socials later."

For once, tonight, this isn't a lie. The restaurant sent over the CCTV footage of her getting assaulted three weeks ago. They were also able to obtain footage from the surrounding businesses, so, including the screen recording I also took, she has a full account of what went down that night. It was awful to watch back, but she has the video pieced together and ready to share the second this show's over, along with pictures of the bruises on her arms, and the cuts on her face and the left side of her body, from where she was pushed over. It'll prove she wasn't arrested and also shed light on the monsters that are out there. So far, people have only talked about the online abuse. The trolling. But when the "be kind" pleas die down, they're told to toughen up and stop being so sensitive. It's a fucking joke.

"Please do. We'd *love* to see it. So what happened to the cruise ship?"

Jack scoffs. "Excellent segue."

"Cruise ship?" Gem asks.

"Yes. Before you were…*buying plants*, you were sailing round the Caribbean, no?"

She shakes her head as if this is the first time she's heard of it.

"So *this*" – he directs her attention to the screen behind him, where one of the projections of a snowy mountain is now showing a picture of Gem taken without her knowledge on the ship – "…isn't you?" He smirks.

Sick fuck.

"Ohh, no. That wasn't me. I never even left the country. But you have found my doppelgänger. Poor girl. Apparently, she lost her job because of all the harassment."

The host freezes, but I can see how hard he's breathing. The picture is taken down immediately.

Strike two.

"So, seeing Pete again – that must be tricky given how things were left between you two. Let's take a look to remind ourselves of what happened." The host tries to buy himself some time, making no attempt to transition smoothly, which means behind the scenes everyone's panicking. I can't even imagine the chaos going on in his earpiece.

A montage plays of Gem and Pete seeming all in love. Pete has his own square on the bottom right now, the producers anticipating their reactions. Jack squeezes my shoulders tight and I force myself to relax. I didn't realise I'd tensed up. I quickly check to see if anyone else noticed me quietly raging even though I know what's onscreen is fake. Harvey's looking anywhere other than at his computer, because no brother should ever see his sister pretending to fuck someone on TV. Nana Harvey's looking my way and smiling.

Keep it together, Parks. For Nana, if not for yourself.

The sound of two cast members arguing steals Gem and Pete's attention away from the clip. The montage disappears and reveals the studio in a frenzy, but Gem and Pete's reaction boxes stay in place. Red faces, pointed fingers, and raised voices. Others struggle to hold the guys back. They swing their fists and argue over everything and nothing. The second the security guys finally get there, ready to intervene and drag them away, the fight ceases and everyone stands as still as a statue. As if they're androids resetting, without another word, all of them sit back down in their seats, leaving the muscled-up guys dressed in black to stand awkwardly by before eventually retreating.

"What the hell is going on?" The host finally snaps.

Gem smiles at him innocently. "It's almost as if you can't believe everything you see on reality TV."

He stares at her blankly with fury in his eyes as his chest heaves.

Strike three.

Suddenly, the feed cuts out completely, and the image is replaced by a blue screen with the words "broadcast interrupted" in bold. All of us cheer in celebration, hugging and high-fiving each other. I look over to see Gem's mom and nan doing a victory lap of the living room with huge smiles on their faces.

She did it.

"Love Lodge" was never a dating show; it was a test of human fortitude, with this as their final exam. And they passed with flying colours.

TWENTY-FIVE

GEMMA

Six weeks. It took me *six weeks* to completely destroy the credibility of the UK's hottest new dating show and turn my life around.

> Is December Fools a thing? Because that's what this feels like
>
> Gemma's cryptic AF. What does that even meaannn???
>
> This is so stupid. It's all made up!

Thanks to members of the live audience secretly filming the drama unfolding once the feed cut out, we didn't have to do anything more for people to start demanding the truth from the creators of the show. Very quickly, the channel cancelled series two. I reinstated my Instagram account and posted the video of what happened to me, along with a "story-time" telling everyone about the year I'd had, keeping specific details of the show out of it but making it clear reality TV and real life are two very different things. The goal was to give people a new perspective, but more than anything, it felt good to get everything off my chest.

Without expecting them to, my castmates – because that's what they are: performers in an unscripted drama, not game-show contestants – flocked to the comments to voice their support, and that gave viewers of the show even more to question. If the people I supposedly hated, fought with, and backstabbed on the show cared that much, surely I couldn't be half the villain I was made out to be. That, plus the reunion, set the wheels in motion, though a lot of people still had it out for me and accused me of playing the victim.

But then Pete insisted on a catch-up.

We both thought going along with his plan on the show would redeem my arrival. It wasn't until we got out that we saw how much worse things got for me by staying. So, being the schemer he is, Pete pitched me a new idea, and the next thing I knew, we were in a bougie London home staging a photoshoot. It was all glamour, both of us dressed to the nines, posing on a sofa in a beautifully decorated living room. We both had duct tape over our mouths, which was what got people to realise this wasn't any ordinary photo. When his fans and my haters zoomed in, they found all kinds of easter eggs alluding to something more going on. We both had our fingers crossed and wore a friendship bracelet on each of our wrists. His said the word "just", and mine said "friends". On the shelf behind us was a stack of books, fake-dating rom-coms mixed in with TV editing tricks, Frankenstein, an inti-macy coordinator handbook, a legal guide to NDAs, and a book on the Meisner acting technique. And if that wasn't enough, there was also a candle on the table with a label that read "smells like bullshit".

What I wasn't expecting was Pete's caption:

Take nothing at face value. This wonderful and kind

woman changed my life, and I owe her everything. She isn't who you think she is. Look past what you see on the surface, and you'll discover that too.

I don't blame Pete for my downfall – I thought faking it with him was a good idea too at the time – but I do give him most of the credit for my vindication. It had to start with me though. I had to believe I was worth saving and be willing to put myself out there again.

It took me too long to speak up and defend myself, but I'm never going to let anything or anyone silence me again.

That picture was the final nail in the coffin and there was nothing the TV execs could do about it, because technically we didn't mention the show directly. They had enough to deal with as it was. After that, huge opportunities, like the ones I'd dreamed of being offered when I chose to take part in the show, started coming in. Modelling agencies and talent management companies tried to convince me to sign with them, promising me the representation I deserved, but I turned them all down. I know how to land brand deals on my own and how to get paid work on my terms, and that's what I've started doing again. No contracts tying me down – nothing but the content I create, post, and own being shared in return for payment. No more feeding plants for me. I don't need an empire; I just want a peaceful life.

Although, there is one contract I'd sign up to over and over again…

"Keep them closed!" Tom covers my eyes and shuffles us inside his cabin. I've barely set foot on the ship, and already he's up to something. "And…open!"

My lashes, still wet with happy tears, blink as they adjust

to the light again. I take in Tom's room. It's exceptionally tidy and decorated with tinsel and fairy lights. Even though I was disappointed not to be back with him in time for Christmas, it meant I got to spend the holiday with my whole family, which we all thought would be a rarity with both me and Oscar working on ships. Then, when Oscar went off to meet Eliza's family for what I'm sure was an incredibly wholesome evening, Tom and I celebrated our first Christmas together virtually, which was…everything other than wholesome.

"Welcome to your new room."

Huh? "But what about Jack?" Surely all three of us can't share. Not full-time. He'd get sick of us.

"He's happy with his new arrangement."

I wrestle with the guilt that I've indirectly evicted him. "But—"

A sly grin spreads across Tom's cheeks and he places his hands on my waist. "There's been a development."

"Care to elaborate on that?"

"I'll tell you later, but right now…" He presses his lips against mine and moans with satisfaction. He does it again, the moan even bigger, as if he's eating his favourite flavour of ice cream. "Oh man, I can't believe I get to do this again." He kisses me once more, his hands roaming to my bum and squeezing me like he was desperately trying not to do at the gangway. "Can't do *this* on FaceTime."

I giggle, pulling him in even closer to me, unable to get enough of him.

"Oh, I should tell you, there are rules that apply to this living set-up. Well, only one, but I take it very seriously."

"Yeah? What's that?"

"No clothes past this point." He walks into the centre of the room and draws an imaginary line on the floor from the end of the desk to the wall on the opposite side. "And the rule is, if you're caught past this line in your clothes, they get taken off for you."

I smile, thinking of all the fun we'll have living together properly. "But you're past the line right now."

"Who said I was the only one the rule applied to?"

And with a smirk as sexy as that, how can I resist? I cross the line and go to him, immediately reaching for the hem of his T-shirt. "As if I need a reason to take your clothes off."

"Can't I…see him tomorrow?" I say through a yawn as I lean on Tom's shoulder. Today has been long enough without the jet lag.

"Push through, Princess. I promise it'll be worth it."

"Why the mystery? Why can't you tell me?"

"You'll see." He squeezes my thigh.

I grumble, and he kisses the top of my head.

I attempt to keep my eyes open by people-watching while we wait for Jack to join us in the bar.

"Stay awake, baby," Tom says softly, and the next thing I know, I'm staring back at my face on his selfie camera. *Oops.* "Smile for the grandkids."

Effortlessly, I do.

Once I braved it and began posting on socials again, Tom finally took the plunge and did the same. After multiple weeks of gigging back on land, he has a huge backlog of content stored up to use. And now he knows what he's doing, he's going to make it stretch over a longer period of time. His plan is to post stand-up clips until he eventually runs out, then he'll go back to "not-vlogging" with me. His online return has been well-received. Of course, we can never fully escape people who want to rain on our parade, but we aren't giving anyone the power to destroy us.

"Here he is!" Tom gets up, and I do the same.

I was expecting a new hairdo, a face tattoo, a piercing, or *something* big, but Jack looks exactly the same as before, except…happier. Almost as if there's a spring in his step. It's not until I look at the girl holding his hand that I realise why he might be okay with not sharing a room with Tom anymore.

"Who's that?" I ask Tom tunefully, excited Jack's opened himself up to love again.

He looks at me with an amused grin. "Sadie."

THANK YOU!

If you enjoyed More Than Clickbait, please consider leaving a review! Any review, however short, helps my books find other readers.

To stay up to date with future releases, sign up to my mailing list.

LEAKED! SCANDALOUS PHONE CALL BETWEEN TOM & GEMMA

Sign up to Philippa Young's mailing list for exclusive access to this steamy transcript:

www.philippayoungauthor.com

ACKNOWLEDGMENTS

More Than Clickbait simply couldn't have happened without the love and support I received for More Than Shipmates. Since publishing my debut novel I've made some amazing friends, both in readers and other writers, and I'm grateful to every single one of you for making me feel less alone. Thank you all for taking a chance on a new author and falling in love with Eliza, Oscar and Tom the way I did.

There are some amazing people who've helped me on this journey and deserve the biggest squeezes ever:

Joe — my fiancé (*squeals inaudibly*) — thank you for making me believe in love again. And our pooch, for being the reason I leave the house, mostly to walk with you, but sometimes to escape you.

Alicia, for cheering me on every step of the way and loving this story from the first draft, despite the state it was in.

Nina, for saving Tom and Gemma from a quad biking accident (don't ask) and for all the late night writing sessions.

D.J. Murphy, I feel so lucky to have met you. Thank you for your incredible feedback. Here's to love triangles and reality TV!

Kirsty & Zoë, for taking time out of your busy lives to voice your valuable opinions once again.

Stephanie, I see you, friend. Thank you for the love and friendship bracelets!

Mazz, for being my ultimate cruise companion.

Ben, for continuing to answer all of my weird-ass questions about ship life.

Tabitha, for being the friendly face I needed and championing my books on my behalf.

And last, but by no means least, my editor Bryony, for all of the amazing work you do behind the scenes to make my words sparkle. I would be a mess without you, as would this book.

Printed in Great Britain
by Amazon